MW01074970

Last Round

A TWISTED FOX NOVEL

USA TODAY BESTSELLING AUTHOR

CHARITY FERRELL

CHAPTER ONE

Silas

"REMEMBER that time you switched his mom's name to his side chick's in his phone, and he ended up sending her nudes instead?"

Something about listening to conversations in bars is intoxicating.

I absorb it like the mixed drinks I create.

People perch on heavy stools and slur their darkest secrets.

Admit their drunken truths.

It's different tonight. I'm not listening to an intoxicated soul pour their heart out. It's three women wedged toward the end of the bar, debating on who had the pettiest ex revenge.

I observe them, pretending to dry a martini glass, and replay the last retaliation in my mind.

He sent nudes to his mom instead of his side chick.

I shudder. I'd jump off a goddamn cliff if I accidentally sexted my mother, let alone sent her a dick selfie.

Yet another reason I steer clear of relationships.

No girlfriend, no revenge.

I learned that lesson in high school when a two-week fling declared her love for me and then keyed my car after I broke up with her. That shit is for the birds.

I set down the glass and grab another. I've never seen them in the three weeks I've bartended at Luna Bar, but that's not unusual. It's a busy bar with different faces coming and going, depending on whatever event the bar is throwing—fight nights, ladies' nights, or bar crawls.

Luna Bar isn't a dreary bar with dimmed lights and classic country tunes blaring from a jukebox. The lights are bright, and the music genre falls somewhere between Hank Williams and Imagine Dragons, so I can hear them decently.

The clock hasn't struck midnight, so plastered coeds aren't packing the place yet. Being the kick-ass employee I am, I ignore customers waving me over with drink requests. I can't tear my eyes away from them.

More specifically, I can't stop staring at *her*.

There are three of them, but I've fastened my focus on the woman who'd swapped the names. We'll call her Name Swapper. She's a dark-haired beauty—a nameless, shit-stirring woman who screams trouble.

But me? I live for fucking trouble.

Stroking my jaw, I admire her sitting perfect-postured on her stool while sipping on a cotton candy–colored cocktail. Her tongue wraps around the tip of the red straw—the same color as her lips—with each drink. Every so often, she fiddles with her straight hair that's as dark as the sky will be when I clock out tonight, and the strands fall to each side of her cleavage. Her skin tone is one people lie out in the sun for hours to achieve, but I'd bet tonight's tips that it's natural.

I've worked at bars long enough to guess people's ages. I'm usually right on the money on who's carrying a fake, who recently hit legal drinking age, and who is decades older than me. My guess is she's in her early twenties.

When admiring her from afar isn't pleasing enough, I approach them. Their conversation ceases as they wait for me to explain myself.

I point at Name Swapper and deliver a confident smile. "You

win. I'll be sure to hide my phone when we're at your place later."

The strawberry-blonde next to her gasps.

The brunette to her right scoffs.

Name Swapper stares at me, unimpressed, and settles her half-full glass onto the sticky bar. Her voice is bored when she says, "What makes you think I'd be interested in you *or* your phone?"

I ignore the racket around me, rest my elbow on the bar, and invade her personal space like an asshole. "How about you give me your number? I'll be sure *you're* the only woman receiving my dick pics."

I should be ashamed of myself for the weak-ass pickup line, but hey, time is limited. The bar will soon grow overcrowded, and my chance to shoot my shot with her will be severed. It's rare for me to hit on women in the workplace. I very much believe in the phrase *don't shit where you eat*. I've witnessed too many coworkers hook up with customers, only to deal with the wrath of them showing up to start drama later.

Hard pass on that shit.

But something about this woman is different. A sense that she won't look for me later or expect anything the next morning.

She stares at me, silent and smirking.

I raise a brow. "You single?"

"No fuckboys with side chicks at the moment." She plays with her straw, still feigning boredom, but that smirk tells me she's enjoying this game.

"Good news for me then." I snap my fingers, pull my phone from my pocket, and shake it in the air. "I do need to put your number in since it seems you can't be trusted around phones."

"Cocky." She squints in concentration and bites the corner of her plump lip. "Cocky is my type, so what the hell?"

Score.

My grin matches the same one I sported the night I lost my virginity to Miranda Smith in the back seat of my dad's old

BMW. Good-slash-embarrassing times. At least now, I last a hell of a lot longer than I did at fifteen.

She recites her number, and I type it into my phone. With her attitude, I predicted she'd put up more of a challenge and not hand her number over like loose change.

"And your name?" I ask when finished.

"Lola."

"Nice to meet you, Lola." I slide the phone back into my pocket. "I'm Silas."

She gestures toward my pocket. "I don't reply to texts, FYI. Call or don't bother."

Weird.

That's the first time I've heard someone say they prefer calls to texts. Hell, I'd rather receive a text than a call any day. You call me, and I'll let it ring fifty times until it goes to voicemail.

I snap my fingers. "I'll be sure to call then, sweetheart."

She rolls her eyes at my sentiment.

This woman is unreadable. One moment, she's acting as if she wants to jab a straw through my eyes, and the next, she's giving me her number.

"Yo! Bartender!" A customer pounds his heavy hand on the bar. "Quit trying to get laid! We need drinks!"

Lola shifts in her stool to look at him. The frat boy waves his arms in the air, anxiously seeking my attention.

She points at him. "You'd better go do your job before they fire you."

"Fuck him." I shrug with confidence I shouldn't have about being unemployed. "What can I get *you?*"

They simultaneously hold up their drinks.

"He already served us." Lola signals to Cohen, the other bartender on duty. He's also my boss.

I slightly frown before nodding. "Let me know when you're ready for your next round."

I wink and walk away even though I'd prefer to stay and chat with her.

Have to play hard to get and all.

I also need to do my job.

I make the frat douchebag and his friends Long Island iced teas and roll my eyes at their lack of tip before strolling toward Cohen. He hired me after I was fired from my last bartending gig. I'd worked at Club Layla a year before I mistakenly slept with a shot girl ... who was also the owner's niece. We'd agreed it would be a one-time thing and there'd be no commitments, but she didn't keep her end of the deal.

Again, don't shit where you eat.

"The three chicks in the corner," I say to Cohen, signaling toward them. "Let me make their drinks from now on. I might break my *no hooking up with customers* rule with her."

The beer he's filling overflows and spills onto the bar. He quickly jerks the glass away and grabs a towel, and regret pours through me. Telling your boss you plan to sleep with a customer is a stupid move.

Cohen wipes up the mess before saying, "Which unfortunate woman is this?" His face is unreadable, unsure about whether he's pissed or amused at my statement.

I discreetly point at Lola. "The mouthy, dark-haired one."

He snorts, snatches a glass, and repours the beer. "Yeah, that hookup won't be her. I'd choose someone else ... or just worry about your job."

"Why?" I pinch the bridge of my nose. "Is she your girl?"

"That's a big *fuck no*." He hands over the beer and cups my shoulder, turning me to face them. "The one on the right is my baby sister, who you by no means want to hook up with. The other two are her best friends."

Phew. At least Lola isn't his sister.

I can't afford to lose this job.

Well, I can, but I don't want to.

"Shit, sorry, man. I had no idea."

"As long as it isn't my sister, I don't give a shit who you pick up." He shrugs and signals a *give me a sec* motion to a customer. "You said the dark-haired girl gave you her number?"

I nod.

"Friendly advice: don't call her."

"What? Why?" I scoff. "You in love with her?"

A deep laugh rumbles from his chest. "On second thought, call her. Give it a chance."

When I peer back over to the three, they're staring at us. Lola sends me a flirty smile and waves.

"Is this some trick?"

"Nah." Cohen shakes his head. "Lola's a good girl ... has a *great* phone voice. Call and ask her out. I think you two would be good together." He jerks his chin toward the waiting crowd. "Now, get your ass to work."

I spend the rest of my night pouring beers, mixing endless drinks, and handing out shots. My opportunities to speak to Lola fade, and she leaves before I get the chance.

At least I have her number.

———

I YAWN three times in a row while parking my car in the garage. It took us twenty minutes to get everyone out of the bar, and then cleanup took another hour.

I kill the engine and walk into my house with Lola on my mind, like it strangely has been all night. I'm typically not a man who stresses over a woman. I'd rather cook rice grains one by one than form an emotional attachment with someone. I tried once—the relationship thing, not the rice—and learned my lesson when it ended in disaster.

As I kick off my shoes, I wonder what calling her would be like. I wasn't the only guy who hit on her tonight. I counted at least five. Five assholes I wanted to sucker punch for doing the same thing I'd done. To get back at them, I overcharged them for their drinks.

It was an asshole move.

Sue me.

Why was I the lucky bastard to score her number?

What made me so goddamn special?

And why do I find her so goddamn special that I've been fixated on her since I stepped behind the bar?

Maybe it was her disinterest in me.

That she was immune to my charm.

Calling Lola might be stupid, it might kick me in the ass later, but I hope it'll be worth it.

———

A RESULT of working all night is sleeping all day.

My parents didn't raise me on the belief of a typical nine-to-five workday. I was taught to work every minute of every day. If you weren't working, you were lazy. My father, Grady Malone, was a workaholic who expected the same from me. I grew up envisioning that as my future, but that mindset changed when disaster hit.

Now, I bartend a few nights a week and host club parties. That provides enough money not to have a life wrapped around working a job I hate.

I open the French doors that lead out to my patio, relax on an outdoor lounge chair, and kick up my feet before calling Lola.

It rings four times.

My back straightens when a deep, masculine voice answers.

The fuck?

Is this her dad?

Brother? Boyfriend?

"Is"—I scratch my head—"Lola there?"

It's like I'm twelve and calling a chick's house phone before cell phones were a thing.

"Motherfucker," the guy hisses into the phone. "She did it

again!"

"Uh … did what?"

He blows out a ragged breath. "I'm Callum, Lola's ex. She thinks it's funny to give my number to the men who ask for hers. It's her revenge, reminding me it was a mistake to cheat on her."

Well played, Name Swapper.

Little does she know, her little trick only makes me want her more.

———

I WALK INTO THE BAR, grab a dirty rag, and sling it at Cohen. "You're an asshole."

The towel lands on his shoulder, and he flicks it off, watching it fall onto the linoleum floor.

"You called her, didn't you?"

"I called *someone* who sure as fuck wasn't Lola." I mock his voice and mimic his stance from the other night. "Lola's a good girl … has a *great* phone voice. Call and ask her out."

"You brought it on yourself, man."

"How? For asking for her number?"

"For being an idiot. Did you honestly think a smart-ass like her would hand over her number that easily?"

I didn't, but I allowed my ego to get in the way and tell me it was my charm that had sealed the deal.

"When is she coming in again?"

"That's none of your business."

I rub at my tired eyes. "As an employee, I should know who's visiting this establishment."

"As your boss, I think you should worry about being an employee and less about weekend hookups."

Our conversation stops when the door opens. It's only three o'clock, so the lunch rush is gone, and the dinner rush hasn't arrived yet.

The door slams shut behind Finn, the bar's bouncer, and he strolls toward us.

"Silas! My dude!" He circles behind the bar and slaps Cohen on the back while keeping his attention on me. "Barbecue tomorrow at Cohen's place. It's his birthday, so don't forget his gift."

Cohen frowns at the word *birthday*. "I don't want gifts."

As a single father, Cohen prefers to do everything himself and never asks for favors. I once offered him and his son free baseball tickets to a game I couldn't attend. He wouldn't take the tickets until I accepted money for them.

"I'll be sure to get you a shitty present for the terrible advice you gave me," I tell Cohen.

Finn shakes his head. "Nah, get him a Pornhub gift card. The dude doesn't get laid much, so he needs good content for his spank bank."

I raise a brow. "They sell Pornhub gift cards?"

Cohen smacks the back of Finn's head, and he winces. "You're uninvited, fucker."

I've heard of Cohen's barbecues before, but I haven't attended one. I've always been good at keeping a distance from others.

An idea hits me, and I perk up.

"Will Lola be there?"

Finn blinks at me. "You know Lola?"

Cohen laughs. "He was lucky enough to get her number."

Finn crookedly grins. "Wait a minute. You got the pleasure of speaking with Callum?"

"Sure did," I mutter.

"Dude, I'd stop there," Finn warns. "Lola would tear you apart and then spit you out."

I eye Cohen, ignoring Finn. "Will she be there?"

He nods. "Oh, she'll be there, but I can't promise she won't kick your ass."

"Challenge accepted."

CHAPTER TWO

Lola

CALLS from your exes carry two different emotions:

Anger that you're no longer together.

Sadness because you're, well, no longer together.

Calls with my ex are an alternative to the standard. Callum is angry, but not because we're no longer together.

"What did I tell you about giving out my number?" he hisses through the phone.

Revenge is best served in the form of receiving calls from the men who hit on the girl you'd cheated on.

"Whoops." I laugh, not bothering to hide my enjoyment of his irritation. "I must've gotten our numbers mixed up again."

"Admit it," he says, and I can imagine the smug smile he's sporting. "You do it because you miss me."

Men and their egos—always thinking revenge is because we still love them.

"Negative." I open my car door, settle my bag into the passenger seat, and balance my phone between my ear and shoulder as I get in the driver's side. "I do it because I'm bored, and you deserve it."

"Bullshit. You still think about me."

"You're right. I think about you when I reflect on how it was to have a shit boyfriend. Have a good day, and I'll be sure to send more phone calls your way." I end the call, toss my phone down next to my bag, and push my black sunglasses up my nose.

Some might consider giving his number out petty. It is. But I don't care because Callum deserves it.

Let me paint the beautiful scene of dating Callum.

Imagine having sex with your boyfriend and him not caring about your big O. Then the asshole has the audacity to pull out, release on your stomach, and smear it across your skin—as if his jizz is a damn gift. He then rolls off the bed and says, "Gotta go clean up, babe." Like *he's* the one with cum on his belly.

As I lay there, brooding over how sticky and gross sperm was, his phone beeped with a text.

Then beeped again.

And again.

Then it rang.

I make no apologies for my nosiness—it could've been an emergency, you know? I grabbed his phone to find a text from *Brittany: Blonde from Club Mania.*

Like an idiot, his passcode was his birthday, so it didn't take a rocket scientist to unlock it.

Brittany: Blonde from Club Mania had texted, asking if he missed licking her vagina … and then sent a close-up picture of said vagina he'd allegedly lapped up.

I scrolled through their past messages to learn they'd licked each other several times while he and I were together.

I proceeded to do what any sane person would. I grabbed his favorite—very expensive and dry-clean-only—shirt to clean his cum off me, pulled my lace panties up my legs, slipped my dress on, and left without a word, certain I'd figure out the best revenge for him later. He texted after his shower, discovering his bed was empty, and I replied that he should spill his cum on someone else because it would no longer be his pleasure to do so on me.

I thought of my revenge the next day while visiting my granny in the nursing home when a guy asked for my number. A guy I'd never be interested in because he'd helped his grandmother cheat during bingo, which caused my grandmother to lose. Knowing I couldn't associate myself with another cheater, I came up with the bright idea of giving him Callum's number.

That was a month ago, and since then, it's become my new go-to.

Ten outta ten, ladies.

Highly recommend it.

———

BARBECUES AT COHEN'S are my favorite.

I'm not much of a barbecue girl per se—considering I'd burn down the entire block if I attempted to even light a grill—but I enjoy *attending* them. I get to sit outside with the girls and munch on calorie-ridden snacks while Cohen grills. It's something we've done since high school.

Cars are packed on Cohen's driveway, so I park on the curb. I step out of my black Porsche and grab his birthday gift—a bottle of Johnnie Walker Blue Label. With him being a bartender and my family owning one of the top liquor distribution companies in the Midwest, we appreciate quality alcohol.

The sun beams down on me as I walk up the drive and then step through the creaky wood gate that leads into the backyard. The air smells of fresh-cut grass, and I make my way toward the round table where everyone is seated. The usual gang is here—my best friends, Georgia and Grace, along with Cohen and Finn. Who isn't usually here is the extra person seated next to Finn.

It's *him.*

Silas.

The guy I gave the wrong number to at the bar.

And the one who most likely called said number, given Callum's call earlier.

Cohen stands at the grill, flipping burgers. The others are wrapped in deep conversation, clueless to my arrival, but not Silas. He's sitting tall in the chair that directly faces the entrance to the backyard. He levels his gaze on me as though he's been anxiously awaiting my arrival.

The shit-eating grin on his face confirms he's not as shocked to see me as I am him. He doesn't appear as angry as I'd expect from someone who was given the wrong number. He knew I'd be here and came with one goal—to mess with my head, not rip it off. If he were that upset about my wrong-number game, Cohen never would've allowed him to come.

I keep a straight face, tighten my hold on the gift bag, and pull my shoulders back before strutting toward them.

Two can play this game, buddy.

I'll also be kicking Cohen's traitorous ass.

Silas's smile grows more arrogant with every step I take toward him.

Today is the first time I've had to face one of my wrong-number victims.

I didn't have to worry about the nursing-home cheater because, luckily, my grandma quit bingo, stating, "That bitch Thelma always wins."

The few others were random men at bars.

"Look who's finally arrived!" Silas shouts, dramatically slapping his knee like my grandfather does when he sees a grandchild walk in, and then stands. "It's Callum."

As much as I wish I didn't, I freeze at him calling me Callum.

Oh, this asshole.

He'll be lucky if he leaves this barbecue alive … or at least with two working legs. He could easily live with only one kneecap … and surely, taking out one leg isn't much prison time.

Shaking away my thoughts of bodily injury, I keep my chin up and stroll forward. Drinking Silas in, I hate that he's exactly the type of man I find attractive. Six-plus feet so that there's still a significant height difference when I wear heels. Thick hair, the color resembling the top-shelf whiskeys I sell to clients on the regular. It's long on the top and shorter on the sides with a slight flip in the front. The black button-up, rolled at the elbows, that he wore at the bar is replaced with a simple black tee. Just like I love wearing black, I find it incredibly attractive when men do too.

That night, I spotted him the moment he walked behind the bar. Unfortunately, I'd sworn off guys after my breakup with Callum. I'm not made for relationships. The first few times I'd cracked open my heart, it'd resulted in nothing but letdowns. The way my love life is looking, I'll be the future Thelma—alone in the nursing home and cheating during bingo.

Another reason I knew Silas was off-limits was his job. Cohen has recounted endless bartender stories—how they're in that line of work for the thrill of the nightlife. They have no issues going home with random women like it's their reward after a long night's work.

I shake my head, getting myself together, and walk toward them. All eyes have turned to me as everyone awaits my response when I reach them.

I ignore Silas and glare at Cohen. "Really? You invited him?" I hold up the gift he no longer deserves. "I'm taking this back. No expensive liquor for traitors."

"Technically, Finn invited him," Cohen corrects before pointing his spatula toward Asshole Bartender. "Silas is cool. You two need to talk out your wrong-number differences."

I flip Cohen the bird while still refusing to glance at Silas.

Finn, smirking wide and proud of providing today's

entertainment, signals back and forth between Silas and me. "How did you two meet?"

I roll my eyes at Finn's terrible job of playing clueless. He definitely knows.

"She gave me her number at the bar," Silas answers smugly. My gaze flashes to him as he takes the few steps separating us. I inhale the rich scent of his cologne. It's familiar and expensive … and my favorite. There's something attractive about a man who wears a strong cologne—a sign that he enjoys being in charge.

"Either the music was too loud or I'm losing my hearing because I heard her name wrong," he continues, his focus solely on me as he holds out his hand. "It's good to see you again, Callum."

I narrow my eyes at him and swat away his hand. "Funny, jackass."

"Aunt Lola said a bad word!" Noah, Cohen's son, shouts before crawling out from underneath the table like an ant who's been waiting for a crumb to drop.

Shit, I hate when he hides down there.

For some strange reason, Noah plays with his toys under the table. Georgia said it's because he likes to listen to grown-up conversations. I now agree with that statement.

"Sorry, Noah," I say, feeling the need to explain myself to a kid who has to be reminded not to eat his boogers. "It was an accident."

He nods, accepting my apology, and runs over to Cohen, asking for a juice box.

I walk around Silas to find a chair, bumping my shoulder into his. Throwing my head back, I groan when I discover the only empty chair is between Georgia and Silas.

Did he set that up too?

It wouldn't surprise me after he came here and put on a show. I contemplate grabbing the chair and dragging it to another spot, but that'd prove his little game is working. I can't have that. While he scoots out his chair and sits, I drop my gift onto the small bench where the others are. I sit down to his right, smacking my elbow against the side of his head, and turn my back to him. He lets out an *oomph*.

"Thanks for the heads-up," I hiss to Georgia.

She lifts her phone from the table. "Check your phone for the fifteen text messages I sent."

"Shit," I mutter, sliding my hand into my crossbody and realizing I left my phone in the car.

"Sorry," she whispers. "I had no idea he was coming. I was surprised too."

I frown, but before I get the chance to reply, Silas taps my shoulder. I peer back at him.

"Did you fall from heaven?" he asks, and I wait for a cheesy comment to follow. "Because so did Satan ... and I think you might be him."

My mouth falls open.

Not what I expected.

I narrow my eyes at him. "Um, that's rude."

"I'm rude?" He scratches the five o'clock shadow along his sharp jawline. "What kind of evil person comes up with an idea like that?"

"I think you mean, what kind of *genius* comes up with an idea like that?" Georgia, the CEO of snooping on conversations, says.

That's my girl.

Silas doesn't even pay her a glance. He leans closer to me and lowers his deep voice. "How are you doing today, fake number-giver? Ruin any other guy's dreams of finding love?"

"Nope." I shake my head. "You were my latest victim."

He chuckles. "I should've known it was a trick when you said to call. Texting is always the way to go." He's amused, almost impressed.

"No, I still think calling is better," I say with honesty. "It's more intimate. Texting is so easy … you can't read emotions or lies through texting."

"Too bad for you we'll never get a chance to have a phone call. I don't talk to people who are Satan's sidekick."

"Yet you're talking to me right now."

"Yes, to get your advice on staying out of hell since it seems you have all the inside information."

"You can start by not hitting on random women every night at work." I finally turn in my chair to face him and ignore the attention on us.

That night at the bar, I was aware of his eavesdropping. When he asked for my number, I debated on whether to give it to him. Since it was the first time in a while I'd been interested in a guy, I was tempted. But my intuition stepped in to tell me he was bad news and most likely had a call log full of Brittany: Blonde from Club Manias in it. I observed him as he worked, witnessing woman after woman hit on him while he flirted back.

No, thank you on that.

I was surprised Cohen vouched for him being a good guy. Cohen is picky over who he brings around Noah and us. If he'd thought Silas was a weirdo, he'd have never let him come today.

Silas scoffs, "You were the first woman whose number I asked for at Luna Bar. Consider that flattering."

I mock his scoff. "Yeah, right."

"Ask Cohen. The last thing I need is some random hookup showing up at my job. I have a strict *no hooking up* policy at work."

I raise a brow. "Does that mean you're celibate then?"

He chuckles. "Why, yes, my darling, that's exactly what it means."

"I believe the people who claim the earth is flat more than that."

"How about this?" He strokes his jaw. "Let's start over. You can tell me why your parents named a beautiful girl like you Callum. If their goal was to steer men away from you, it wasn't necessary since you're evil. And I'll tell you why it was a mistake, giving me the wrong number."

"*Fine.* Since Cohen invited you, I'll believe you're a halfway-decent person."

"A whole-way decent person. Now, tell me your *real* name."

"Lola. I didn't lie about that."

"Your *full* name." His dark eyes study me.

"Why?"

He shrugs. "Just curious."

"What makes you think I'd give you my full name when I wouldn't give you my number?"

"Good point." He snaps his fingers. "I wouldn't believe you anyway."

"It's Lola Delgado." I suddenly feel the urge to prove him wrong. "Exactly what I told you at the bar. I'm not a liar."

He eyes me skeptically. "You gave me the wrong number."

"Believe me or don't. I don't care either way."

"It's just hard to trust the Princess of Darkness."

"Is Silas *your* real name?"

"Sure is. You see, I'm an honest person."

Georgia laughs. "I think this guy might actually give Lola a run for her money. That's a first."

"You know …" Silas says, obnoxiously smiling while ignoring everyone else—even Noah zooming around the yard, his arms in the air, proclaiming to be an airplane. "If your goal is to make your ex jealous, I have better ways of doing so."

"Perfect!" I exclaim with overemphasized enthusiasm. "Let me give you his address. I forgot my favorite sweater there and would love to get it back. It's black … super cute. Would you mind grabbing it for me? It was pretty expensive."

"Black sweater. Got it. Anything else? Your anger management books? Nice pills? A way to remove the stick up your ass?"

Oh, wow, he definitely deserves a busted kneecap.

As bad as it sounds, arguing with him is fun. It's nice to talk to someone with a similar sense of humor.

I rest my elbows on the arms of the chair. "If it makes you feel any better, my ex called and yelled at me."

"Sweetheart, I don't give two fucks about your ex. He probably deserved it. You should've just pulled that game on another guy and given me the real one because I'm much more deserving."

"I'm not sleeping with you … if that's what you think you're *deserving* of."

He snorts. "My wanting to sleep with you and the offer to do so are gone. Knowing you, you'd go all praying mantis on me and bite my head off afterward … or Lorena Bobbitt me."

CHAPTER THREE

Silas

"FOOD IS READY!" Cohen shouts, interrupting my discussion with Lola.

My stomach growls, but I couldn't give two shits about a cheeseburger. I'd rather keep talking to Lola and learn the hints she provides about herself between the sarcasm and insults. I've never had so much interest in someone before. It scares yet excites me that for the first time in years, that sense of craving to know someone has returned.

If Lola hadn't attended, I'm not sure I would've come today. Even though I have endless *acquaintances*, I don't have many people I consider good friends. I keep people at a distance, which usually surprises others because I'm a jokester and easy to talk to.

Lola and I are the last people to rise and make our way to the picnic table covered with food—burgers, hot dogs, chips, a large chopped salad, and desserts out the ass. Lola goes first, placing a burger onto her plate—no bun and instead wrapped in lettuce. She grabs a bag of barbecue chips and scoops a beer from the cooler. I do the same, copying her selections but choose a water instead of beer.

Georgia snorts when she glances from Lola's plate to mine. "I see the both of you are current bread haters."

Lola peeks at my plate and blows out a noisy breath. "Really?"

"I wondered why you were copying my meal." I smirk before bringing the burger to my lips and biting off a chunk.

She rolls her eyes and reaches toward my plate.

Uncertain of her next move, I swiftly slide it out of her reach. "Nuh-uh. I don't trust you around my food."

She rolls those wide brown eyes. "Oh God, are you going to make a comment like that every time we're around each other?"

"Are you saying we'll see each other again? An invite? Do I get to go to your birthday party?"

"As long as you bring an amazing gift."

"Noted. When is your birthday?"

"June twenty-third. The best day of the year."

I drop my burger, the fear of that one bite making its way back up my stomach, and a chill runs through me.

"What?" She blinks, cocking her head. "Is that your birthday too?"

"Nah." I shake my head while also hoping to shake away the memories. I clear my throat before continuing, "I tend to steer clear of Cancers. They're usually trouble."

"Look at you, a man who knows his horoscopes."

I nod, hating that while it's a good day for her, it's fucking tainted for me.

Maybe that's a sign Lola isn't the best person to be around.

All she'd be is a reminder of my past.

"Dad! My hot dog is all gone!" Noah yells from the kiddie table inches from us, intruding my grim thoughts. "Time for a yummy cupcake!"

"Really?" Cohen replies, staring at the ground.

I follow Cohen's gaze and see Noah's hot dog, now covered with grass, next to the table.

"He technically isn't lying," Georgia says.

"No, he is lying," Cohen says, his voice stern and parent-like. "What did I tell you about fibbing, Noah?"

"That it'll make my tongue fall out," Noah replies with a frown before sticking out his tongue. His eyes grow wide. "Oh no! Is it going to fall out? I can't eat any cupcakes then!"

Lola shifts in her chair to look at Noah. "You get three lies before it does. So, you'd better choose them wisely."

"Really, Lola?" Cohen asks.

"What?" She shrugs. "The kid is going to know *you're* lying if it doesn't fall out now. I'm actually saving your ass."

"Aunt Lola said ass!" Noah says, pointing at her.

"Listen, kid, I was just sticking up for you," Lola replies before dramatically staring up at the sky. "God, take the boy's tongue away."

Noah smacks his hand over his mouth. "No!"

Cohen stands. "I'm going to make you another hot dog. You eat it or no cupcakes for a week."

"Fine," Noah mutters, crossing his arms and pouting.

"Cancers also have a potty mouth," I whisper to Lola, leaning into her. "I wonder what else that mouth does."

"Talks shit." She grabs a chip and nibbles at the edge of it. "Eats guys like you for breakfast."

My thoughts of her birthday crumble as we return to our game of jest.

"Looks like no cupcakes for you either, liar." I smirk. "Are you going to return the question and ask what my mouth does?"

She grins wildly. "Fails to give women orgasms?"

I slide my finger over my bottom lip. "Too bad for you, you'll never get the luxury of finding that out."

"And too bad for you, you'll never get the luxury of going anywhere near my vagina."

"I didn't know demons had vaginas."

Her smile doesn't falter. It only grows.

"You two do know my kid repeats everything he hears?"

Cohen interjects, spoiling our fun. "The less he hears *the word,* the better."

It seems anytime Lola and I get wrapped up in conversation, everyone around us fades.

Relaxing into my chair, I tune in to the surrounding exchanges to learn about everyone. I shut my eyes, fighting away recollections of when I had something similar. Maybe this is what I need—friendship again. I told myself I didn't deserve it, but this group makes me reconsider that punishment I set upon myself.

———

"ARE you going to give me your real number yet?" I ask Lola as we eat birthday cupcakes. "Or will it be your priest's ... therapist's ... attorney's? I'm almost certain you have all three on speed dial."

I don't want her number to hook up with her now. I want it because A.) it won't make me feel like too much of a schmuck, and B.) I want to see her again.

Lola laughs, wiping frosting from the side of her lip. "I can provide you with all three if you'd like?"

I lick my finger before reaching out and sweeping the tip over the frosting she missed. She sucks in a breath, and I grin, proud of myself for obtaining that reaction from her. When I pull away, she snatches her drink and chugs it as if wanting to wash away the response her body gave me.

"Are you still in love with your ex?" I ask.

"Am I in love with a cheating prick? That'd be a negative." She grins. "I just enjoy a good revenge and need a little entertainment for the rainy days."

"How about you let me be the entertainment on those rainy days?"

"Fine. You give me *your* number, and when I have a rainy

day, I'll *think* about calling. But I'll most likely depend on Netflix."

When she pulls out her phone, clad in a bright neon-green case, I beam while reciting numbers.

"Call. Don't text." I grin and can't wait until she calls because she'll be the one getting the surprise this time.

CHAPTER FOUR

Lola

"NOW THAT BUSINESS is taken care of, when are you free for me to take you out?"

I deliver the generic smile I regularly do when this happens. "It's against company policy to date clients."

The man grins, unfazed by my response—unsurprisingly—and runs a hand down his expensive black suit. He's a guy who thinks the rules don't apply to him even though I'm sure he has a similar policy at his company.

Vince Billings owns the largest chain of liquor stores in Iowa and has ordered his liquor from 21st Amendment—my family's business—for years. I acquired their account last year. Initially, I worked with his son, who is my age, but then Vince came to the office one day and saw me. He immediately switched the contact information to himself.

Vince is nice—don't get me wrong—and good-looking for a man my father's age. Other than him asking me out, he hasn't given off any creep vibes. His invitation would thrill most women.

But me? I vowed never to date a client.

Or a man in power, like him, who sees rules as speed bumps, not roadblocks.

My grandfather, Robert Delgado, founded 21st Amendment decades ago. It's now a wholesale liquor distribution company whose clientele spans over fifteen states. My father, Robert Delgado II, was promoted to president ten years ago, and soon, he'll pass the company down to my brother, Robby, and me.

Growing up around the business, I've witnessed men with authority have no problem breaking marriage vows for other lovers.

I guess my distrust started when I was sixteen, newly licensed, and skipped school to surprise my father at his office. His secretary attempting to stop me should have been a sign to abort mission. Instead, I was the one surprised when I burst into his office and found a woman half his age blowing him. Not only did I want to acid-wash my eyes, but I was also furious. His immediate response was to push her to the floor, buckle his pants, and bribe me to keep it a secret. I got a new Audi ... and then tattled to my mother the next day.

That was when our family relocated from the city to a small Iowa town an hour away. My mother saw Anchor Ridge, Iowa, as a fresh start and a way to restrain my father from cheating. Her grand plan failed.

My father was caught with another mistress not too long after—not by me, thank God. My mother divorced him, and I refused to speak to him for six months. After forced therapy together, I understood the divorce was for the best. They were happier apart, and the reality is, some people aren't made for marriage.

Now, my mother is happily married to a faithful man, and my father's still unhappily chasing his next screw. So, I blame him, along with the few fuckboys I've attempted to date, for ruining my trust in the male species.

Vince laughs, shoving his hands into his pockets. "I spend enough money with 21st Amendment for them to overlook that. Trust me."

I shyly smile, hoping to appear almost clueless. "I don't want to lose my job."

My father wouldn't fire me, but if I start dating clients who share the same birth year as him, he'd question whether I was responsible enough to run 21st Amendment when he retires. With all his affairs, not one has been with someone involved in the company. He's not a fan of mixing business with pleasure.

Vince plays with a bottle of a new and overpriced tequila that's all the rage with millennials. "How about this? If you lose your job, I'll match your salary without you even lifting a finger."

No, thank you on the sugar-daddy offer.

I check my watch. "Oh shoot, I'm running late for my next appointment."

He chuckles. "Ah, I get the hint, Lola."

I stay quiet.

He motions toward the table. "The same time in two weeks?"

"I'll schedule you in."

"Give me more of these products. Campus liquor stores sell this trendy shit like it's candy. The coeds see it on social media and will pay anything to post a selfie with it."

"Will do." I salute him. "I'll make a list and have it ready."

"You're the best. And let me know if you change your mind and want to go to dinner ... a movie ... hell, I'll even take you on a vacation if you want."

"I'll keep that in mind."

———

THE FIRST THING I do when I get home from work is take off my heels. As much as I love my black Jimmy Choos, they're a bitch to stand in all day.

But with heels comes power.

With power comes higher sales.

Some say I had it easy.

That nepotism gave me my position.

Yes, I got my job because my family owns the company, but I've also proven my worth there. My sales numbers exceed others every month. I don't sit in the office and call potential clients. No, I go to businesses and convince them why we're the distributor for them. Then when I acquire the customer, I upsell them.

It also helps that most of my clients are men—liquor store, bar, and club owners. I don't mind doing a little flirting to get them to buy an eighty-dollar bottle of vodka instead of a twenty.

All's fair in the love of sales and marketing.

I trek to my bedroom, change into sweats and a tee, and unlock my phone to order takeout. Just as I'm opening the app, my phone rings.

Georgia.

"Hey, babe," I answer at the same time my stomach growls.

"You. Me. Grace. Drinks tonight."

"It's not girls' night."

We have a weekly mandatory girls' night.

"Yeah … and? We don't only get together on girls' nights."

"I know." I yawn. "I changed into comfy clothes and was about to order food and call it a night."

"Lame," she sings out. "Let's go out. Eat bad food. Then we can call it a night."

"Fine," I groan. "But I'm not dressing up, so pick somewhere chill."

"That makes two of us. Wear sweats. Wear jeans. Wear a onesie. I'll pick you up. Drinks and dinner are on me."

I change into leggings and a sweatshirt, throw my hair into a ponytail, and wait for Georgia to pick me up.

Georgia and Grace have been my best friends since I moved to Anchor Ridge in high school. I was the new girl at their school. We met at a party, where I witnessed Grace turn a guy down. He gave her a hard time, so I stood up for her. After that, we became inseparable, forming our best-friend trio. I don't know what I'd do without them.

We come from different backgrounds, and our personalities are diverse, but I could never see myself without them in my life. I'm private yet mouthy and sarcastic while Georgia is in your face and loud. Grace is quiet, soft-spoken, the girl-next-door type. Our differences balance each other out.

———

"SERIOUSLY?" I ask when Georgia pulls into Luna Bar's parking lot.

She whips into a space, shifts the car into park, and peers over at me. "What?"

I've never had an issue with Luna Bar. We've hung out in what I'd consider the mid-grade bar a few times. Cohen always discounts our food and liquor, and there's a sense of security with him watching over us. But after the Silas situation, I'm not sure how seeing him will be. Since he works at Luna, I should've thought twice before giving him a fake number. After our conversation the other day, there's no doubt he'll give me shit if he's working tonight.

I hold back the urge to ask Georgia if he is. She'll think I'm interested.

"Oh, nothing," I mutter. "I just thought we'd mix it up tonight."

"You said casual, and this is pretty casual."

Fingers crossed that Silas isn't working tonight.

Too bad, deep down, I'm secretly hoping he is.

CHAPTER FIVE

Silas

I GRIN cheesier than I should when Lola plops down on a stool at the bar. Like last time, I ignore customers and head directly to her. "Aw, babe. You came to see your boy."

Screw tips.

I'd rather hang out with her.

The desire to sleep with her is now off the table. I want to keep it strictly platonic. Not only do I not want her to hate me, but I'm also a little scared of her being around my dick. She might chop it off or some shit.

Thou shall not risk your manhood for crazy chicks, even if you think they'd be an amazing lay.

Grace and Georgia take the seats on each side of her. They were cool at the barbecue, much nicer than Name Swapper. Grace is a bit shy, and her striped dress fits her personality. Georgia is quite the smart-ass but not as evil as Lola and reminds me of a damn flower child every time I see her.

But I have no desire toward them—only Lola. I guess evil is my type. I'd be the first to die in a horror movie. I'd go straight to the serial killer if she had dark hair, a glare that I found sexy as fuck, and a body that put an hourglass to shame.

That excitement rises at the realization she's sitting on my side of the bar, not Cohen's. Technically, there aren't any available stools on Cohen's side, but I won't allow that detail to ruin my Lola high. I'd bet tonight's tips that she could ask any dude to give up his stool for her, and he would.

She laughs at my greeting. "You wish."

I nod toward her messy ponytail and casual outfit. "I see you dressed up for the occasion too."

That comment results in her flipping me off.

The night we met, she was in a short black dress.

She wore black shorts, a crop top, and wedges at the barbecue.

And tonight, even in her baggy sweatshirt and tangled hair, she's just as gorgeous.

I motion toward Cohen, who's busy shaking a martini. "Why are you not sitting over there then?"

"Faster drinks. We figured fewer people would be on this side of the bar." She bites into the corner of her plump lip. "Word is, you make watered-down margaritas, and Noah could mix up better drinks than you. I'm steering clear of that, and I'll have a simple glass of wine. Surely, you can't mess that up."

"An order of hot wings and onion rings for each of us too," Georgia adds, draping her purse along the back of her stool. "We're starving, and Lola gets meaner when she's hungry. You've been forewarned."

"First off," I say, pointing at Lola, "I'm frightened of a meaner version of you. Second, even though I've concluded that you three are monsters, I will not allow wings and onion rings to be served alongside wine." I shudder at the horrific combination.

"Wings and onion rings go well with margaritas. I'll prove your drink slander wrong."

Lola shrugs. "Fine, but don't let us down."

"I've never been known to let a woman down." I wink.

Georgia scoffs, "Pickup lines that lame won't work on her. Do better than that. Assholes are Lola's kink."

Grace nods in agreement.

"Yep," Lola says. "Cutesy isn't my thing."

I smirk. "Lucky for you, I'm not cutesy, sweetheart."

"Sweetheart is a cutesy sentiment," she fires back.

"Fine, I'll make your pain-in-the-ass self a drink. How's that for cutesy?"

"Doing better."

I walk away to start their drinks. It's a weeknight, so we're slower. Slower means fewer tips but more time to bullshit with Lola.

You can't have the best of both worlds.

I use every skill I learned during bartending school to make their margaritas and spend more time on them than I should. Hell, I didn't try this hard when I made last year's Super Bowl MVP a drink.

There are a few secrets to creating the perfect margarita: chill the glass for five minutes, use fresh lime juice—none of that imitation shit—and always add top-shelf silver tequila. To spruce it up, I add strawberry, grapefruit, and basil.

Pride rolls through me as I hand them over, giving Lola hers first. I stand in anticipation, waiting for her to taste it.

She takes a slow sip, shuts one eye as if in deep concentration, and then takes another. Licking her lips, she says, "Not too bad."

"Not too bad?" I make a *chef's kiss* gesture. "It's perfection."

"Aw," Lola says mockingly, her eyes meeting mine in amusement. "Does that upset your ego?"

"It does actually because there are two things I'm known for —my drinks and making women come back for more."

She scrunches up her face. "Cheesy and cutesy. Ew."

I chuckle, facing my palms toward her. "Sorry, sorry."

"Dude, she isn't going to sleep with you!" an overweight and balding man across the bar shouts. "We need another round, *and* my wife is up for a threesome if you want to get laid."

Grace, who just took her first drink of my delicious

margarita, spits it out at the man's remark. "Did he really say that?"

Lola snorts, jerking her head toward the man, now joined by his thin, red-haired wife, and they're making out. "If you can't sleep with me, might as well bang a middle-aged couple."

"Piss off," I grumble. "That just shows how many people want me." I hook a thumb toward myself.

"A man wants to watch you fuck his wife." She chews on the tip of her red nail, hiding a smile. "That won't make me jealous."

"Eh, I'm declining their offer, *but* if you ever reconcile with Callum, I'm up for it. He can watch the two of us together."

She dramatically gags. "You just stated two things that will never happen."

"Your loss, Name Swapper." I slap the bar. "Now, I'll be back to hear you admit that's the best drink you've ever had. Onion rings and wings, coming right up."

———

"JUST SAY YOU CAN'T GO," Georgia tells Lola. "Blame it on cramps. The flu. The universe is in retrograde."

I pause mid-pour, ready to eavesdrop on my next Lola conversation. It seems to be a new hobby of mine. Not one of the conversations I've snooped on of hers has been boring. I help a customer, peek a glance at Lola, pour a drink, sneak a stare at Lola. She coincides with every job duty tonight.

They've devoured their food, and for someone only mildly impressed with my margarita, Lola sure had no problem ordering another round.

Lola groans. "He'll make some speech about being present if I want to be in charge someday." She knocks back the remainder of her margarita.

Grace sighs, sliding her straw in and out of her glass. "Let's brainstorm on excuses for you to bail."

"The only excuses I have are death or hospitalization." Lola throws her head back before jerking it up suddenly, as if a thought hit her. She playfully smacks Grace's shoulder. "Break my foot. Use the stool."

"What?" Grace gapes at her. "You want me to cause bodily harm to get you out of a work social?"

Georgia shakes her head. "That wouldn't work. He'd tell her to grab crutches and not be late."

Deciding it's my time to shine, I finish the drink I was making, pass it to the customer, and walk to them. "What are you trying to dodge?"

"Nothing," Lola answers, waving me away.

I stay put. "I'm the king of dodging shit." I press a hand to my chest. "Tell me what it is, and I'll give you an escape plan."

Lola half-shrugs. "Just some stupid work thing."

I crack a smile. "I'm sure being the Princess of Darkness is a hard job."

She snatches her napkin and tosses it at me. "Funny."

"What's the deal?" Propping my elbows onto the bar, I lean into her space. "Why don't you want to go? Do they make you grow horns during the initiation into hell? I'd probably want to skip out on that day too."

She grins, half-shrugging. "If that were the case, I'd go so that I could find a demon to haunt you."

"Please make sure she's hot." Tingles shoot up my neck as I move in closer, taking in the sweet smell of her perfume. It's sexy and bold, just like her. "What's so bad about it?"

"It always ends up being a big couples thing." Lola frowns before slapping both of her friends' arms. "And these two have other plans because they're bad friends at the moment."

"Call Callum," I suggest. "You have his number memorized … or I can do it for you? We've chatted before. We'll exchange Lola horror stories."

"He'll be there," Lola says. "And most likely with some random date he found the night before."

"Whoa, you work with your ex?" I guess I'm the only one with the *don't shit where you eat* rule.

Lola massages her temples. "Unfortunately."

"Rookie mistake, Lola." I shake my head as if I were her coach and she just lost a game. "Rookie mistake."

She scowls at me. "Like you haven't slept with anyone you work with."

Just like she wants to dodge that event, I avoid that comment and don't answer.

I slide my elbows off the bar and stand straight. "I'll go with you. I'll be your date."

Lola blinks at me. "What?"

I'm as surprised as she is at my date offer. I'm not a man who meets coworkers, families, friends, any of that shit. It's not like I'd ever see them again, so it's pointless.

Georgia perks up in excitement as if she were five and it was Christmas. "That would stick it to Callum."

I snap my fingers, unsure of why I'm not telling them I was only kidding. "Awesome point."

Lola eyes me suspiciously.

My gaze doesn't leave hers. "I make for a great fake date, I promise."

"Is this something you've done before?" Lola clips a loose strand of hair behind her ear while eyeing me in uncertainty. "You seem pretty confident in yourself."

"I usually charge for my services"—I pause and fake bow—"but for you, I'll make an exception."

She stares at me deep as if attempting to read my mind. "You're crazy."

"Just offering my services. Take it or leave it. It's up to you." I smirk at her and walk away.

CHAPTER SIX

Lola

I'M CONSIDERING HAVING a man pretend to be my boyfriend.

What is wrong with me?

A responsible adult would suck it up and go solo, but I've never been a fan of my father's work events. And it's not that I can't get a date. I don't want one.

Dating apps, Snapchat, and website after website offering ninety-day trials to find your perfect match or your money back have made dating a nightmare. If Silas is comfortable with playing pretend boyfriend, why not? He's fun, and he won't try to date me afterward.

I nearly fell off my stool when he suggested the idea. After taming my shock, I pulled myself together and played it cool. In the back of my mind, I knew I'd take him up on his offer.

I pick up my phone to text him but remember what he told me.

Call. Don't text.

Giving me a taste of my own medicine.

It rings twice before a boasting voice answers, "Anger Management Hotline. How may I assist you today?"

I'm quiet for a moment, replaying the words in my mind.

"Hello?" the man says. "Is someone there, or are you in the process of sucker punching a guy, breaking a poor man's heart, or kicking puppies?"

I laugh. "Is that the best you've got?"

Props to Silas for attempting to alter his voice, but there's no erasing the cockiness that bleeds through it.

"What was that?" he asks, unfazed by my calling him out. "You need to schedule another appointment since you canceled your last one to attend your weekly visit to the underworld?"

"First off, I'd kick *you* before I ever kicked a puppy."

He breaks character, his tone returning to normal. "Good to know you'd protect an animal over me."

"You're not as cute. Sorry, not sorry."

"There you go, battering another heart."

"Keep talking shit, and I'll batter your balls next." I sit down on one of the overpriced leather dining room chairs I purchased with my first bonus check, rip off my strawberry yogurt lid, and shove a bite into my mouth.

"I take it you're calling to ask me out on an apology date? *Or* is this you requesting me to be your eye candy to your work event?"

I can imagine the smug expression on his face. "Eye candy? More like desperation candy. You're the Peeps of sweets."

"Keep telling yourself that, sweetheart. *And* Peeps is the number one–selling Easter candy, by the way."

"I'm not even going to waste my time fact-checking that because Peeps could grant immortality with just one taste, and I still wouldn't eat them." I'm mid-bite when something dawns on me. "Wait. How did you know I was calling? I never gave you my real number."

"Thank you for providing the reminder that you gave me some schmuck's number, who you kicked to the curb, instead of yours."

"You're welcome." I crack a smile before licking my spoon clean. "I figured you needed some entertainment."

"Cohen gave me your number."

I move the phone from one ear to the other. "That little shit."

"Technically, he's a half-shit. He only gave me the first three numbers and then told me it was my job to figure out the rest. When you called, the first three matched up, and I took a guess that it was you."

"What if it wasn't me?"

"I guess I'd have had to spend my day talking someone through an anger issue. I think I have a soothing voice. Don't you agree?"

"Nope. The cockiness triggers a migraine with me every time."

"You know what's good for migraines?"

"Not talking to you?"

"Orgasms." He emphasizes each syllable of that word. "That is an area of expertise I excel in. They used to call me Orgasm Rx."

I cover my face and hold in a laugh. "I'm seriously reconsidering this whole fake-date idea."

"When and where do I need to pick you up?" He clicks his tongue against the roof of his mouth. "Is there a certain route I need to take to the gateways of hell?"

"I think you mispronounced *heaven.*"

"And I think you mispronounced, *Thank you, Silas. I'm so happy you'll bless me with your time and presence.*"

I finish my yogurt, toss the empty container into the trash, and stroll into my living room. "Thank you, Silas. I'm writing an editorial the next day on what it's like to go out with a dude with an ego the size of the ocean. I appreciate you giving me plenty of material to work with."

"Aw." He chuckles. "My little number-changing rebel is writing a diary entry about me."

I scoff, "You wish."

"On the plus side, it'll give me another opportunity to talk to Callum. I have a list of things to ask him. The first being, how can I avoid dying when I'm around you?"

"That's it. I'm bailing."

"Nah, we have a hot date. Send me the details and your address, and I'll see you then. Catch you later, Princess of Darkness."

He ends the call.

What did I get myself into?

CHAPTER SEVEN

Silas

FAKING a relationship isn't a hobby of mine.

I've never done it.

I'm not sure how I got myself into this mess.

Lola.

That's how.

I'm not a relationship guy.

I tried it once, and it decayed the life I'd always known.

It ruined others' lives too.

All because I thought I knew what love was, thought I could pull off some *Romeo and Juliet* shit. Over the years, I've grown up and learned that love is merely an infatuation with someone you want. Sometimes, that infatuation can survive marriage, children, and the mundane of life. Others see love as a shiny, new toy, but then the desire slowly wears off. They cheat and fall out of love, and everyone around you suffers. Then it's off to the next obsession. Love is a fantasy that I want nothing to do with.

Lola and I are almost strangers, and I have no idea why the fake-date idea popped into my head. I allowed it to drop to my lips and spill from them. She'd pulled me into her web from the moment I overheard her and her fellow psychos talk about the demise of their ex-boyfriends.

GPS announces I've arrived at my location, and I park my car in front of the one-story townhome with a manicured lawn. The bright red door is fitting for the owner, but I expected a black home that looked straight out of a horror movie.

I hesitate before stepping out of my Audi, unsure if I should text her and say I'm here. Or if I should walk to the door, date-style ... even though today is sure as fuck not a date.

I enjoy out-of-the-box shit like this. Call it a field trip, if you will.

"Ah, fuck it," I grumble.

It's Lola I'm picking up. She won't assume it's a date if I go to her door. I'm also curious what the inside of her place looks like.

Waiting until a spandex shorts–wearing woman passes us with her petite, dressed-up dog, I head toward the front door, passing a black Porsche on the way up the drive. My knuckles meet the red paint on her door when I knock, and I take a step back, waiting for her to answer.

"Damn, you look hot," I say when the door swings open and Lola stands in front of me.

A black dress hugs her hourglass shape, and her black heels are the tallest I've seen her sport. She texted me last night to remind me of the dress code, so I pulled out the suit I'd worn only a few times from the back of my closet.

I step forward and walk in, not waiting for an invite.

"Come on in," she grumbles, moving to the side to allow me better access.

The open floor plan of her home provides me with a hint of Lola's life—the plush white couch that few would dare to have in their home, for fear of staining. Three red paintings hangon the living room wall. The place is so clean that it looks almost unlived in.

I slip my hands into the pockets of my black pants. "You ready to do this?"

She shoves her phone into her bag. "Nope."

"We can ditch and do something better?"

"I wish," she groans, her shoulders slumping. "My father would kill me."

"Father?" I cock my head. "I thought this was a work event?" Meeting the parents isn't what I expected tonight. If I'd known that was the case, I'd have called in sick to tonight's festivities. Acting like her boyfriend around her coworkers is one thing, but around her family? Nah, that produces more difficulty and effort. I'm great at pretending. I've done it nearly the past decade of my life, but it's not easy to act like you're dating a woman without doing the shit couples do—kiss, hold hands, look at each other with stars in your eyes. Lola would probably castrate me if I tried to kiss her.

"My father works at the company." She snatches her keys from the hook hanging on the wall.

"Works at the company … or *owns* the company?" I'm uncertain why this thought creeps into my mind. Maybe because there's no way an entry-level employee could afford this home and the car sitting in the driveway.

"Um … owns."

"What company?"

"It's 21st Amendment."

"The alcohol distribution company?"

"The one and only."

Impressive.

Anyone involved in the liquor business knows 21st Amendment is one of the best you can go with. They supply alcohol for the biggest clubs, liquor stores, and bars in the state.

"What do you do there?"

"Sales."

I smile, mentally picturing her showing off her products. Hell, if she came to Luna Bar and I oversaw orders, I'd purchase whatever she told me to.

She sighs. "You ready to play the lying game?"

"Definitely, but we need to get our stories straight on the way. It's necessary to know how evil my date is."

She holds up a finger. "Fake date."

"Fake date." I nod.

We leave her house, silently walking side by side, and her heels make a *click-click* against the pavement. She doesn't argue about me driving. The sweet smell of her perfume overtakes the evergreen air freshener hanging from my rearview mirror.

I plug the address into my GPS and hit her with questions as soon as I shift the car into drive. "Favorite food?"

Lola buckles her seat belt and relaxes into the seat. "This is a business party. Why do you need to know my favorite food?"

"What if I'm asked personal questions?" I tap my fingers along the steering wheel. "You want me to tell them I only fuck you on the regular but know nothing about you?"

She shrugs. "Sounds like a good plan to me."

"Cool." I turn at a light and merge with traffic. "I can't wait to tell your father that." I cast a quick glance at her, raising a brow. "Should I go into explicit detail ... try to sell him on the idea that I fuck your brains out?"

"Funny." She stretches out her legs and moves her head side to side as if stretching it too. "Um ... you can say hummus if you're asked?"

"Bullshit. No one's favorite food is fucking hummus. Try again, Satan. I'd have pictured your response to be more along the lines of *the broken hearts of men* or *the poisonous apple given to Adam.*"

She crosses her arms, unaware that it accentuates her cleavage, and I lick my lips. "I'll retract that statement and say it's your head if you keep talking shit because I'm going to bite it off."

"Kinky ... I like it."

She snorts. "If you say hummus, my father will believe you."

"If I say hummus, your father will never believe I've wined and dined you, making me a shit boyfriend. Now, hit me with something believable." I'm not about to pretend to be a bad boyfriend. I want to be the best damn fake boyfriend ever.

"Strawberry cheesecake."

"That's more like it."

"Glad my favorite food is now more to your liking." Her response bleeds sarcasm.

As much as I want to pay her a glance, I keep my eyes on the road. Responsible driver over here. "You going to ask what mine is?"

"Nope. I figured I'd make it up as we went."

"So ... if someone asks you that, what will you say?"

"Hummus," she quips with no delay.

"Oh, fuck off," I say around a laugh.

She returns the laugh while pulling a tube of lipstick from her Louis Vuitton bag. "You asked."

"All right, all right. Favorite sex position." I hope she doesn't shove my face into the steering wheel for that question, but messing with her is fun. A pretend boyfriend doesn't need to know that tidbit of information.

She doesn't shove my face into the steering wheel, but she does push my shoulder. "None of your business."

"Ah, that's my favorite too. It really hits the G-spot. Girls crave it."

Pulling down the visor, she refreshes her lipstick and smacks her lips together when she's finished. "You wouldn't know what a G-spot was if it smacked you in the face."

"Your type of man?"

"One who doesn't talk as much as you."

"Hey now." I reach out and tap her thigh. "Be nice to the guy doing you a favor. Otherwise, we can call Callum. You two can make up, and I'll drive home."

"Ugh, fine," she groans. "I will provide all the intel you need to my life. I'm just nervous to see him."

"You still have feelings for him?" I frown, hating the idea of that.

"No, I'm nervous because I want to kick him in the balls,

and my father would kill me for assaulting one of his employees." She sighs and stares straight ahead. "And for some reason, I want to know why he cheated."

She's nearing the line of vulnerability with me, and I don't want to run for the hills. I want to drag more of it out of her.

"He did it because he's a cheating bastard who can't keep it in his pants," I state matter-of-factly. "It had everything to do with him and nothing to do with you."

She sends me a skeptical glance. "How are you so certain?"

I grip the steering wheel. "Because any man in his right mind would be stupid to betray your trust, to play a dangerous game that'd leave him without you. Callum is an idiot. That's why he did what he did. Sometimes, it takes men losing something to realize they made a mistake."

She stares at me, impressed. "Look at you, all wise guy. Who would've thought you could come up with something like that?"

"That's why we're playing the *get to know you* game, Name Swapper. You'll find out I'm cool as hell and a better man than the one who played you."

"Shockingly, I'm starting to like this Silas you're giving me."

I grin at the compliment as if it were the equivalent of hitting the lottery. "Wait until I play the boyfriend role. You'll fucking love me."

———

VALET PARKING IS a bonus we don't talk about enough. Probably because it's always a lazy and unnecessary perk. You don't have to search for a spot or walk whatever distance to your destination.

A kid I went to school with argued with a man over a parking spot once. The fight escalated, and my classmate shot the man. He's now serving time for attempted murder. Not only did he lose his spot but his dinner reservation was also canceled.

He sacrificed freedom and a filet over a parking spot.

Fucking idiot.

I toss my keys to the valet and dash to Lola's side to beat the valet from opening her door. Tonight's job is to be the chivalrous and well-mannered boyfriend. She stands, running her hands down her dress, and I hold my elbow toward her. She peers at me in surprise before slipping her arm around it, and we walk into the century-old building.

Tonight's event is being held at Lady Emporium, a deserted library that the state had planned to tear down until a developer stepped in and purchased the rickety building. He remodeled, loaded cash into it, and now, people pay top dollar to hold their parties, weddings, and proms there.

I've bartended and attended events at Lady Emporium, but there's always something new to appreciate here. The high ceilings, crystal chandeliers dangling from them, and expensive marble beneath our feet. The ballroom is crowded with people, huddled in their little cliques, extending every age range.

No wonder Lola didn't want to come solo.

"Lola." A man stands in front of us, blocking our path, and eyes Lola with deep regret. He's tall, slender, and dressed in a stiff suit.

Lola clears her throat and tightens her elbow hold on me. "Callum."

Ah, so this is the lovely Callum.

Had she given it a few minutes before saying his name, I might've picked up on the familiarity of his voice.

His gaze cuts to me before snapping back to her—no doubt an attempt to act like I'm not a threat to him. *Act* being the key word. I know when a man is jealous of another. Even though I shouldn't be, I'm the same with Lola. I can only imagine how territorial I'd turn if we slept together, dated, and then I lost her.

His lips tighten. "We need to talk."

"Hard pass," Lola replies.

"Come on." He presses his hands into a pleading gesture. "You owe me that."

I arch a brow and hold back the urge to tell him she doesn't owe him shit. But I know Lola, and she has a spine as strong as a diamond. The revenge stories I've heard from her prove she won't need any help with putting Callum in his place.

"I don't owe you a goddamn thing." Her voice is powerful and firm as if she were presenting a million-dollar deal. "You lost the right to talk to me when you cheated."

"Please," he begs. "Let me explain."

"No," is her only response.

His eyes widen at the realization she won't fall into the trap of his ways, so he turns his attention my way. "I see you've already replaced me, huh? You didn't seem like the type who'd automatically jump into another man's bed."

And as strong as Lola is, now's my time to step in.

"Whoa," I say, breaking our connection to pull Lola slightly behind me. "Don't talk to her like that."

He's not helping me be the perfect fake boyfriend. If we end up fighting within five minutes of arriving, that'd be the ultimate fail.

Callum thrusts out his chest so hard that it's almost comical. "Or what?"

Lola was smart for leaving this idiot. She's just as smart when she cups my elbow and tugs me back from stepping toward Callum.

"He's wasted," Lola says, "if you can't tell by the smell of his breath. Ignore him, and we'll move on to speaking to someone who isn't an asshole."

"If you don't want to talk here, can we do it another time?" Callum asks, shooting a woman a dirty look when she runs into his shoulder. "We can do coffee, dinner, whatever you want." Desperation fills his voice and face, but I don't feel sorry for him. He chose to cheat and end their relationship.

Lola peers away from him as if she's lost all interest she ever had. "I'm good."

"Why do you give my number to random guys then?" He scrubs his hand over his reddened face. "It's further proof you miss me."

"Or I'm just a spiteful bitch." Lola raises a brow, not even caring that she just referred to herself as a bitch. She takes my hand. "I need to go find my father ... you know, *your boss*. He could easily create an excuse to fire you if you kept talking like this to his daughter."

"That's some bullshit," Callum grumbles.

"Don't worry. I won't say anything as long as you leave me alone." Lola turns away, so she's no longer facing him and he's talking to her side. "We're broken up. I'll stop giving your number out. It's over."

"I'll see you around, babe." His voice wavers with the last word.

Lola cracks a smile. "Not if I can help it."

I smirk, jerking my chin up at Callum as we pass him, and squeeze Lola's hand. I ignore people as we make our way through the crowd. "I'm surprised he didn't fire Callum when you broke up."

"He never knew we were dating. I kept it a secret." She comes to a halt. "And you're about to meet the boss."

"How did we meet?" I rush out, realizing we didn't discuss the important details on the drive here.

"Make up something off the top of your head, and I'll agree." She shoots me a quick look. "Don't make it something sexual."

"In front of your father? Gross."

We haven't even reached the ten-minute mark, and I've already met the ex and now the father. I wasn't prepared to be bombarded like this straight from the get-go. Hell, I didn't even know that her father would be present until she told me when I picked her up, and I couldn't bail then.

The man walks with wide steps and approaches us with ease. Lola stands tall, matching his posture, and I understand where she got her perfect one from.

"Lola," he says, a gleam in his eyes when he reaches us.

She breaks away from me to hug him and kiss his cheek.

"You look nice, honey," he says when they part, and then his gaze flashes to me. "And who is this?"

"This is …" Lola pauses, searching for the correct way to label us.

"Her date," I answer for her, holding out my hand.

He shakes it, his grip strong. "Robert Delgado II."

"Silas Malone. It's nice to meet you, sir."

Lola raises a brow at my saying *sir*.

He smiles. "This is the first time Lola has brought a date. You must be special to her."

"Yes, sir. I think she's falling in love." I cringe when Lola's heel meets my shin.

Robert chuckles at her response. "Come on. We have an incredible lineup of spirits tonight. We'll have a drink and get to know each other."

It takes all my strength not to tell them I have an emergency and need to leave. Since I don't want to embarrass Lola, I push forward and follow them, maneuvering around people holding loud conversations while sipping on champagne and cocktails. Compliments and hellos are thrown to Robert every few minutes.

Robert stops at a four-person table, and just as I pull Lola's chair out for her, a blond woman around Lola's age joins us.

"Hey, honey." Her tone is full of pep—the kind they always give the preppy girls in movies. She runs her hand along Robert's shoulder and then down his arm before enveloping his hand. "I thought you ran off on me."

Robert smacks a kiss to her cheek. "Of course not, baby."

Lola's eyes harden in their direction as she settles into her seat. I run my hand along her shoulder—like what Blondie did to Robert, only not as desperate.

"Hey, Lola," Blondie says in almost a squeal. Her eyes widen when she sees me taking the chair next to Lola. "Who's your friend?"

I wave. "I'm Silas."

The woman presses her hand to her deep cleavage. "I'm Kelli, Robert's girlfriend."

Robert stands proud at the statement—no doubt loving having an attractive and young woman at his side.

Lola settles her elbow onto the table, turns her head, and covers her mouth as if holding words in.

I smile, making sure it's not overly friendly so Lola doesn't kick my ass for it later. "It's nice to meet you." I'd look like a straight prick in front of Robert if I reacted how Lola was and didn't say a word to her.

"You too," Kelli says as Robert pulls out her chair, and they sit.

Robert rubs his hands together. "I have a rare whiskey coming our way."

As if on cue, a server stops at our table with a tray of drinks in crystal glasses. She carefully starts placing the glasses in front of us.

"I'll just have a water," I say, stopping her when she comes to me.

Her gaze pings from me to Robert, clueless on what to do.

Robert shakes his head. "Have one drink with us. I promise it'll be worth it." He holds up his glass. "This is five hundred a bottle."

"I'm driving tonight, and I want to make sure your daughter gets home safe."

I smile at him. If Robert argues, it'll make him look like an asshole now. I used to dread this part when I went out. People would stare at me in shock and throw out question after question about why I didn't drink. I'm a bartender, a regular at clubs, and I fit the image of a party guy.

"It's a relief you worry about my daughter's safety," Robert says, smiling before his eyes meet Lola's. "I like him. How long have you two been dating?"

CHAPTER EIGHT

Lola

THERE ARE two reasons I don't bring men around my father:

I haven't had a boyfriend serious enough for him to meet.

He works too much and has hardly been around since my mother divorced him.

Shock accompanied my father's arrival when he saw Silas. He and my mother have been bringing up marriage more lately as if trying to find out where my future is headed. Now that my father assumes I have a boyfriend, he'll ask about Silas, so I'll have to create a breakup story.

I shift in my seat. "Not long."

"Yeah," Silas says with a nod.

"I'll be back with your water," the server tells Silas.

The night is full of conversation with no quiet gaps at our table. I don't say much, but my father says plenty. Kelli throws in remarks here and there, a smile on her injection-filled lips. I tend to tolerate my father's women, but I'm not a Kelli fan. She mistakenly talked shit about my mother in front of me, and we haven't gotten along since. It's not like she'll last long anyway.

Everyone at the table stared at Silas, dazed, when he declined the whiskey. I had grown up around liquor, and I can taste quality with one sip. Any other bartender would never turn down a whiskey like this. Some would consider it a once-in-a-lifetime opportunity because it's not something you can buy in stores. You have to know someone who knows someone to get it. I'm thankful that Silas keeps my father entertained with conversation so I don't have to do the job. The smartest thing I did tonight was have him come.

———

"HOW DID I DO TONIGHT, Name Swapper?" Silas asks as we pull out of Lady Emporium's parking lot.

An overplayed song drones in the background of the car. It's after ten o'clock. Later than I wanted to stay and earlier than my father wanted me to leave.

I stretch out my legs and yawn. "Surprisingly, you did a great job. You might want to take up a career in fake dating."

If I were to ever bring a real boyfriend around my father, I'd hope his and Silas's mannerisms and behavior were similar. By the end of the night, my father loved him, the coworkers he introduced Silas to found it easy to chat with him, and Kelli eyed him as if ready to seduce him the moment my father kicked her to the curb.

When I'd answered my door at the beginning of the night, I had been impressed at the view of him standing there. I'd told him to dress somewhat formal, and he had taken my direction seriously. His black suit fit as if God had approved every stitch to its perfection.

"Nah, it's too stressful." He stops at a red light and places his hand over his heart. "I try to live an honest man's life, Lola."

"That's nice to know," I say around another yawn.

We make small talk on the drive back to my house. He asks what it's like, working at 21st Amendment, and I drill him on bartending life.

"Are you not a drinker?" I ask.

He sighs as if this is a regular conversation for him. "Nope."

"If you don't mind me asking, why?"

Saying *if you don't mind me asking* is stupid. I already asked him if he was a drinker. That pretty much is the opening to asking questions. Since I'm a private person, I don't usually dive into people's personal business.

His attention stays on the road. "It's not my thing."

"But you're a bartender," I state like *duh*. "No wonder people say your drinks suck."

That was actually a rumor I made up that night at the bar. Cohen had mentioned Silas was one of the top bartenders at Luna Bar. I just enjoy giving him a hard time about it.

"You, of all people, should know my drinks don't suck." He hits the blinker and turns onto my road. "Drinking is not required of bartenders. We just need to know what mixes well together." He stops in front of my house, shifts the car into park, and unbuckles his seat belt. "I'll walk you in."

I clamp my mouth shut. Even though I want to ask twenty more questions, I can tell he doesn't want to talk about it any longer. I wouldn't want someone I'd only met a few times—fake date or not—to intrude on my life like that.

I dart my arm out, stopping him from opening his door. "You don't have to do that. Tonight wasn't a real date."

He takes my hand, squeezes it, and returns it to my lap. "This fake date is a gentleman, so I'm walking you up. I won't try to make out with you—even if you asked me. You, my favorite devil, are no longer a woman I want to sleep with."

I suck in a breath of rejection and fidget with the chain of my purse. "What do you want to do with me then?"

Why does him saying he no longer wants to sleep with me have my heart thudding dully in my chest?

My stomach clenches as nausea hits me.

"A friend," he clearly states, opening his door. "I want us to be friends." He stops and peers back at me. "I'd love for you to want that too."

"Of course." I force a smile, my eyes meeting his friendly ones. "Friends."

He walks me to my door, and before he leaves, I give him a little wave.

And that short conversation cements my relationship with Silas.

My *friendship* with him.

RELEASING A DEEP SIGH, I rest my back against the door and drop my purse onto the floor when I walk into my townhome.

I flip on a light and then press my hand to the wall, balancing myself to remove one strappy heel and then the other. Though it's unusual for me to leave stuff around my home—I'm a type A—I step over them and trudge down the hallway toward my bedroom.

I bought the open-concept townhome a year ago. My parents provided the down payment after I graduated from college, but I'm responsible for everything else. The fluffy white carpet feels comforting against my bare feet as I move through the room. The interior is nearly monochrome—mainly black and white with pops of color spread along the home. There's also a lack of patterns—all the pillows, furniture, and décor stick to solid colors.

It's a one-bedroom—what my parents told Robby and me they'd provide each of us until we needed something larger. I think it was their plan to prevent us from having roommates. My father has made it clear that he only sees them as distractions —even though the man apparently doesn't consider throwing events and sipping on expensive alcohol with his flavor of the month isn't.

I step out of my dress when I land in my bedroom and am slipping on a lace teddy when Georgia calls.

"How was the big date?" she asks as soon as I answer.

"It was *not* a date," I reply, pulling down the comforter and fluffing out my pillow.

"Fine. How was your *fake* date?"

"It was fun."

"Is he there with you now?"

"Um, no. Home all alone."

Unfortunately.

Had Silas not made the whole *I want us to be friends* speech, there was a possibility I'd have asked him to come in. Not even for sex, just to hang out for a while longer.

"Did he try to come in for a nightcap?"

"Surprisingly, no." I head toward the bathroom to brush my teeth and do my eighteen-step skincare routine. "He said he no longer wants to sleep with me and instead wants to be my friend."

"Hmm ..." She pauses, thinking. "He'd be a nice addition to our friend group. I like him, and Cohen seems to think he's a good guy."

I shrug. "Fine with me."

"Grace has Finn. You'll have Silas. It's time for me to find myself a guy bestie."

"You have your brother."

"Eh, so not the same." She goes quiet for a moment, and her voice lowers. "Noah, buddy, I told you, it's past your bedtime." She sighs. "I have to figure out a way to bribe the kid back to bed. Call me tomorrow, okay? We can do lunch and chat. Love ya."

"Love you too." I end the call after hearing her tell Noah he can have a candy bar if he promises not to tell his dad.

A half hour later, I'm back in my bedroom and plugging my phone into the charger. As I slip into the chilly sheets, my phone beeps with a text.

Silas: I enjoyed our fake date. Good night, my little devil.

Smiling wide, I immediately reply.

Me: Thank you for coming, my little fake date.

His response is just as quick.

Silas: I'd prefer a better nickname than that boring-ass one.

Me: MINE IS THE DEVIL!

Silas: Devil suits you. Fake Date isn't flattering enough for me. We're going to be so much more than that. Brainstorm tonight and let me know in the morning. I just wanted to say good night.

Me: Good night ... my soon-to-be nicknamed friend.

Silas: *kissy face emoji*

This is something unexpected.

I didn't think this would happen.

When I got ready for the event tonight, I thought it could go one of three ways.

1. Silas wouldn't show.
2. It'd end up in disaster.
3. He'd try to sleep with me at the end of the night.

None of those happened.

Instead, it only turned into so much more.

It made me want to know more about this man, give him more of me, and have a few more *fake* dates.

I slap a hand over my forehead.

This man might ruin my hard-ass persona I have going on here.

He also might ruin me.

CHAPTER NINE

Silas

Two Years Later

"HEY THERE, BIG SHOT," Lola shouts over the music, pressing her lips to my cheek and stopping at my table. "This place is packed."

I grin, pride beaming through me, and kiss the top of her hair. "The turnout is amazing."

Wrapping my arms around her, I squeeze her side. She's my biggest cheerleader and the support system I never knew I needed. The night we met forever changed my life for the better, and I can't imagine not having her around. It'd be a boring and depressed life without Lola.

Cohen finally got his dream—owning a bar. He and Archer, a guy who worked with us, partnered up to start Twisted Fox—a small-town bar in Anchor Ridge, Iowa. He worked his ass off to get the place ready. The girls helped with the design and decorating. I volunteered to kick off the place with a night to be remembered grand opening.

I enjoy bartending, but I love throwing events more. I told the guys I'd bartend part-time at Twisted Fox, so I could be involved with everyone. They immediately offered Finn the bouncer position, and he gladly accepted.

Twisted Fox might be smaller than what I'm used to, but I put in more work with the opening than I have with large clubs with thousands of partygoers. I have *friends in high places* connections, and it's easy for me to ask influencers to post where they're hanging out for the night. They post, and the people will follow, hoping for their chance to see the influencers and to also hang out where *the cool people* do. Social media is the key to marketing these days.

What was once an old diner has been remodeled. There's a large bar, TVs on every wall, and sports memorabilia Cohen picked up on the days he went to the flea market. It's something he and Noah like to do together.

Lola squeezes my arm. "I'm going to go tell the guys congrats. This is so exciting!"

I raise a brow. "Don't act like you didn't play a large part."

She spent hours and sleepless nights with Grace and Georgia here. That's something I've loved since I slid into being in this group of friends. They are die-hard ride or dies. If you need something, they're there. If someone needs help, they'll spend every minute doing it. It's an entire network of people who you know will always have your back.

"Dude, is that your girlfriend?" Eric, a guy recently drafted into the NBA, asks. His question is directed toward me, but his eyes are on Lola as she makes her way through the crowd, swinging her hips with every step.

"Nah," I reply, shaking my head. "Best friend."

Eric's teammate shakes his head. "How can you be best friends with someone that hot and not want more?"

It's a frequent question sent my way. Lola is gorgeous—exactly what drew me to her. And the more we become friends, the more beautiful she gets to me. Even if she doesn't try, eyes follow her in desire everywhere we go. Just like I made sure the bar's opening was perfect, Lola made sure she looked fucking perfect to celebrate it.

A short dress that flares out at her thighs shows off her toned tan legs. Her black hair is down but clipped back on each side, keeping it out of her eyes.

I rub my chin. "I don't date."

"Not even *her*?" Eric asks, gripping his beer bottle around the neck. "Man, I say that, too, but I'd break that rule in a heartbeat for her."

"If I dated her, I'd fuck it up and lose her." I scrub a hand over my face, the reality of that smacking into me. It's something I remind myself of every day.

Even though I get along with everyone in the group, Lola is my person. We click. We're there for each other anytime it's needed—whether it's taking care of the other when one of us has the flu, being the first one in line when the other has reached a new life achievement, or just having someone at our side. She's the first person I call anytime I have good news.

Always.

That's why Lola is my best friend, and we can never be anything more.

———

"YOU DID IT, GUYS," I say around a yawn.

It's been a successful night. The Twisted Fox grand opening went great. We fucking killed it, and with Cohen and Archer running it, I know the bar will be successful. Everyone is gone, and for the past hour, we've said we need to get the place cleaned up and then go home to get some sleep. But instead, we've been sitting here, bullshitting and having our own private celebration for our friends' achievement.

Cohen has always been the patriarch of our friend group, and Archer recently joined us. Although I don't think it's something he'd planned on doing. He's a loner—prime example:

he's behind the bar, doing shit, while we've all been sitting around, talking. The past few months he's worked with us, opening the bar, he and Georgia have bickered like two kids on the playground. Archer is a man who doesn't say much, but most of his words are talking shit to her.

No one knows why they hate each other—well, none of us guys. The girls act like they do, and while Lola and I are close, she refuses to gossip about her friends.

"*We* did it," Cohen corrects. "Twisted Fox wouldn't be here if it wasn't for everyone's help. I appreciate it so much."

Finn smirks, holding up his beer. "Does that mean free alcohol for life?"

"No," Archer grunts. "You can have an employee discount on food, though."

"Always the rude one," Georgia comments, shaking her head.

He shoots her a deep glare, and she shrugs.

Lola leans into me, resting her head on my shoulder. "I love the entertainment they provide."

I slide my fingers through her thick locks. "I have a feeling we're going to get so much more of it too."

"We're a team," Grace says, perched up in her stool. "A family. We'll always have each other's backs."

CHAPTER TEN

Lola

THINGS I'LL DO before getting in another relationship:

Chew leather.

Fight a cobra, blindfolded.

Swallow a dozen wasps.

I slump onto my couch and tug my phone from my jacket pocket. Just as I'm about to text the girls *Code Red*, I stop, remembering they have plans tonight. Georgia has a shift at the boutique, and Grace is at dinner with her parents.

Silas invited me to dinner with him tonight, but I stupidly declined because I had a date. A ridiculous date where the guy took me to a dinner with his friends … and his ex. His ex was a nightmare, making comments and giving me the stink eye all night. I'm almost positive I caught her friend confiscating her knife, so she didn't do anything stupid. After she called me a dumb whore and the guy not standing up for me, I booked an Uber and hightailed it out of there. It wasn't a night for a stabbing.

Maybe tomorrow, after I've had a little more vodka.

Or if I could be the one doing the stabbing.

The guy didn't attempt to stop me from leaving.

One of his friends did follow me out and apologized, asking me to come back in.

Like that was going to happen.

So, now, I'm home, unstabbed and annoyed.

That's the last time I find a guy on a dating app. I'd steered clear of them for so long, but a coworker found the love of her life on one, so I thought, *Why not?*

To make my shitty night better, I grab my phone and text Silas.

Me: May Day! May Day! Root beer floats, stat.

My *May Day* texts are always different. Sometimes, it's root beer floats or tacos, milkshakes, sushi, pizza—whatever my frustrated heart desires.

My phone rings.

"Fucking May Day *again?*" Silas asks, yelling over the loud noise in his background.

"Yep." I sigh. "Again." Another sigh—this one more dramatic.

"Fine, I guess I'll bail on this orgy I was about to have so you can hang out with a *real* man."

"I'm slapping you in the face for lying about participating in an orgy when I'm sure you're at Twisted Fox with the guys. And as for the *real man* comment, only guys with small cocks refer to themselves that way."

He chuckles. "I'm looking forward to it. Let me kick all these people out of my bed. Be there in fifteen." He doesn't hang up fast enough for me not to overhear him telling the guys he has to go.

While waiting for Silas, I change into sweats and one of his tees that I stole from him during a trip a few months ago. He keeps asking for it back, but he should know once I confiscate an item of clothing from him, it belongs to me.

Possession is nine-tenths of the law, people.

Right on time, there's a knock on my door, and Silas walks in with a grocery bag, the handles tangled around his wrist.

I eyeball him, my lips curling into a smile, and gesture to his clothing. "You really look like a man who was about to orgy it on." I step closer and slap his stomach.

"Jesus," he hisses, his knees buckling, but he quickly steadies himself. "The fuck was that for?"

I play with the door handle. "I told you I was slapping you."

"I thought you were only shit-talking," he mutters before lifting his arms. "I've got the goods ... and the goods will be on the floor in a minute if you don't move your sexy ass out of the way."

I step back, allowing him to slide between me and the doorway, and we make a beeline toward the kitchen. His sneakers squeak with each step he takes across the bamboo flooring. Settling the bags on the counter, he pulls out a tub of vanilla ice cream and a two-liter of root beer. I open a cabinet, pluck two glasses, and place them next to him.

"Tell Silas what happened," he says, dragging the ice cream lid off the container.

"Ugh," I say while gathering two spoons and the scooper.

"Was it better or worse than the guy who invited you over, stocked his fridge full of food, and then told you to make him dinner?" He scoops out perfect ice cream globes and drops them into the glasses.

"Oh my God, I totally forgot about that little prick." I grip the two-liter, twist open the lid, and pour it over the ice cream, watching the bubbles dance at the top of our glasses. "I texted you to have bail money handy in case I poisoned the food I didn't end up making."

"Didn't he say he did it because he wanted to see how you'd be as a housewife?"

I nod. "And I told him I'd be a black widow."

"You have to give the guy some credit, though." He tosses the scooper into the sink and pushes the ice cream into the freezer. "That took some balls."

"Balls I was close to cutting off and frying in a skillet for his dinner."

"Balls are balls, baby doll."

With our glasses in our hands, we migrate to my living room, popping a squat on the couch. I dunk my spoon into my glass, scoop up ice cream and root beer, and shove it into my mouth.

"Mmm," I moan into my spoon.

"Are you ever going to tell me why you keep going out with these assholes?" he asks, settling back against a pillow. "You don't even like to date."

"Are you ever going to tell me why you don't drink?"

I inhale a short gasp, dropping my spoon into the glass, and it's as if everything stops. Looking away from him, I direct my gaze to my lap. Those words weren't supposed to tumble from my lips. They were supposed to remain suppressed in my mind and never be released in the open around him.

I haven't mentioned Silas's sobriety like that since our fake date years ago. At first, I was concerned he had a problem, but as time passed, I've learned that's not the case. Silas is private about his sobriety for a reason, and it'd be selfish of me to pester him for what that reason is. Some people want to conceal why they make the decisions they do, and I respect that.

I hope he'll tell me one day, but I don't push him.

Our friends also asked, and like me, after he blew us off the first time, they retreated. We might be nosy, but we're also respectful toward each other—except for Archer and Georgia.

That's why my brain is processing how I managed to allow myself to go there tonight. I had *one* vodka tonic at dinner, so it wasn't a drunken question.

Silas clears his throat, and I tilt my head up, staring at him with apologetic eyes.

"It's not my thing," he replies, scratching his shoulder with the handle of his clean spoon. He hasn't dipped into his float yet. "I like to be in control ... something you can't do when you're drunk." His words are restrained as he recites his answer like a prepared speech.

"Have you ever been drunk before?" I ask, putting my foot in my mouth again. My throat tickles as I wait for him to either tell me or change the subject.

His Adam's apple bobs. "Yes."

"So, what changed?" I've already opened the can, so might as well see how much I can yank out. "Did you have a bad experience? Piss yourself in front of the popular girls?" A forced laugh rolls up my throat.

He eyes me suspiciously. "I grew up. Decided it wasn't for me."

"But being around drunk people is?"

"We want what we can't have." He winces—a sign he didn't mean to tell me that. Shock flashes across his face like a burn.

"Can't have?"

He repeatedly shakes his head, his shoulders tightening. "I didn't mean it like that." Shoving his spoon into the float, he moves it around, the sound familiar to someone stirring their morning coffee. "Tell me about how your date went wrong." He squeezes his eyes shut and continues to play with his drink.

"It was awkward," I reply, that same sense returning. "He invited me to a dinner for his friend's birthday but never warned me that I'd be meeting his friends twenty minutes after meeting him."

Silas loosens his shoulders, and his body begins to relax. "Sounds bad but not terrible. Were his friends weird?"

"His friends were nice, but his ex, not so much."

"He brought his ex?"

"He didn't *bring* her, but they have the same circle of friends. He knew she'd be there and still invited me. Probably thinking it'd make her jealous."

He settles his glass on a coaster on the coffee table, the ice cream melting. "You need to stop dating losers. None of them are worthy of you."

A weight forms in my chest—a heavy burden of the truth that I love when my best friend says stuff like that to me when he shouldn't. When it only complicates things further.

Silas and I joke around about dating other people, but we never go into deep details, and we most definitely don't discuss hooking up with anyone else. We're human, and just because we can't form an emotional connection with someone doesn't mean we don't want intimacy—even if only for a night. I don't expect Silas to keep his dick in his pants since we're only friends, just like he doesn't expect me to keep my vagina under lock and key.

I scoot closer to him, afraid my question changed tonight. He's acting—*faking*—like he's the same Silas, but his muscles are tight, and he's looking everywhere but at me. I need to rewind to where I didn't slide into a territory I had known I shouldn't.

"One of these days, I'm going to find me a normal guy who takes me on normal dates," I say, forcing some pep in my tone.

His gaze slowly returns to me. "Doubt it."

"I'd better."

"Why?"

"I'd prefer not to be alone for the rest of my life, thank you."

"You'll have me."

"I don't want to be *romantically* alone, so unless you plan on marrying and screwing me for the rest of your life, then I still need someone."

We're falling back into the old Lola and Silas, and that brief awkwardness is dissolving.

"You want to get married someday? I thought you hated marriage?"

"I don't *hate it* … I just have a hard time believing in it."

"Because of your father?"

I nod and shove another bite into my mouth. He knows about my father's infidelities, just as I know about his mother's. We've confided in each other that it's hard to believe in people and relationships after we've seen the ones closest to us become toxic.

"Damn Robert Delgado," he mutters with a chuckle. "Always fucking everything up."

I lick my spoon clean and point at him with it. "Uh-oh, you'd better not let him hear you say that. He loves you."

Silas has attended countless work events with me since our fake date. We told my father we decided we were better as friends. He was skeptical at first, but with how many years have passed, he finally believes us. Or at least, he says he does, but he still mentions Silas anytime I tell someone I'm single.

I set my glass to the side, shift, and face him, crossing my legs. "Would we change if I got into a serious relationship?"

Anxiety swirls through me at the question—at the thought of losing him.

He grimaces, his back straightening. "I hope not but probably. All I ever want is for you to be happy, Lola. If you get into a relationship, as much as I'd hate for that to happen, we'll adjust and stay friends."

"You know, some guys wouldn't be comfortable with their girlfriend having a guy best friend."

"Then I'd hope you'd kick them to the curb because I'd pick you over a woman any day. If they couldn't accept our friendship, which is a large part of my life, that's not accepting me. You're too special for me to lose."

"You think you'll ever find someone you'll eventually want to be with?"

He draws in a deep breath, and his dark brows furrow. "Even if I did, I don't know if I could open myself up to them like they'd want. I don't have enough heart to give someone a chunk of it. Nor do I think I have enough hands to accept someone giving me theirs. I don't think I'd be as careful with it as I should."

Silas's relationship logic is hard to understand because he's such a good man.

Any girl would be lucky to have him, so why does he think he'd be better off alone?

I haven't seen him toy with women's emotions or promise them something he couldn't provide.

There are two explanations of why someone fears love:

1. They've witnessed heartbreak from others.
2. They've experienced heartbreak themselves.

My tone is hesitant, the words nearly choked out, when I ask, "Have you ever been in love?"

He flinches, staring at me uneasily. "What?"

"Have you ever been in love?" I repeat. "Do you hate it because it's something you've experienced that didn't work out?"

"Love is for fools, Lola," he replies with a huff.

"All right, were *you* one of those fools who fell in love?"

He blows out a long breath. "Once ... I thought I was."

My mouth falls open, a knot forming in my stomach.

Years of friendship, and we've never ventured into this talk before.

"Who was the girl?" I rush out, wanting to get every piece of him he's willing to give before he returns to hiding his secrets.

I also already hate the girl before he's even given me details. She made Silas resentful of love, and from the change in his demeanor at my question, whatever happened really affected him.

He looks away from me, peering straight ahead to nothing. "That's not important."

"Oh, come on. We're best friends." I slap his leg—an attempt to appear playful, but it only creates more tension.

He stares at me with vulnerable eyes, but I can see he's trying to fight it. "It was in high school. It wasn't a big deal."

I jump when he suddenly reaches forward and snatches the remote from the table. His action causes our glasses to shake, and one of them nearly falls off the coaster. He snags it before my white rug is stained and levels it, giving it a second to make sure it's staying.

He flips on the TV. "I'm not talking about this."

This is the first time Silas has acted like this.

To where I've seen something that affects him this deeply.

There was once a time when this man who doesn't believe in love found love.

And whatever he experienced ruined him for anyone in his future ... even me.

CHAPTER ELEVEN

Silas

LOLA'S QUESTIONS haunt me on my drive home.

Have I ever been in love?

It's a question I can't answer because I don't know.

Years ago, I thought I was, but what did I know at eighteen? I still had a curfew, was applying to colleges, and was a disrespectful prick.

How did I know what love was when I didn't even know who I was yet?

Even if it was what people call *real love*, I don't deserve to have it now.

I'm not a man for love.

I'm a man who destroys the faith you ever had in it.

That's why I don't take it … don't ask for it … don't want it.

A woman's heart is safer in the hands of someone else.

It was a dagger to the heart as I listened to Lola talk about eventually getting married. The cut was deep, and it hurt, but it's what's best for her. I wouldn't wish a lonely, miserable life on anyone, although I dread the day that comes. Whoever that someone is won't deserve her.

My feelings toward Lola confuse the shit out of me. She's my best friend, but sometimes, my selfish heart craves more.

Sometimes, when I look at her, my mind wanders—a mental torture of trying out love again with her—but I fight those feelings.

It's not right for us.

It'd taint our friendship, our lives, and hell, everyone around us too.

No disrespect, but fuck love.

Fuck love for ruining my life and locking my heart up in a steel cage.

And fuck situations where you end up wanting more with your best friend.

But just like I've stayed away from liquor, I'm strong-willed, and I have the power not to let anything go further with Lola. We will always be friends—nothing more.

I'm a good actor. It's easy to be the fun guy who throws parties and lives life to the fullest. I'm so fucking fake.

I don't have a life to live to the fullest.

I don't deserve it.

I don't deserve to get wasted, to drink with my friends, to feel the high of liquor.

I don't deserve a lifetime of happiness ... and that's why I'll never get it.

I GROAN when I see my father's name flash across the phone screen. It's a jackass move, but we don't always see eye to eye.

"Hello?" I answer.

"You sound like you just woke up," he says, his voice loud.

"I work nights."

"You didn't RSVP to Janet's birthday party."

Janet was my father's mistress. During my senior year of high school, he left my mother to be with her. My mother, embarrassed by my father's actions, left town to stay with her family in Colorado. I didn't want to leave my senior year of school, so I stayed with my father. A month later, he married Janet, and she moved into our home with her son, Trent.

I move my phone from one ear to the other. "Will Trent be there?"

I hated Trent from the first time my father introduced us, and the hatred grew worse when he transferred to my high school. I've let go of my resentment toward Janet, but that'll never happen with Trent. Months after he moved in, he did something unspeakable. That grudge will always be there.

He hesitates before answering, "Yes." His tone tells me he briefly considered lying.

"Then no." Unlike him, I don't hesitate.

"Silas. It's been *years*. Don't you think it's time to move on?"

I grit my teeth, hating that he was brought up this early in my day. He's like a thunderstorm during a special event—no matter what, he ruins the entire thing.

"Time doesn't erase what happened." I clear my throat, shutting my eyes, hoping the memories don't pop through. "It won't fix what he did."

His voice deepens. "He's your brother."

"Stepbrother. There's no shared blood. Even if there were, it wouldn't make a difference."

"What am I supposed to do then? Tell Janet you can't come because you're still upset with her son?"

"Upset?" I force my words through clenched teeth. "He didn't steal the last Oreo from the pantry, Dad. He ruined not only my life but others' lives too. I'm not just upset with him. I despise him."

"That's not true, nor is it fair to pin that on him. You were all teenagers."

"We were old enough to know better."

"It seems we need to make separate plans." He pauses and releases a deep breath. "Again."

"Sorry," I grumble.

"If you were sorry, you'd stop holding this grudge."

"I'm sorry that you and Janet are stuck in the middle of this. I'm *not* sorry for never wanting to see the asshole again."

There's a moment of silence. This is a regular conversation between us. It's hard for him and Janet to deal with having children who can't stand each other. But that's Trent's fault, not mine. Regardless, I'd never tell anyone to choose sides. All I ask is for her to celebrate shit with us separately and keep that bastard away from me.

You know that saying, Your life can change at any moment?

My life is proof of that.

A proven tale that it's the truth.

In the span of ten minutes, everything I thought was pure in my life was taken from me.

In such a short time, I lost my life and myself.

CHAPTER TWELVE

Silas

High School—Senior Year

I'D NEVER SEEN a dead person before.

And quite frankly, I wish that were still the truth.

I could've gone my entire life without witnessing it—the splatters of blood, the smoke mixing with the darkness of the night, and the car alarm screaming as if it were signaling for help on its own.

I gulp, my breathing ragged, my hands shaking, as I stare down at them. My head spins as I attempt to calm it down, unsure of what to do, as sirens blare in the distance. They grow louder and louder, closer and closer, as my heart rams against my rib cage, as if it wanted to burst out and observe the scene itself.

Soon, others will join me.

They'll survey the scene as the alarm rings through their ears.

Will they blame it on me?

Will they slap handcuffs around my wrists and say what a rotten bastard I am?

Or will people feel sorry for me, but I'll still live with the guilt for the rest of my life?

My body throbs, and as much as I want to act tough, sobs break through my façade.

Police cars, a fire truck, and an ambulance swerve around me, circling me in and giving me no chance to escape even if I wanted to. But they ignore me, one firefighter pushing me down onto the pavement as he rushes toward the burning car. They ignore my Camaro, still running but in park with the driver's door thrown open.

"I'm sorry," I whisper, not having the strength to pull myself to my feet. "I'm so fucking sorry."

Pain and guilt tighten around my neck like a noose.

Some will say it's my fault, but was it?

I didn't hit their car.

I was only on the road, speeding around the turns, to stop them.

To protect them.

But I failed.

CHAPTER THIRTEEN

Lola

"HOW LONG HAVE you known about them?" Silas asks, giving me the stink eye.

We're sitting in Cohen's backyard, the sun setting in front of us. Today was Cohen and his girlfriend, Jamie's, gender reveal party. And boy, was it eventful.

They found out they were having a baby girl. *Yay!*

Then Cohen discovered Archer and Georgia had slept together. *Not yay!*

It was once, years ago, before they knew who each other was, but they'd kept it from him—for understandable reasons. They'd been doing a great job of hiding it until Georgia started flirting with Archer's brother, Lincoln, and all hell broke loose. What was supposed to be a friendly little party has turned into a shit show.

Good times.

Never a dull moment in this circle of friends.

Grace and I were the only ones who knew about them sleeping together, and it was supposed to stay that way. Silas endlessly questioned me on why they hated each other, but I always acted clueless. I love the guy, but I would never break Georgia's trust.

But maybe it'll bring the two of them to finally admit they have feelings for each other. Although Archer will have some groveling to do after what he pulled the morning after they slept together.

"Oh, please," I reply with a snort. "Anyone with a brain knew there was history between them. I'm surprised it took this long to come out."

Silas flicks his finger against the table. "Those two are in love with each other. They'll be dating by the end of the year."

"Isn't it strange how two people who hate each other can also be in love?" I sigh. "Maybe that's what I need."

Silas stops his finger, peering at me and raising a brow. "Huh?"

"To fall in love with someone I hate."

"Do you even hate anyone?"

"Yes." I nod. "Paul Lemmings. In fifth grade, the asshole pulled my hair and called my dog ugly." I tap my chin. "Oh! And Britney Spears' father."

"Tell me I'm not going to have to stop you from hunting down Paul Lemmings in hopes of falling in love with him."

"Maybe." A playful smile passes over my lips. "Maybe he can pull my hair a different way now."

"Shut your damn mouth." He confiscates the glass of red wine in my hand. "No more for you, young lady."

I laugh. "If Archer, the brooding jerk, can convince someone to fall in love with him, there's hope for us all." I gesture toward him. "Even you."

He stares ahead. "Nah, I don't think so."

"You know, every time I bring up relationships around you, you act like they're the male version of menstrual cramps."

"Never had menstrual cramps, but I'm sure with what I've heard, it is."

"*But*"—I stretch that word out—"let's say you did get into a relationship. What's your type, Silas Malone?"

Nearly a year has passed since I asked Silas if he'd ever been in love. Since his reaction was so out of character, I've steered clear of the conversation until tonight.

He plays with my wineglass, moving it in circles, and the wine splashes against the rim. "That's an irrelevant question because it'll never happen."

"This is a what-if game. It doesn't mean it'll happen."

He sets my glass down, reclines in his chair, and crosses his arms behind his neck. "You don't want to know, trust me."

"Oh my God!" I swing my arm out to smack his chest. "Is it some weird kink? Like axillism?"

He drops his arms, and they fall slack onto his lap. "The fuck is axillism?"

"It's when someone likes to have sex with people's armpits."

His mouth falls open as if he's about to speak, and then he shuts it and holds his finger up as he comes up with the right words. When he does, they leave his lips slowly. "You think my type is … *armpits*? Like body odor is a turn-on for me?"

"Hey, buddy. You're the one who said body odor, not me."

"Please, for the love of God, tell me you made up that word."

"Nope. My brother had this friend who showed us armpit porn once. He explained it to us *in detail*." I shudder, remembering how fascinated he seemed by it. *No offense to his fellow axillism peeps, though.* "It's a real thing."

"To clear the record, my type is not armpits."

"Good to know. Then *what is* your type?"

Turning his head, he stares at me, eyes wide. "You."

This time, it's my mouth dropping. "What?" That one word comes out in six stutters.

"Don't act so shocked, Devilina."

I'm keeping my composure, but *holy shit*. Warmth infuses my body.

Get your shit together, Lola.

I smile confidently. "You like me. How cute." Throwing my

head back, I dramatically speak up to the sky. "I'm Silas's type, God. Did you hear that?"

He playfully cups the back of my head and tips it back down. "Whoa, hold up. Let me clarify. Someone *like you.*"

"Meaning me, sucker." I snatch my wine, chug it, slide out of my chair, and jump to my feet as if I'd just been called down on *The Price is Right.* "I mean, it doesn't exactly surprise me, considering I'm cool as hell. Some might even say I'm semi-attractive."

Since my dumbass didn't consider wine and jumping don't go well together, I wobble, and before I fall into the table, Silas pulls me onto his lap. Our faces—*our lips*—are only inches apart when I raise my head. I get a hint of the mint gum he was chewing earlier, and that, along with him, sobers me up. I didn't expect him to say that, and even though this isn't the first time I've sat on his lap, it's never been this intimate. It's not something we've ever done alone—always around friends and *always* playful. This, right here, is the opposite of that.

I'm not the only one who is shocked. Just like I didn't expect him to say that, I don't think he expected to either. It dropped from his lips so effortlessly, though, as if it'd been locked up for years and finally just broke from its cage. It seemed as if hurling the truth at me almost pained him.

There have been times I've thought about what a different relationship with Silas would be like. But then those thoughts go crashing down. Silas has been clear that attempting any relationship with him would be like giving written consent for him to crush your heart, injure it, and then hand it back with an *I told you so* look on his face.

I clear my throat and rest my elbow on his shoulder. "It appears we're alike because you're also my type. I mean ... not you, but someone *like you.*" I mock the voice he used when telling me that.

He's no longer playful, not with the pained expression on his face when he looks at me. "If that were the case, then why'd you give me a fake number when we met?"

I wince at the memory of me turning him down. "I didn't know you."

Even though he's quiet, I take in his change of breathing as well—a sign that I'm not the only one who's nervous about discussing this.

"I thought you were a fuckboy," I state, going forward. "A guy who only wanted to get in my panties."

He starts to talk, most likely to deny it, but I talk over him.

"Which I wasn't mad about because it was who you were: a player wanting a quick screw. Then I saw you at Cohen's, and we clicked and became best friends. And, hey, consider yourself lucky because my friendship slots are very limited. But as for what we were talking about, my type is someone who wants a relationship as strong and fun as we have."

He fixes his stare on me, and I can hear the movement of his chest heaving in and out. He grips my waist and slowly moves me, so my back is against the arm of the chair, and I'm not so much on him. It's almost like a rejection—that we were too close and we needed space.

"But there are plenty of ways you're not my type," I say, quickly recovering from looking like a fool.

He scratches his head. "Hmm? How?"

"You don't want a relationship."

He nods. "I'd be a boyfriend from hell. You know … where you're from."

"Oh, please. I see the front you put on." I lean back against the arm more, slightly raising my chest, and Silas's eyes drop to my cleavage. "There's so much more to you than the whole player persona you put on."

His eyes don't stay on my chest long, and he diverts his attention to me. He's looking at me, but it's half-assed—not fully there as if his eyes are on me but his mind is somewhere else.

"Bad guys don't attend parties and act like fake boyfriends," I go on. "They don't show up with snacks when a girl is sad, and they most definitely don't know said woman's take-out orders by heart." I dig my nails into his shoulder. "That kind of man—I hate to tell you—is made for relationships."

If my words hit him, he doesn't offer a reaction to it.

His face is blank. "You're the only woman I do that with. Ask me Georgia's take-out order, and I'd be clueless."

"Exactly! That's why you're *my type*."

His eyes finally meet mine, deep-set, drinking me in like I'm liquor—a drink that's off-limits to him. He clears his throat as if clearing his mind, and his words are raspy when he says, "Maybe once upon a time, I could have been that guy for you, but now? Babe, it'd never happen." He squeezes my thigh. "I'll never be your prince in shining armor. I'd be the one who broke you so hard that it'd be impossible for you to be rescued by someone else. You'd never want that fairy-tale love because I'd have broken every dream you had in it."

There's a finality in his voice with each word, and it causes the hair on my arms to stand. He speaks as if he truly believes he'd be the villain in any story.

Well, little does he know, I love villains.

"I'm the Devil's spawn, remember? I don't want fairy tales. I'd gladly take a broken man, a man hiding in the darkness, who feels as if he's not worthy. You know me well enough to know I don't and will never look for a Prince Charming. I'd rather have the dragon who sets fire to anyone who tries to get to me."

"I'd set *you* on fire and leave you to burn. Trust me when I say I'm toxic."

Cupping his strong chin, I jerk him closer to me. "Why do you talk about yourself like that? Why do you think you're so fucked up?"

I know plenty of people I'd consider fucked up. He is not one of those people.

Broken? Definitely.

Fucked up? Definitely not.

He's this gorgeous man who's had something tragic happen to him—something that threw a curveball, destroying any hope he had for being someone's lover.

"I don't think I'm fucked up. I *know* I am." His body trembles beneath mine—every damn part of him. His lips. His arms. His legs.

"No, Silas, you're not," I whisper, settling my hand on his thigh—the one my ass isn't halfway on. "You just went through something."

"I'm fucked up, and me wanting to kiss you right now proves that more."

I hold in a breath.

"Would I want to slide my hands through your hair and devour your mouth with mine?" he says it so low I can barely hear it.

But I heard it, and my body is reacting to every word he said.

What he said lights me up in ways I've never felt before.

"Then do it," I say boldly without giving myself the time to consider what his reaction to my statement might be.

He presses a finger to my lips like he knows he can't cross that line, but he needs to touch my lips in some way, and bows his head. "It'd be the kiss of death to our friendship."

My lips slowly part, and as I speak, his finger glides down my chin. "Or the start of something new."

Licking his lips, he cups my face tight as if it were the shield holding him back. Then he drops his hand, as if he's lost the restraint, and curls his hand around the back of my neck, pulling my face closer to his.

I gulp, inhaling a breath.

Then the sound of a door slamming shut rings through the air.

Silas pulls back.

I gasp.

Cohen comes stomping through the backyard like a kid whose party got ruined … because, well, it sorta did.

And now, he just ruined mine.

Silas scoots the chair back, grips my waist, and slides out from under me. As he does this, his waist—*his erection*—brushes against the back of my thigh, stealing my breath. His eyes shoot to me in fear, and I look from one side of the yard to the other, so I don't push him back down and straddle him.

Silas moves faster and plops down in my abandoned chair—the chair I probably should've stayed my happy ass in—and he grips the arms of the chair as if trying to talk himself down. He won't even look at me.

"All right," Cohen says when he reaches us. He's so absorbed in his predicament that he doesn't notice how awkward Silas and I are acting. "Which one of you knew about my sister and Archer?"

"Not this guy," Silas says before immediately pointing at me, his fun-guy front returning. "There's your culprit right there."

I glare at him for throwing me under the bus.

He ignores me, so Cohen is the next victim of my glare.

"Look, Archer didn't know who Georgia was, and vice versa."

"Then what happened? When did it happen?"

"Before you introduced them, and if you want to know more, ask Georgia. It's her story, not mine. But for now, the secret stays here." I tap the side of my head, wishing I could do it to Silas, only a little harder.

Maybe it'll knock some sense into me too.

I went into Cohen's backyard, knowing Silas was my best friend.

Now, I'm more confused about our relationship than ever.

CHAPTER FOURTEEN

Silas

IF I HAD to compare myself to any animal, I'd say I was a chameleon. I'm able to blend myself in with whatever environment I'm thrown into.

I only allow people to see what I want them to see. I'm seen as a people person, the jokester, the one who never takes anything seriously. But it's all an act. No one, other than my family, knows the real me and the burdens I hide deep within my soul.

I toss my shit across the bathroom floor and step into the shower, the hot water burning as it slides down my skin.

What the fuck was that with Lola tonight?

Sure, we flirt with each other, but our conversations have never turned so intimate.

Thinking about her and her words, I lower my hand, wrap it around my cock, and stroke myself. There's so much I find attractive about Lola ... so much I love about her. Not only physically but also her attitude, her personality, and the way she plays hard while also having a heart of gold.

We're the same but opposite.

She acts tough but is soft.

I act normal but am really rough on the inside.

Lola has never gotten so real with me like she did tonight.

I stroke myself faster, the buildup growing stronger, and when I release, it's her name I moan. Since we met, anytime I jack off, I always think about her.

I step out of the shower, wipe off my face, and shake off my hair.

Cohen interrupting us was a sign that we need to be careful —that whatever ideas we have cluttering our friendship need to be laid to rest.

———

I CLENCH my jaw while reading the text.

Trent: Want to grab a drink? Talk about shit before my mother's party?

I fight with myself on how to respond. I hate when he reaches out. I decline, and then he looks like the good guy who tried.

He's not the good guy.

Like me, he's the villain.

I'd never voluntarily sit down and have a drink with him. The few times we've been around each other at family occasions, he attempts conversation, but I can't stand the sight of him. When he transferred to my school, we had almost a rivalry. I hated his mother for breaking apart my parents' marriage. He hated my father because he was the reason he had to move schools his senior year.

Then the party happened.

He did something no one can take back—all because he's a selfish bastard who doesn't care about anyone but himself. He didn't have to do what he did that night. His beef was only with me, and he should've left the others out of it. His decision ruined everyone's lives … except his because the asshole acts like it never happened, like he didn't create tragedy.

Instead of replying, I delete his text, hoping to forget he even exists.

CHAPTER FIFTEEN

Lola

"AND THEN THERE WERE TWO," I tell Silas, plopping down on the couch and patting the empty space next to me.

He takes a sip of his water before sitting. "Because the others scurried off to their bedrooms to most likely bang."

"Bitches," I grumble. "How dare they."

We're at Archer and Lincoln's grandparents' lake house, which is about two hours from Anchor Ridge, with Archer, Georgia, and Lincoln's girlfriend, Cassidy. We ordered pizza and hung out. Then it was time for the couples to ditch us. Georgia was the first to fake a yawn, telling us she and Archer were going to bed. Shortly after, Lincoln and Cassidy did the same.

Silas snatches the remote. "What's your movie of choice for tonight?"

I shrug. "You pick."

He shakes his head. "Nuh-uh. Last time I picked, all you did was comment on how unrealistic every scene was."

"The guy jumped off a bajillion-story window, landed on his feet, and then ran as fast as the car he was chasing." I throw out my arm. "If you think that's realistic, we need to get that brain of yours checked."

"It's an *action* movie. That's what they do."

"You know what I do? I call bullshit on that."

He drops his head back. "Exactly why I told you to pick what we're watching. No Hallmark shit, though."

"When—and I stress, *when*—have I ever picked Hallmark?"

Silas opens his mouth, most likely to make some ridiculous comment, but stops when a moan comes from down the hallway. His gaze shoots straight to me, and I slap a hand over my mouth to hold in my laughter but fail.

"Oh my God," I choke out between laughs. "Two of them are totally hooking up."

Silas places his hand to his ear as if trying to get a better listen. "Who do you think it is?"

"Georgia," I say with certainty. "That girl has a loud mouth, even if she tries to be quiet."

Silas rests his hand on the arm of the couch. "Should I go tell them to keep it down?"

I rub my nose. "I'd feel terrible, ruining their … mood."

"They're ruining our mood, though." He gestures toward the TV. "We can't watch a movie when there's porn playing in the background."

"We can turn the volume up." I stare at him timidly. "This is also Archer's place. Is it cool to tell people not to bang in their own house?"

Technically, it's his grandparents' but same difference.

Silas rubs his hand over the leg of his sweats. "We'll just crank up the volume." He hands me the remote. "Pick a movie."

This is the first time we've ever been in a situation like this. Not much time has passed since our friends started coupling up. They also used to be less in our faces about it, but I guess those days are over. When Georgia invited me to come, I made sure Silas was coming so I wouldn't be the odd one out.

Now, I think sitting here with the background noise of sex might be more awkward. And just when I think it can't get weirder, there's action coming from Lincoln's room.

"Jesus, fuck," Silas hisses, scrubbing a hand over his face

before gesturing toward the remote. "Pick something, pronto, please."

I flip through the different Netflix options and decide on a suspense movie. That will make both of us happy—Silas gets a little bit of action, and I get a little bit of mystery. Win-win.

Before hitting play, I snag the blanket folded over the end of the couch, prop a pillow up, and make myself comfortable. Silas doesn't care when I rest my feet on his lap.

"Blanket?" I ask. "I *guess* I'll share."

He shakes his head. "I'm good."

The couples are still at it, and it gets worse when we hear the echoes of what I'm sure is a bed hitting the wall, reverberating through the house.

Thump-thump-thump.

I fake gag. "All right, I'm about ten seconds from changing my mind on telling the porn stars to relax. There are people trying to live sexless lives over here."

Silas chuckles. "Play the movie. It'll drown them out."

The movie starts, and not even five minutes in, a sex scene begins.

It's been a while since I've hooked up with anyone, and now, sex is all that's happening around me. Silas and I refuse to look at each other. We've watched movies with sex scenes before but never when also surrounded by people having sex, never when we're hearing moans and groans and beds shaking and intimacy.

The man—a main character—is banging a flight attendant hard in the back of a private plane. And I mean, *she's most likely going to be sporting some bruises and she might not be able to walk off the plane* kind of screwing.

It was dumb of me to choose an R-rated movie. I should've thought ahead. I figured there'd be some violence, some blood, but I didn't consider there'd be soft-core porn.

I stare at the screen, nearly bug-eyed as my breath catches in my throat.

This could be us.

Having sex.

Me throwing my head back as he pleasured me.

No, no, no.

Bad Lola.

It's affecting Silas too. He shifts on the couch, adjusting his pants, and hits my foot in the process, as if he forgot it was there. I lick my lips at the outline of his hardening cock through his sweats. The view and feel of it against the edge of my foot is mesmerizing.

I can't exactly smack my face to rid of the thoughts, so I suck in a deep breath and decide to go about this a different way.

"I'm going to call this one out as unrealistic too," I comment, my voice raspy. "There is no way a man makes a woman come that quick. No way."

Silas's gaze darts to me, but he doesn't utter a word. Our eyes meet, and I should divert my attention because I have a feeling that I'm staring at him in a similar way. His breathing is heavy, and he rests his arm over his waist, shielding my view of how aroused he is. My tongue darts out, licking my lips, and I have to fight the urge to lower my hand and dip them into my panties.

We're not supposed to want each other like this.

It isn't what our friendship allows.

I want my best friend in ways I shouldn't.

"We could do it one time," I say.

"What?"

"Hook up." I pray that he doesn't turn me down. "Just once because we're both obviously … turned on."

He stares at me, stunned. "You're turned on?"

I shoot him a *really* look.

"I can leave the room if you want to take care of that."

I deliver that same *really* look as before, slowly dragging my foot over his lap and rubbing it over his erection. My chest is heavy, and I'm practically panting. He shudders underneath me, and I can feel my pulse against my throat.

We both want this.

"This is dangerous," he mutters as the room grows hot. Or maybe it's just me.

"It is," I whisper.

He carefully moves my feet off his lap and bends my knees. I stay quiet when he starts to get up. Gulping, I wait for it—the rejection—for him to leave the room because at least one of us is thinking rationally.

But he doesn't stand.

Instead, he settles himself on his knees next to me. I maneuver, so I'm on my side, staring down at him. Stretching forward, he caresses my cheek. I tremble when his fingertips slip down to between my lips. I stop myself from opening wider, from sucking on his finger, scared that might be too much.

He peers down at me with hooded eyes in what appears to be admiration. "Are you sure about this?"

I urgently nod. "Positive."

Briefly, though, those thoughts hit me.

Is this selfish?

To put our friendship on the line for one night? One time?

Tipping his head down, he briefly kisses me. I open my mouth, allowing him entrance, and he sucks on the end of my tongue before pulling away. I curl my hand around his neck, attempting to bring him back, but he doesn't allow it.

But right now, in the emptiness of this room, with the background of passion playing around us, I want him more than ever.

Every inch of my body craves him.

And if I sink my hand deep into my heart and drag out the contents, the truth of how I feel will be thrown out for all to see. I've craved Silas for so long, but I've been afraid to admit it. Admitting your feelings for someone could lead to rejection and embarrassment.

And once I admitted it to myself, how was I supposed to not look at him and hope for more?

He rests his hand on the waist of my sleep shorts, his finger toying with the loop of the tied strings. All it would take is him untying the strings, and we'd be opening a door we've kept closed for so long.

And when he does, everything changes.

"Rise up a little for me," he demands.

I do as I was told, and he jerks my shorts down. I peer down to find Silas's gaze leveled on my black lace panties. He wastes no time, as if he knows how desperate I am, before he slips my panties to the side. Moving closer, nearly halfway hovering over me, he jerks one of my legs up.

And without warning, he slides two fingers inside me.

They fill me perfectly. His thumb presses against my clit—not gentle, but not too rough. He plays with it while slipping his fingers in and out of me. He's focused on his fingers, not taking a break to look at my face, as if this is his life's biggest goal. I writhe underneath him, growing breathless, and his breathing comes out ragged.

I'm staring at him as he works me with full concentration as if he needs his performance to be perfect, and then my back is arching, and I'm moaning his name. It's quiet, only for our ears —unlike my friends. Our little secret means hushed moans.

It's quick, like I shut my eyes for a few seconds and then it's over. As I'm catching my breath, Silas stands, pulling at the bottom of his tee with the same fingers he had inside me.

"Do you want me to …?" I burst the words out, my brain only halfway functioning, and point at the bulge in his pants.

He shakes his head, standing tall. "Tonight was about you."

I do a circle motion with my hand toward his cock. "But what about *you*?"

"Tonight was about you," he repeats, his voice firm, and he jerks his thumb over his shoulder. "Do you want something from the kitchen? I'm going to grab a water."

"No," I say, my voice trembling. "I'm okay."

I watch him turn, giving me his back, as my heart batters

against my chest, telling me to call him back. Silas isn't the first man who's pleasured me ... but he's the first guy who's ever made me feel a passion like that by only fingering me.

And now, he's shut down.

He made me orgasm and then mentally left.

Our relationship has changed.

Whether it's good or bad, I'm unsure.

All I know is, we'll never be *just friends* any longer.

Silas is scared of ruining our friendship.

But is he more scared of being in love with me than losing me?

CHAPTER SIXTEEN

Silas

WHEN I MAKE it to the kitchen, I throw open the fridge door and frantically grab a water.

What were you thinking?

You weren't supposed to touch her.

You were supposed to keep your relationship platonic.

Lola is more than just a friend.

She's my world.

And now, I might lose her.

I chug the water, open the fridge for another, and gulp that one down too. Jerking a chair out, I slump down onto it, dropping my head between my open legs.

"What did I do?" I whisper to myself, my voice cracking.

I'm not sure how long I sit in the kitchen, reminding myself what a mistake I just made. It was a spur-of-the-moment thing, and the way Lola was rubbing my cock and licking her lips had already gotten me riled up.

"We could do it one time."

Those words were my undoing.

I force myself out of the chair and sluggishly return to the living room. The sounds of our friends' lovemaking have dissipated. The only noise is the movie Lola picked. I shouldn't have allowed that. I should've scrolled through the shows and found the most PG-rated one I could.

Lola is facing me, her eyes shut, her hand resting underneath her cheek as she sleeps. A rush of relief leaves me because I have time to work out what I'm going to say before I have to face her again.

This can't happen again.

We need to stop it before it gets too deep.

I'm going to fight like hell to make sure nothing changes with Lola after what happened tonight.

Hopefully, this wasn't a life-changing mistake.

I need to get out of here.

CHAPTER SEVENTEEN

Lola

IT'S silent when I wake up alone with a blanket tucked around my body—most likely Silas's doing. Rising, I move my neck from side to side, working out the crick I already feel coming. The silence tells me Silas is most likely gone.

After giving me an amazing orgasm, when he said he was getting a water from the kitchen, I didn't expect him to be there nearly all night, as if he were pumping the water from the well in there. Had I known he'd scurry off, scared, I'd have run to the guest bedroom and at least been comfortable in my sleep of shame.

When did he leave?

Why did he leave?

Did last night ruin us?

Yawning, I snatch my phone from the coffee table and find a text from the couch evacuator.

Silas: Had an emergency. Archer said you can ride home with them.

What the fuck?

I clench my hand around my phone.

There's nothing like being ditched by the man who fingered you last night.

The text was sent six hours ago—one a.m.

What an ass.

Silas could've easily woken me up and told me since he somehow communicated with Archer to take me home.

Shivering, I wrap the blanket tighter around me and reply, unsure of how long it'll take him to see my text since it's early. He drove two hours home late at night, and Silas isn't an early riser.

Me: You could've woken me up and told me.

His response comes moments later, shocking me.

Silas: Sorry. You looked so peaceful, sleeping. I would've felt like an asshole.

Yeah, bullshit. He's not getting out of this that easy.

Me: I wouldn't have been mad.

My message goes through, and my fingers hover over the screen as I chew on the edge of my lip. It needs to be brought up, and I have a feeling he won't do it.

Me: After that orgasm, you could've woken me up every hour of the night, and I wouldn't have said a damn thing.

Three bubbles form on the screen. Then disappear. Then form again. I jump when my phone beeps with his message.

Silas: I've told you for years that I have mad skills.

At least he's being playful.

That has to count for something, right?

———

BY THE TIME the others join me in the kitchen, I'm showered, dressed, and searching for something decent to drink.

"Archer, you're rich. You need to invest in an espresso machine here. If there's no Starbucks, you have to make up for it somehow," I say, leaning back against the cabinets and frowning at the hot muck in my cup.

"I've been telling him that," Georgia says, skipping down the stairs and slapping Archer's stomach. "I don't even know how to work a normal coffee maker. Everyone drinks iced coffee now."

"Not me," Lincoln says. "I'm not picky about my coffee."

"That's because you got used to that prison coffee," Cassidy says, running her hand through her straight blond hair. "I don't know how you haven't gone back to your Starbucks ways."

Lincoln shrugs. "Don't knock it until you try it."

I raise a brow. "Prison or shit coffee?"

"Eh"—Lincoln smirks—"both."

"Let's hit the road and grab some decent coffee … and a McMuffin," Georgia says.

"Sounds good to me," I mutter, ready to get out of here as fast as I can.

Even though no one said anything, I saw the curious eyes when they didn't see Silas. I'm sure Archer told Georgia I was riding with them, and since Lincoln and Cassidy are somewhat newer to the group, they don't get deep into our business. Silas said he had an emergency, so that's all I'll say if they ask.

———

JUST AS I'M shoving the last bite of my McMuffin into my mouth, I get another text from Silas.

Silas: You make it home okay?

I debate on whether to answer him, so I set my phone down and sing out about how my loneliness is killing me with Georgia to our favorite Britney jam. Silas bailed on me in the middle of the night, so he can wait for a response.

———

AN HOUR LATER, I strip off my clothes, throw them in the laundry basket, and step into the shower. Tipping my head back, I allow the water to sprinkle down my face as I think about last night.

It changed my friendship with Silas.

When I get out, I finally reply to him.

Me: Nope. I'm currently walking home because someone left me stranded.

He replies to me minutes later when I'm trudging into the kitchen.

Silas: Funny, you pain in the ass. I made sure Archer could take you home before I left.

Me: You woke him up but not me?

He didn't wake me up because he knew he'd have to face me after making me orgasm. One thing I hadn't discovered about Silas before is that he's a chickenshit.

Silas: I didn't want to piss you off. Him? I don't really care if I do.

Me: Why'd you bail?

Silas: I had some family shit come up that I needed to take care of. Sorry.

I don't believe him, but I'm also not in the mood to call him out for the second time today.

CHAPTER EIGHTEEN

Silas

EVEN THOUGH I'M concerned it might be awkward, I smile when Lola walks toward the bar at Twisted Fox. It's the first time we've seen each other since the lake house.

That was a week ago, and it's rare for us to go that long without seeing each other. We also haven't talked to each other as much as we used to. I'm blaming it on us both being busy with work so that I don't have to meet the reality that we caused this distance between us—Lola saying only one time and me going through with it.

"Hey you," I greet when she tugs a stool back and plops onto it.

"Hey, ditcher," she replies with a playful smile.

I chuckle, shaking my head. "Always a pain in my ass."

So far, not as awkward as I feared.

She shrugs, tossing her dark hair over her shoulder. "Better to be a pain in the ass than someone who bails on their friend in the middle of the night."

All right, so she's choosing awkward for tonight actually.

"Oh, come on," I groan, throwing my head back. "I told you, it was an emergency."

"What was the emergency then?"

"It was a family thing. My mom needed something." I slam my eyes shut, hating that I just lied to her.

I left because of myself. My hands shook as I covered up Lola, grabbed my keys, charged to my car, and left the lake house. After driving around for hours, contemplating whether to go back, I went home. Not that I got any sleep.

Once, I ran to the bathroom, worried that I'd puke because my anxiety was so goddamn high. Another minute, I sat at the edge of my bed, my palm against my chest as my heart raced.

"I'll make it up to you." I grab a square white bar napkin and drop it in front of her. "I promise."

She taps her black nails against the bar. "I take gifts, food, or cash."

I smile at her remark, and it puts me a little more at ease. But no matter what, we both know what happened. I knelt beside her, helped her push down her shorts, and pressed my fingers inside her warmth. I stroked her and played with her clit until she came apart below me. And it is a memory that I'll never forget.

Lola grunts when a woman shoves herself between Lola and the man sitting next to her. She turns, glaring at the woman, and jerks her shoulder back, slightly hitting the rude woman, who's paying her no mind.

"Hey, hottie," the woman around Lola's age greets, and Lola snorts at her little name for me. "Can I get a sex on the beach?"

The woman tries to straighten herself out, but there isn't room, and Lola isn't moving for her.

I salute her, trying not to laugh at Lola mean-mugging the girl. "I got you."

"And your number," she adds.

"No, you can't." Lola answers for me, her voice sharp. "He'll get you your ridiculous drink, and then you can go on your way."

I retreat a step, shocked at Lola's words, and the woman shifts to look at her.

"Are you his girlfriend?" she snarls.

Lola hesitates, her eyes squinting. "I'm his boss, and he can't give his number to thirsty customers."

"I can only give thirsty customers drinks," I say with a nod of confirmation.

I've never given a woman my number in front of Lola, no matter where it is. And she's returned the favor.

"Whatever," the woman grumbles, her flirty voice now hard. "I'll just take the drink then."

She steps back, moving around Lola and between an open stool and a burly man, who calls her sweetheart and asks if she wants him to buy her drink. I quickly make the drink, some of the OJ splashing as I finish it off, and hand it to her. She delivers a look as dirty as the one Lola gave her, snatches it from me, throws some cash down, and leaves—no tip included.

Damn, that sure took a quick turn.

I open the drawer, shove the cash in, and return to Lola. "I love it when you get all territorial."

She laughs, now chewing on her nail. "Don't act like you're not the same with me."

"I do it to protect you." I gesture to the bar. "Are you not hanging with the girls tonight?"

"Nope. Grace has been weird lately—absent and secretive. Georgia is forcing Archer to go shopping. So, I came to see Cassidy."

I curl my hands around my mouth. "Bullshit."

She flips me off.

I rest my elbows on the bar, on each side of her, and lean in closer. "You came to see me, your favorite person in the world."

She rolls her eyes. "Whatever." She groans. "I need a drink to keep my mind off this douchebag at work."

My muscles tighten, and my back straightens. "Whose ass do I need to kick?"

"No one's." She cringes. "Some guy at work is giving me a hard time and trying to turn everyone against me by telling them I'm given the easy-to-close and bigwig clients because of who my dad is. In reality, I'm given the harder clients because I'm better at closing the deals."

I snarl and give myself a reminder to have her point him out the next time I attend a work event with her. "Who cares what him or what a few people think? Your dad knows what you're capable of, and that's all that matters."

"I know. It just sucks, having people talk shit about you." Her shoulders slump. "Especially when it's not true."

I brush my hand over hers but pull away when she trembles at my touch. "Tell me what I can do to make it better."

Her attention is pinned to her hand as if she can still feel my touch there. "Make me the best damn drink you can … and don't let me yell at any girls who hit on you."

Is this how it's always going to be now?

Are the simple touches we once had—which were playful and we didn't read too much into them—finished? Do we have to be careful, be nervous, with the way we are around each other now? Do we have to change the friendship we once had?

CHAPTER NINETEEN

Lola

WHEN I WALK into Twisted Fox with Georgia, Cassidy, and Grace, I spot Silas at our favorite table waving us over. Since our talk at the bar, our relationship has returned to normalcy—for the most part. We act like the incident at the lake house never happened. It's better for our friendship that way. Plus, it's not like we haven't had hookups that didn't result in relationships. Ours should be the same way.

Silas kisses my forehead when I reach him, stands, and jerks the stool out for me to sit next to him.

Georgia plops down and dances in her stool as she slaps her hand on the bar. "All right, give me your margarita orders."

"Strawberry," I say.

"Make that two strawberries," Cassidy adds.

"Just a water for me," Grace replies in a soft voice.

All eyes direct to Grace.

"No margarita?" Georgia asks, raising a brow.

Not only are margaritas Grace's favorite, but she also looks stressed. She's a teacher, so I usually blame it on being around crazy children all day, but it's something deeper. I don't want to ask in front of everyone because I tend to pry into people's personal business privately.

"I wish." Grace slaps a hand over her mouth, shutting her eyes as if she let out a secret she hadn't intended to. She lowers her hand and tone at the same time. "I work in the morning."

She and Georgia both work at an elementary school. Georgia is the school counselor, and Grace is a teacher.

Raising my wrist, I peer down at my watch. "Babe, you look like you've had a hell of a day. Have a drink, scarf down some greasy bar food, and don't give a shit about calories. Consider it a serotonin booster." I wink at her. "Trust me, I'm a pro at this stuff."

Grace drops her hand underneath the table, resting it on her stomach. "Maybe another time."

"Whoa," Silas says. "You knocked up or something?"

The table turns quiet as if Silas released a secret he wasn't supposed to. Well, everyone, except for Cassidy, who breaks out into coughs. If she were actually choking, I'd swat Silas to give her the Heimlich. But that's not why she's coughing. It's to hide the truth she knows about what's going on with Grace.

And from Silas's question, my guess is, there's a bun in Grace's oven.

Grace chews on her bottom lip, not yet denying it. Grace doesn't lie because she's terrible at it. Girl gives herself away in minutes. No matter what, you immediately know.

She fidgets with her hands as everyone awaits her secret.

Then she slowly nods and shuts her eyes.

I stare at her, unblinking, while everyone else has their own reactions.

"Who's the father?" Finn asks, and my eyes shoot to him. There's a deep cut of pain not only in his voice but also evident on his face.

Finn is in love with Grace. Grace is in love with Finn.

I had no idea Grace was dating someone, and she isn't the type for random hookups. I'd expect a pregnancy announcement from Georgia or Cassidy, sure, but not Grace.

I thought Silas and I had some friendship turmoil brewing.

Grace's pregnancy just beat that out. If there's a baby daddy in the picture, that man might push Finn out of Grace's life. It's the same concern I've had with Silas if one of us gets into a serious relationship.

Grace clears her throat. "I don't want to talk about that."

Our friends start throwing out questions, and Grace's face twists in unease. The poor girl appears freaked out enough about being pregnant. The last thing she needs is to be interrogated when she can't even have a drop of liquor.

I hold up my hand to stop them. "She'll talk about it when she's ready." I send Finn a *shut it* look.

"Do your parents know?" Georgia asks as if she needs just one question to appease her for the night.

"Not yet," Grace croaks out.

Grace's parents are strict—not asshole strict, but more *we expected better out of you* strict. Her parents are pretty much perfect, so Grace can't call them hypocrites for wanting that out of their children.

My parents? They have no right to question my ways when my dad humps anything with a vagina. At least his infidelity gives me an excuse not to be a golden child.

Georgia grabs Grace's hand and squeezes it. "Do you want me to go with you when you tell them? I mean, I'm down for being a second mom."

This is why our friendship works so well. While I'm good at sticking up for my friends and telling people to shut up, Georgia is the positive and comforting friend. Those traits are probably what made Archer fall in love with her. He was a broken man, fighting an internal war with himself, and she helped him through it.

Grace doesn't look back at Finn. She tells us she doesn't have a plan and doesn't know what she's doing yet since she just recently found out. The bar isn't the place to make her dive into what secrets she has. Grace needs privacy right now.

When I sneak a peek at Silas, I find him staring at Finn in

concern—most likely having the same worry for him that I'm having for Grace. They'll both need support systems through this new development in their lives.

For years—longer than Silas and me—Grace and Finn have run away from their feelings in fear of losing each other. But now, it seems almost too late for them.

Grace is having another man's baby.

Finn looks like he no longer has a beating heart.

My chest hurts because I'm scared this might be my future with Silas.

————

I DRANK one too many margaritas tonight.

In my defense, so did Georgia.

"You okay?" Silas asks when he parks in front of my house.

I rode to Twisted Fox with Georgia, but since we decided to take a trip to Tipsy Town, Archer drove her home, and Silas is my ride.

I'm not drunk. I can say my ABCs. I know my birthday. I'm not seeing triple. I just had a little too much. I rest my head against the headrest and think about Grace and what she's going through. She has us, but I still can't imagine the fear and loneliness inside her.

If her baby daddy were a decent guy, we'd have already met him. She would've had more enthusiasm because Grace is one of the most positive people I know. She always sees the light at the end of the tunnel. Whoever the father is, it's someone she doesn't want it to be. And from the way she looked at Finn, my guess is, she wishes it were him.

I know Silas's question meant to be more along the lines of, *Tell me you're not about to puke in my car*, but that's not what's on my mind.

"Do you ever get lonely?" I ask.

He shifts to look at me, the dim light above us providing the only illumination in the car, but he doesn't answer.

"Because sometimes, I do."

Silas strokes his jaw. "Sometimes … but when it happens, I call you."

A hint of a smile forms on my lips. "Same."

My emotional side rarely makes an appearance in the outside world. I keep that bitch hostage most of the time because I don't want people to ever see me as weak. For years, I watched my mother sit in the kitchen and cry after my father was caught cheating again. I'd stand in the hallway, peeking around the corner, as she begged him to stop. She was broken and sad, explaining that to him between sobs.

But even with all that pleading, my father couldn't commit to her. She threw out every emotion she felt, but nothing changed. All he saw was a woman he could walk all over, and all I saw was that emotions made you look weak. On the outside, my mother was a strong woman. You'd never know she was breaking behind closed doors.

She was lonely—I saw it in her eyes every morning after my father stayed out late. I'd hear her crying at night, masking her whimpers into a tissue. And as much as I hated it, when I snuck around and stared at her, I knew I'd never allow that to be me.

I love my mother, and her going through that hell made me decide I never would. No one, except myself, would ever break me with their actions.

The car goes silent, the outside traffic the only noise around us.

Silas jerks his chin toward my house. "Do you want me to come in and keep you company?"

I shake my head. "No, I'm okay."

"You sure?"

"Positive."

I gulp. *Hide those emotions.*

"Lola." Reaching out, he cups my chin and strokes it, the

action giving me goose bumps. "You call me anytime you feel lonely, do you hear me? I'll be there for you, no matter what."

I nod, and for some reason, my chin trembles in his hold. "I know."

And I do know that. If I call, Silas is always there.

His hand leaves my chin to stroke my jawline. "You know you're the most important person in my life, right?"

"I know." My words are barely audible.

"You know that I love you?"

I nod again, unable to form words.

"That means, you'll never be alone. *Never.*" He puts so much stress on his last word, making it heavy, making it a fact. "I'm sure seeing Grace and Finn tonight has you worried about us. It crossed my mind too. But they're not us. Even something like that couldn't break our bond. You're the best thing in my life."

I wrap my hand around the wrist of his hand stroking my face—not to stop him, but to keep his touch there.

He smacks a loud kiss on my forehead. "Let's get you inside."

My heart drops into my stomach when he pulls away. He turns, stepping out of the car, and I do the same.

His hand rests on the arch of my back as we walk to my front door. "You sure you don't want me to come in?"

I shake my head, fetching my keys from my purse. "I work in the morning. You probably need to talk to Finn tonight and make sure he's okay."

He squeezes my waist. "Call me if you need anything."

I feel like my mother as I cringe when he pulls away. "Okay."

"Love you." He places a kiss on my cheek, only inches from my lips.

I turn my back to him, unlocking my door, and he stands there, making sure I'm safely inside before leaving. After shutting the door, I rest my back against it, the wood cold against my bare shoulders. As much as I don't want it to, as much as it surprises me, a single tear falls down my cheek.

It's the alcohol.

It has to be—because this isn't me.

Or is it?

I've never had to show my emotions because I've never been close to losing someone I care so deeply for, never feared how empty my life would be without them.

That dread, that desperation, is now close to bleeding through me.

I want a bond like Cohen has with Jamie, like Archer and Georgia, and Lincoln and Cassidy. And seeing Grace and Finn reminded me that might never happen with the only person I think it could.

But why?

Each one of them had difficult journeys but pushed their way through them because their love for the other was worth it. Cohen hated Jamie and her family for years, and she's his baby mama's sister. Georgia and Archer had a bad beginning, but they're making up for it now. And Lincoln is a felon, dating a woman with family in law enforcement. Maybe my mother's pleas weren't enough for my father, and her love wasn't enough to keep him, but my friends are examples that, sometimes, love is enough.

They chose each other, chose their hearts and happiness.

They opened themselves up, their broken and dark parts.

Can Silas and I do the same?

Or will one of us be my mother, pleading for something the other will never give?

CHAPTER TWENTY

Silas

LOLA'S WORDS haunt me as I walk back to my car. Shrinking into my seat, I replay them in my head.

She has no idea how lonely I get.

No one does.

I rest my head against the steering wheel. I'm lonely, but I do everything in my power to blanket that loneliness—hang out with my friends, *Lola*, and work nonstop. It doesn't work all the time, though. When the loneliness does creep through, I allow it to eat at me because I deserve it.

Lola is changing. It could be our friends coupling up and starting lives together. It could be Finn's reaction to Grace's news tonight. Eventually, Lola will want that too.

———

TWISTED FOX IS STILL OPEN, and I dodge people on my way to the bar. I fall on a stool in the corner and give myself a moment to reflect on tonight and what it means for our group.

As soon as the last customer leaves, Finn races behind the bar, snatches a bottle of whiskey, and pours himself a double.

After draining it, he slams it down on the bar, and I'm shocked the thing doesn't shatter.

I join him, slapping his back. "You good, man?"

It's a dumb question because it's obvious he isn't, but I wasn't sure how to approach the situation.

"All good." To wash away his lie, he pours another drink.

I steal the bottle from him. "Don't bullshit me."

"Would you be pissed if you found out Lola was pregnant?"

I look away, hoping he doesn't see how that statement affects me. "I don't know."

"Bullshit. You would."

I sigh. "Let me drive you home."

Instead of replying, he swipes the bottle back and takes a long chug. It's nearly empty when he hands it back.

"Let's go," he says, wiping his mouth with the back of his arm.

Like with Lola, our ride is quiet. He spends most of it on his phone, frantically texting, and my guess is, he's texting Grace. After dropping him off, I drive to the one place I shouldn't. I call myself an idiot when I park my car and sit there, knowing I won't have the guts to get out.

I go here when I need a reminder that I don't deserve the good life.

Lola is lonely, and the reality of my friendship not being enough of what she needs frightens me to the core. I'm going to lose her just like I lost the reason I can't step out of my car.

———

"I'VE MISSED YOU, HONEY," my mother says, her voice musical while staring at me from the other side of the table at her favorite restaurant.

I clutch the menu and smile at her. "I've missed you too."

I love my mother. Mona Malone—she kept the last name because she said it had a certain ring to it—is the strongest woman I know. After my father left, she allowed herself a year to mourn their marriage, then she returned to Anchor Ridge and moved on with her life. She and my father are cordial to each other, and she's forgiven but not forgotten what he and Janet did.

She clasps her hands in front of her, resting them on the white tablecloth. "What have you been up to?"

"Not much. Working." I shrug. "The usual."

"Girlfriend?" It's a question she always asks.

I cringe. "You know there will never be a girlfriend."

I hoped the topic wouldn't come up, but each time, she tends to find a way to weave it into the conversation. If I didn't love her so much, I'd bail every time for that very reason. I already know what's coming next.

"Silas, honey," she starts, "I know what happened all those years ago was tragic and devastating, but eventually, you'll need to accept it and move on."

I wince at her words. I don't know why since it's always the same speech.

Reaching out, she rests her hand over mine. "You deserve happiness regardless of what you tell yourself. What happened wasn't your fault." She sighs. "I just want my son back."

I abruptly pull away, staring at her blankly. "You lost that son years ago."

There's hope in her eyes. "But we can bring him back."

I stay quiet.

"I talked to your father. He said Trent has been reaching out to make things right between you." She's so mellow, so calm, while my heart is racing in my chest.

"Trent can kiss my ass," I bite out.

"Silas—"

"Don't *Silas* me," I interrupt before unraveling my napkin and smoothing it out onto my lap. "Let's talk about something else."

The server cuts into our conversation when she takes our

order, and we move on to a lighter chat—one that doesn't have my stomach curling, threatening to puke up lunch. Something that doesn't remind me of the mistakes I once made.

———

"HOW WAS LUNCH WITH YOUR MOM?" Lola asks over the phone.

"Not bad," I reply, scratching my cheek.

Not bad after she stopped trying to lecture me.

"Did you get that chicken dish I'd told you to try?"

"Yeah, and it was meh."

"Ugh, you need better taste buds."

I chuckle. "What did you do today?"

"I started narrowing down what to do for my birthday. You know, the best day of the year."

My chest caves in, and I force myself to sound excited. "Oh yeah … what are you thinking you want to do?"

Either Lola doesn't catch on to the dread in my voice or she chooses to ignore it. "One of my clients offered me a table at Sixes. It's been a while since we've been there, so I figured, why not?"

"Hmm."

"And you'd better be there this year."

"I will." An ache forms in the back of my throat.

"I'm serious, Silas. No bailing, do you hear me?"

"I hear you."

Today has been nothing but somber reminders of my past. First my mother and now Lola—even though Lola has no idea why. Every year, this happens, and every year, I wish I could ask Lola to change her birthday. No matter how hard I try, I can't bring myself to be in a celebratory mood. So, I don't show.

It's the only time we've had issues in our friendship.

Her birthday.

I'm always a no-show. I make up for it later, and it's not like

I purposely lie. I plan to go, I hype myself up, but when it comes time to leave, I can't step out my front door. It's too hard.

"Promise me," she says, breaking me away from my thoughts. "Promise me you won't ditch me on my birthday."

"I promise as long as nothing comes up."

"Oh, bullshit. I don't want any excuses. You know when my birthday is every year, yet no matter what day of the week it falls on, you go MIA. I'm always there for your birthday and make sure it's special for you."

Forgetting her birthday isn't the issue.

It's the only day of the year that I dread.

———

"IF JAMIE and I can make it with two little ones at home, your no-kid-having ass can too," Cohen says, sternly staring at me from across the bar.

"What's the deal with Lola's birthday anyway?" Finn asks. "You never miss anyone's but hers."

"Will you be there?" I ask him, hoping he'll say no because Grace is pregnant, which will pull the attention away from me.

Finn nods.

So, everyone but me will be in attendance. *Fuck my life.*

I kick my feet against the stool legs. "How's it going with Grace?"

"It's weird, having a girl roommate," Finn says. "It'll take some adjusting, but I'm happy to be there for her."

"*There for her* is an understatement," Lincoln says. "My man is understanding the damn assignment of playing baby daddy."

Not surprisingly, we found out Grace's baby daddy is a married piece of shit. Oh, a married, *also expecting a baby on the way with his wife* piece of shit. Grace wants nothing to do with him, but she also didn't want to tell people she got pregnant by a taken man. To help with her problem, we came up with a plan —Finn will act like her baby daddy. He was reluctant at first, given it's a weird job, but he agreed to it, knowing it'd help Grace.

He also agreed to move in with Grace to make it more believable. Cassidy gave him her bedroom and is staying at Lincoln's penthouse.

Finn shrugs. "I want to be there for Grace any way I can." I shut my eyes, wishing I could be the same for Lola every single damn day of the year.

"And the new job?" Cohen asks.

"Yeah, traitor," Lincoln says, tossing a beer cap at Finn, "how's the new job?"

"It's different." Finn runs his hand over his stressed face. "The hours have taken some getting used to as well as not being here and hanging out with you assholes."

Grace's brother-in-law owns a luxury car dealership and offered Finn a job, so he could be more available to Grace. Finn was reluctant to take it, worried that Cohen and Archer would be upset with him for leaving them, but they couldn't have been happier for him. At the dealership, he'll make more money and have better benefits. At the end of the day, we always want our friends to do their best and be happy.

After an hour of hanging out at the bar, Finn leaves to be with Grace. Cohen and Lincoln linger to their side of the bar for their shifts. And Archer, who maybe said five words while we hung out, stops me before I leave.

"The war going on in your head," he says out of the blue, "let Lola drag you out of it before you lose her. You'd better show up at the party because if you keep bailing, she'll stop inviting. Your invite will go to another man. Remember that." He slaps me on the shoulder. "Don't fuck it up."

Without waiting for a reply, he turns around and walks toward the Employees Only door.

Not fucking it up is easier said than done.

CHAPTER TWENTY-ONE

Lola

SILAS IS the most dependable person I know.

Except for on my birthday.

I almost didn't invite him this year, so I wouldn't get my hopes up. I've questioned him numerous times on why he seems to have an issue with my birthday, but he says it's nothing. He promises to show, but then he goes MIA every year.

"Do you think Silas will show tonight?" Georgia asks, eyeing a black dress before returning it to the rack at the boutique we're shopping in.

"Who knows?" I grumble, shrugging to play it off like I couldn't care less. Fingers crossed that I look convincing. "He said he would, but if he doesn't show, then he doesn't."

My stomach knots. Worrying about Silas showing up for my birthday has been a nonstop thought.

She gives me a disapproving frown. "There you go again."

I twirl a strand of hair around my finger. "What again?"

"Acting like you don't care if he's a no-show."

"Silas doesn't owe me anything." The words hurt as they come out of my mouth.

"Except he's one of your best friends—behind me, of course.

He can't bail on your birthday with no explanation again. It's weird and rude."

"Sometimes, people have stuff that comes up."

"Every single year?"

I turn away from her, pretending to focus on a rack of lingerie. "Maybe he's not a birthday kind of guy."

"He shows up for everyone else's birthdays, just not yours."

She steps to my side and grabs my hand to stop me. "Sorry, babe. I'm not trying to be a downer, but it sucks to see you sad on your birthday when he bails. If he doesn't show this year, he'd better explain himself this time."

I nod, digesting her words, but I'm unsure of how my reaction will be if he doesn't. At least I chose a place where I could drink this year.

Georgia means well, but I hate hearing it. I try to tell myself that Silas doesn't owe me anything. He's not my boyfriend or lover, so I can't get angry with him. I don't expect people to show up to my party. I told Grace and Finn they could skip it with everything they have going on.

"What about this one?" I hear Georgia say around a gasp, and I realize she left my side. When I shift to look at her two racks away from me, she's holding up a short red dress.

"Hello, birthday dress," I say, staring it down.

"Now, off to find some shoes," Georgia says, perking up at my approval of her choice.

I find the perfect pair of strapless black heels and then stop at the salon for a blowout.

Don't feel sorry for yourself, Lola.

It's not cute, and it doesn't go with your new dress.

———

BIRTHDAYS ARE a big deal to me.

Yes, I'm one of those girls.

Judge me all you want.

It's not about the gifts or the attention. It's how I was raised.

For as long as I can remember, my family has always gone all out for birthdays. No matter what anyone has going on, we always make sure to celebrate. I had lunch with my mother and Robby earlier today. Tomorrow morning, I'll have brunch with the girls.

"There's the birthday girl," Harry, Sixes' club owner, shouts, throwing out his arms when he sees me.

I rode to the club with Lincoln and Cassidy since they live the closest to me. I almost asked Silas for a ride, but the last thing I wanted on my birthday was to wait around, only for him not to show, like a bad '90s flick where the cool guy asks the girl to prom as a joke and ditches her. With perfect timing, Georgia, Archer, Cohen, and Jamie pulled up to the valet behind us. We waited for Maliki and Sierra, our friends from Blue Beech—a town a few counties over—and then went inside.

Harry waves us forward in a follow-me gesture. I grab Georgia's hand, and we form a human chain, careful not to lose anyone while filing through people. Harry leads us up wide stairs and gestures to the security guard to move to the side, giving us entry into the VIP section.

"We have birthday-girl shooters and bottles coming your way," Harry says as a server approaches us, staying at his side. He jerks his thumb toward her. "This is Abby. She's your server for tonight. Abby, whatever she orders is on the house."

Abby eagerly nods, pulling at her sequined skirt that she's paired with a crop top, the bar's logo in the center. "I'll take good care of them."

The bouncer strolls over to Harry, whispering in his ear, and he tells us to have a good time. Abby asks which drinks I'd prefer and says she'll be back.

As soon as she leaves, everyone takes their seats. I check my phone, hoping to find something from Silas, but nothing. He texted me *Happy Birthday* this morning and had breakfast and flowers delivered. When I asked if he'd be here, he replied with a simple, *Of course.* I almost called him but didn't want to look desperate. That was six hours ago, and as much as I want to, I have too much pride to ask again.

If he shows, he shows. If he doesn't, then I'll act like it doesn't affect me. I've given up trying to figure out why my birthday is such a burden to him.

Abby returns with a bottle of Grey Goose, cocktail shooters, and mixers. I grab the vodka, unscrew the lid, and drink it straight. It burns, like acid falling down my throat, and I nearly gag. I haven't had straight vodka in years.

"Jesus, Lols," Georgia says. "I know it's your birthday, but you might want to calm it down. The night is still young."

"The night is still young, but I'm not getting any younger." I hold up the bottle. "Might as well live it up now."

Loud club music plays around us, but it's not so in your face in the VIP area, so we can still hear each other speak. I'm not sure if that's a good or bad thing tonight. Maybe I need some chaos to drown out my thoughts of spending yet another birthday without Silas.

"If Silas doesn't show up, it's not going to be pretty," Georgia attempts to whisper to Archer, but since Georgia can't exactly whisper, I hear her.

I check my phone again.

Nothing.

That calls for a cocktail shooter. It's tastier than the vodka, so I take another. Every time I stupidly look at my phone, I take another shot.

This is what happens when I get my hopes up even though I said I wouldn't. As I'm taking my whatever number shot, I stop in my tracks.

Silas is walking toward us, sluggishly inching toward the table, with intent on his face. His powerful figure stands out among the lingering people, and I can nearly hear the echo of my heart as I bolt toward him.

He's here.

Too bad he's not as happy to see me as I am him.

CHAPTER TWENTY-TWO

Silas

THREE HUNDRED AND sixty-four days of the year, I live a normal day-to-day life. I have no problem with rolling out of bed, leaving my house, and acting like an adult.

But there's one day that I can't, when I can barely function. When every time I attempt to do my mundane actions, I'm hit with the memories. In fear of them, I don't want to get out of bed. And that day just so happens to fall on Lola's birthday. Not going to lie, I've even considered asking her to change her birthday before. I'm that desperate to steer clear of it. It's scribbled out of my calendar in bright-red permanent marker. It's my personal doomsday.

My head is already throbbing when I walk into Sixes. If I had it my way, I'd be at my house, ignoring everyone and waiting for this day to end. But Archer's words smacked some sense into me. If I keep this up, I'll lose Lola. We're already treading into those dangerous waters. My absence would just pull us deeper into it. I can't let that happen.

Curse words leave my mouth, low and barely audible, as I make my way toward our friends. I ran into Harry as soon as I walked in, and since I knew him from throwing events at his club, he pointed me in their direction. My mouth is dry even though I chugged a bottle of water before exiting my car and tossing my keys to the valet. Tonight will be the hardest night I've had to pretend.

Lola's gaze meets mine. She grins as if I'm the birthday present she's been waiting for. Seeing her this happy is why I dragged myself out of my misery and came to the club. Like one of those people who darts toward their loved ones at the airport, she jumps into my arms. I capture her around the waist, holding her up, and her hair drops into my face.

"You actually came!" Her voice is slurred, and alcohol lingers from her red lips as she peers down at me.

I carefully set her on her feet, taking in how stunning she looks in her red dress and heels. "I actually came."

"I didn't think you would." Her face softens. "I figured it'd be another year of Silas ditching me and then apologizing for it tomorrow."

"I'm here." I kiss the top of her head, knowing my words will be limited tonight.

"Thank you." Her words are nearly a whisper—a sharp contrast to the slur she gave me earlier.

She snatches my hand, erasing the distance between our friends and us, and their expressions are filled with approval when I join them.

Damn, it feels good not to be a letdown this year.

"How much have you had to drink?" I ask Lola, squeezing her hand.

She spins to face me and holds up her thumb and pointer finger, leaving some space between them. "Just a teensy-weensy bit."

"What's a *teensy-weensy* bit?" I raise a brow while jerking my head toward the table covered in liquor bottles. "An entire bottle?"

"I'm not sure." She shrugs. "I figured if I got drunk, I wouldn't think about you ditching me."

Her words sting, and I drop my head in shame. She's this drunk because of what I did in the past.

Is this how she looked every year when she realized I was a no-show?

This isn't Lola. She doesn't wear her heart on her sleeve like some of our other friends. A crowbar is needed to crack her open to even draw out shards of obscured pieces. I've also never seen her this drunk. Sure, I've heard stories of her wild college days with the girls, but nowadays, she always stops after a few drinks. She said she got that out of her system.

And even though I shouldn't be, I'm annoyed with her behavior. Almost pissed.

"He actually came," Georgia tells Archer, attempting to keep her voice down, but as usual, she doesn't.

I brace a hand around Lola's waist before she topples over and point at her. "She's drunk as hell."

Archer nods. "That she is."

"I've never seen her like this."

Lola is now talking to Maliki about different liquors he needs to start carrying at his bar, Down Home Pub.

"Blame yourself for that," Archer says, never caring to filter his words.

I huff. "You're blaming me for her being plastered? Maybe blame yourself for not stopping her."

"No," Georgia says, answering for her boyfriend. "We're blaming you for playing head games with her all these years. She drank because she figured you wouldn't show. It's as simple as that."

Lola, now done with her conversation with Maliki, separates herself from me. "Let's dance." She holds out her hand toward Georgia.

I scrub a hand over my face. "Or let's find you some water."

"I choose dancing," she chirps, not even considering my idea.

"How about you choose not to drink anymore?" I almost

feel like her father. "You were worried I wouldn't make it, and I get it, but I'm here now. You don't have to act like this."

She winces as if I slapped her in the face and grabs Georgia's hand. "We're dancing."

Georgia allows her to pull her up from the couch, and they hold hands while walking away from us, dancing to the beat of the music. I scrub a hand over my face, wishing I hadn't come.

"Nice going." I fall back into a chair next to Archer and glare at him. "You could've stopped her from chugging liquor like it was water."

Archer shrugs his broad shoulders. "Not my circus, not my monkeys."

My glare deepens. "No, she's just your girlfriend's best friend."

"It's her birthday. I'm not going to play babysitter. Let her enjoy herself."

"There's the baby daddy and baby mama," Lincoln calls out.

Our conversation ends, all attention cutting to Grace and Finn strolling in our direction. Even though Finn said he was coming, I wasn't sure if Grace would. Which was stupid because the girls are always there for each other.

"Grace!" Lola shouts, stopping her dancing to stumble toward them. "My bestie carrying my future godchild. Thank you for being here!"

"Um, excuse you," Georgia says from behind her. "I'm the future godmother."

Lola wrinkles her nose. "We can *all* be a godparent."

Georgia shrugs. "I'll accept that."

"Happy birthday," Grace says, hugging Lola before Finn guides her to the couch. They sit down at the end of it, making themselves comfortable.

"I haven't seen you this wasted since college," Grace says, her eyes on Lola.

"I've *never* seen her this wasted, period," I add. Even though I'm replying to Grace's comment, I'm studying Lola.

"Agreed." Georgia nods. "Did something happen today?"

Georgia knows why Lola drank so much, so I don't know if her question is a cover, so other people don't know. My guess is, it is.

Unlike me staring at her, Lola hasn't glanced in my direction since Grace and Finn arrived.

"It's my birthday. I was gifted a complimentary bottle from the club since I'm the owner's alcohol rep. He also sent over some bubblegum shooters." Lola motions to the tray of shooters, then snags one and knocks it back.

I run a hand through my hair in frustration. "I'll be sure to tell Harry you're cut off."

"Hey, guys. Can I get you anything else?" the server says, interrupting the birthday shit show.

Grace and Finn order what Lola should be ordering—seltzer water.

I consider leaving. I can apologize to Lola when I'm not a depressed dick and she's sober.

I start to stand, but Lola saying, "My best friend," causes me to freeze.

She collapses onto my lap, the weight of her a sudden shock, and sits sideways. Her breathing is ragged as she wraps her arms around my neck.

I inhale her sweet perfume, almost getting as drunk on it as Lola is, and my mind races. This isn't the first time she's sat on my lap, but it is the first time since I fingered her on the couch. If it were beforehand and if she wasn't drunk off her ass, I would find it normal.

She tips her head down, and her black hair curtains our faces as if giving us privacy from everyone. I groan, hating that my dick hardens when she shifts to straddle me. Just like all her other actions tonight, the expression covering her face isn't one I'm used to. This is a different woman with different emotions and a different mindset tonight.

"I want to fuck you," she whispers into my ear. Unlike

earlier, her words aren't slurred. They're clear as if she hadn't had one sip of liquor.

There's no hint of humor in her voice.

None of our usual playfulness.

I shut my eyes, a pain squeezing at my heart. "You're drunk."

"And?" She slowly slides against me, rubbing her core against my erection, and I groan. "We can leave and finish where we left off at the cabin. This time, I can touch you, tease you, *fuck you*."

Every muscle in my body tightens.

This can't be fucking happening.

This isn't the time or the place to have a conversation like this.

This isn't the time or the place for me to have to stand my ground and most likely have to be a dick to her on her birthday.

She's making a fool of herself. A fool out of me because whatever I do, it will be a show in front of our friends. I can allow her to dry-hump me, which she kinda, sorta is. I can leave with her and have sex with her. Or I can kick her off my lap.

I shut my eyes, growing more and more turned on at the feel of her body against mine. My cock aches, calling me a dumbass at the idea of turning her down. It's been a minute since I've had sex.

"Lola," I grind out, "this isn't the place."

"Then let's leave," she breathes out. "Get out of here. No one will care. They'll probably be happy for us."

My head is spinning. I clamp my hands around her waist, halting her from grinding, thinking it'll solve the problem.

Lola snatches my wrist, plucking it off her waist, and drags it down to her thigh.

And that's when I do something stupid. Without thinking, I abruptly stand.

And Lola drops to the floor.

CHAPTER TWENTY-THREE

Lola

I'VE NEVER BEEN this humiliated in my life.

As I'm on the floor, staring at Silas in shock, I think about my mother. All those times I saw her as weak, as ridiculous, for begging my father to be with her.

I'm my mother.

I finally understand her pain.

Our situations are different, yes, because my father married her. Promised her until death do they part. But Silas swore to never hurt me, and he did.

On my birthday.

In front of all our friends.

Embarrassment hits me from every angle. I was nearly dry-humping him in public. He dropped me on my ass. It was the alcohol's fault to begin with along with my emotions and the lack of eating since I hadn't had an appetite. The thought of Silas not coming made me disgusted at the thought of food.

My gaze is pinned on him, my eyes watery, and my dress is damp from a vodka glass that dumped over in what I'll always refer to as *the fall of my ass*. Hurt and tears are in my eyes. Unreadable emotions are in his. If he didn't want me in his lap, he could've moved me off more casually … carefully … not as if

I were a dirty T-shirt being tossed on the floor after a long day at work.

"Goddammit, Lola," he says around a huff before raising his voice. "Drink some water because you're being a sloppy fucking drunk." As soon as the words leave his mouth, regret flashes across his face.

Everyone's eyes are on us.

He's never talked to me like that.

Then it's almost like what happened just dawned on him.

"Come on." He reaches out, holding out his hand, but I swat it away.

"No, I don't want your help." I sniffle, blinking back tears, and pull myself to my feet. With how tipsy I am, I'm surprised I'm able to. My head spins, my world turning upside down, and the noise around us fades away.

"I'm sorry," Silas croaks.

"I think you should go," I demand.

He was the first person I wanted here, and now, he's the last person I want to see.

I adjust my dress, failing to look at anyone, and fold my arms over my stomach. "That's what I want from you for my birthday. To leave." This is the most broken I've ever felt in my life.

"Fine." Silas pinches the bridge of his nose. "I'll go."

We stare at each other. He looks at me as if begging me to change my mind about asking him to leave … and I want to. I'm holding in sobs when he turns to walk away.

"Well, well, look what we have here," a man calls out.

Silas freezes, and I look forward and see a guy standing in front of us. He's staring straight at Silas while running his hands together. Two men stand behind him, but I quickly dart my gaze back to the man who called Silas's name. He's tall, clean-shaven, and attractive.

"Silas fucking Malone," the guy says, his tone a mixture of excitement and cockiness.

Silas stares him down, his glare colder than he looked when I was practically dry-humping him. He steps in front of me, blocking the man's view of me.

The guy strokes his jaw while coming closer. "I haven't seen you in forever. You act like your family doesn't exist."

Whoa.

Who is this man?

Is he related to Silas?

It dawns on me that I've never met anyone from Silas's family.

"I'm a busy man," Silas says, his voice full of warning.

"Busy, huh?" The guy does a once-over of our friends and scoffs. "Enough time for a birthday party, though, huh? Who's the birthday someone?"

This is where I can get my revenge on Silas.

He obviously doesn't want this guy to see me.

I walk around Silas, revealing myself, and all this commotion sobers me up. Holding up my hand, I say, "Me."

"Goddamn, the birthday girl is hot." Cocky Boy extends his hand, staring at me instead of Silas now. "I'm Trent, Silas's brother."

"Stepbrother," Silas corrects with a snarl. "No blood relation. Thank fucking God."

"Oh, come on, brother," Trent says. "Let's forget about the past. How about this? Let's share a drink. We can go to my table —which is larger and surrounded by NBA and NFL players and other high-profile people—or stay here."

Silas works his jaw. "Nah, we're good. Go hang out with your high-profile friends and beat feet."

"At least let me buy the birthday girl a drink," Trent says.

"She's had enough," Silas snaps, popping his knuckles.

Archer and Lincoln stand and join Silas, and Trent chuckles.

"I wouldn't mind a birthday Sprite," I say, chewing on my lower lip. "I don't want to be hungover tomorrow." I cringe at the thought of consuming anything containing alcohol. I cringe more at the thought of turning around and facing everyone after what Silas just did.

"I think you've already crossed that line," Silas snarls.

Trent snaps his fingers. "A birthday Sprite it is." He does a sweeping gesture toward the table. "Any of these guys your boyfriend?"

His eyes fasten on Silas as if he wonders if it's him and that's the only one he cares about.

"Nope," I quickly say, not bothering to look at Silas.

Screw that.

He did what he did, so I'm not going to worry about how he feels about me being around Trent. Plus, the faster I can get away from here, the better.

Silas curses under his breath and wipes his forehead with the back of his arm.

If Silas hadn't done what he did, I'd have turned Trent down. Hell, I'd have turned any guy down. But now, all I want to do is escape. His rejection killed me.

Before I grab Trent's hand, Abby scurries toward us, holding a tray of glasses. "Sorry! I got caught up at a table." She hands Finn and Grace their drinks, and when she sees Trent, her face brightens, and she giggles. "Hey, Trent. Can I get you something?"

"Nah, I'm good, Abby." Trent gestures to me, and Abby frowns. "I'm going to escort the birthday girl to the bar and get her a drink, so we can talk more privately."

He drops his hand, and this time, he holds out his elbow. I put mine through the open space, connecting us. We walk away, and I don't glance back at Silas once.

Call me a bitch.

Call me whatever.

But at this point, I don't care.

CHAPTER TWENTY-FOUR

Silas

I GO to follow Lola and Trent because, well, fuck that shit, but Archer snags my elbow, pulling me back.

"Unless you plan on making things right with Lola this minute, sit your ass down," he practically snarls. "You just humiliated the girl in front of everyone on her fucking birthday. Don't do it a second time."

I wince at his words, fire burning through me. I'm pissed at Trent for showing up and speaking to me. I'm pissed at Lola for leaving with him. I'm pissed at myself for my behavior.

"Let him get her a drink while you think about your weird asshole actions," Georgia adds, looking like she wants to rip my head off as much as I want to do to Trent's.

She's protective of her friends—as they all are. I've witnessed her kick guys in the shin for less.

I plop down on the chair—the same one where Lola told me she wanted to fuck me. The same one where I turned her down and embarrassed her. I want to stand up and kick it, punch it, do something. As I sit there, I inhale deep breaths in hopes that it calms my racing heart.

This is my punishment for coming tonight, for thinking I could get away with having a good time. Nothing good ever comes out of this day. Not only did Lola and I have a disaster, but Trent, out of all people, also had to show up. My past keeps coming back to haunt me.

Instead of being as miserable as I am about this day, he's now hanging out with Lola, saving her from me—the big, bad best friend who embarrassed her. I dropped her off my lap—one of the worst things I could've possibly done—but I didn't know what else to do. And I hadn't thought before standing.

I slump my shoulders, opening my legs, and drop my head between them.

I'm losing my best friend because I can't get over my past.

"What the hell was that about?" Cohen asks, causing me to raise my head. "Why would you do that shit to Lola?"

I'm asking myself the same question, buddy.

"I'm so confused," I mutter.

"We all are," Cassidy says. "Lola was looking at Silas with stars and horniness in her eyes. Instead of nicely turning her down, he pushed her off his lap." She shakes her head. "That has to do something to a girl's ego. Especially when Silas acts like he's in love with her."

"Acts like?" Finn snorts. "Silas *is* in love with her."

They're talking about me now as if I weren't even here. As bad as I want to tell them to shut up, all that's on my mind is Lola and what I did.

"I hate that motherfucker," I hiss, balling up my fists. "I'm doing everything I can not to storm down there and beat his ass."

"Why do you hate him?" Jamie asks, her voice careful and soft. As a doctor, she's used to handling tough situations.

I tap my foot. "He's shady as fuck."

Always has been.

Always will be.

I will never trust Trent.

He can't be trusted with secrets, with friends, with people's lives.

He can't be trusted with Lola.

"He's shady as fuck because he's really shady as fuck, or he's shady as fuck because he's flirting with Lola?" Lincoln asks.

"Both." I grimace, hating their names being said together.

"Are you going to finally admit you two have hooked up?" Georgia asks.

I stare at my tapping foot—an action to stop me from jumping up and beating Trent's ass. "Nah, we've never had sex." That's the truth. Georgia asked if we've hooked up, and I said we've never had sex. It's not lying.

"But have you *hooked up?*" Sierra clarifies.

I stay quiet. I'd never say anything about what happened the night at the lake unless Lola said it was okay. But then I don't know if I would want people to know because it'd make our friends give us hell about being together.

"How about this?" Finn states with confidence. "Grow some balls and go apologize and tell Lola how you feel."

My face burns, a slash of anger crawling through me, and I glare at Finn. "I could say the same shit to you, brother."

He doesn't have room to talk. He's loved Grace for years, and he hasn't done anything about it. Finn is as terrified of losing Grace as I am with Lola.

"Don't take your anger out on me, man," Finn snaps, hunching forward.

I stand and point at Grace. I shouldn't say the words, but they blurt out from my loose lips. "Grace wouldn't be pregnant with another man's baby had you grown some balls."

My stomach churns. I said that to get back at Finn, but I stupidly hadn't thought about how it'd affect Grace.

Finn bares his teeth as if he's ready to beat my ass. "Watch your goddamn mouth."

At this point, a fight sounds good to me.

I need this.

Someone to take my anger out on … my hurt … my regret. It shouldn't be a friend, though.

I stare at Finn with hard eyes. "Does the truth hurt?"

Everyone watches us, glaring at me as if they want to kick my ass.

Archer stands, preparing to jump in if he has to.

Finn wipes the edge of his mouth. "Like you're doing with Lola. Instead, she's going to hook up with your stepbrother."

Oh, fuck no.

Those words should've never left his mouth.

I rear my fist back, but before it can make contact with Finn's face, Archer pulls me away the same way he did when I tried to stop Lola. He shoots me a warning glare.

"Whoa," Georgia says when Archer has the situation handled. "We all know Lola isn't hooking up with anyone tonight."

Grace grabs Finn's wrist, stopping him from standing to beat my ass. "This is not the place. Let's go."

I slam my eyes shut, the sound of Grace's voice causing more guilt to build inside me. "Shit, Grace. I'm sorry. I was pissed and—"

"It's fine," she rushes out, but I can tell it's not. "I just … it's time for us to go."

I fold my hands together and bow my head. "Really, Grace—"

She talks over me. "You're sorry. Okay. I get it."

Her lower lip trembles, making me hate myself more. Add Grace to another person I humiliated tonight. I'm not even drunk, and I'm acting like an imbecile. Instead of creating more damage, I turn around and walk away. On my way out the door, as I pass the bar, I hesitate.

Maybe it's time for me to break my sobriety.

Maybe it's time I started numbing myself.

CHAPTER TWENTY-FIVE

Lola

"THE BIRTHDAY GIRL doesn't look like she's having a good time," Trent says as the bartender hands over our Sprites.

Yes, he also ordered a Sprite.

"She is most definitely not," I reply, circling my straw through my drink.

He runs his hand over his smooth cheek. "Who pissed you off?"

I wave off his question. "It doesn't matter."

He shifts to face me. "It was Silas, wasn't it?"

I take a sip of my drink.

"Let me make up for whatever he did."

Gripping his Sprite with one hand, he holds the other out to me. I grab it, and we mosey through the crowd toward the subdued section of the bar, where two-top tables are scattered throughout and the music is softer. I've never been in this area of the club, but I've heard about it. It's for the VIPs of the VIPs who like the club but prefer to be on the tamer side of things. It's quite contradicting to go to a club but not want the club experience.

I retreat a step, our hands still clasped, as I flit my gaze over the section. "Are we allowed to be here?"

Maybe I'll ask Harry for a table here next time.

Who am I kidding? I will never celebrate a birthday here again.

Trent offers a reassuring smile. "I didn't reserve a table, but it's okay. I know Harry." He motions toward the other side of the club, close to where my table is. "I was with my friends over there, but you look like you'd rather drink swamp water than socialize. I figured we could drink our Sprites and chat. Sober you up. Get you away from whatever has you upset."

My friends won't mind if I take a minute for myself, away from everyone. I don't want to be around Silas, and I don't know if he's gone.

He leads me to a table near the back of the room, grabs my Sprite, and places our drinks on the table before pulling out a stool for me.

Trent is attractive—tall, dark-haired, and handsome. Not as handsome as Silas, but it was no surprise that Abby was nearly drooling when she saw him. Not only does he look good, but he's also made me feel comfortable tonight.

"Why does Silas hate your guts?" I ask, sitting down and hoping my question takes the attention off me.

Trent scoots his chair closer to mine before plopping down. "His dad left his mom for mine. It was a messy situation, and as stepsiblings, we didn't get along because of it. We were immature teenage boys. I let it go. Silas hasn't."

Silas has mentioned his father leaving his mother, but he never said anything about a stepbrother.

"Have you tried speaking to him privately?"

Trent nods. "All the time. I've invited him to meet up, have coffee, talk, anything, but he won't. He even refuses to attend family events if I'll be there."

"Oh."

That doesn't sound like Silas, and I don't want to talk bad about him, especially not knowing the entire story. But no matter what, my loyalty remains with Silas—even if I want to punch him right now.

Trent pats my hand, catching on to my silence. "Enough about him. Let's talk about *you*."

"Well … it's my birthday."

My brain isn't exactly on its A game right now. I took too many shots, fought with my best friend, and am now with a man said best friend hates.

I'm tipsy.

Okay, maybe a little beyond tipsy.

I can't drive home, but I can recite my full name.

"I got that part, babe." Trent chuckles. "What do you do?"

Simple question. My gool ole drunken brain can also answer that.

Props to me.

"Alcohol sales."

"Oh, cool." He grips his glass and taps his fingers against it. "What company?"

"It's 21st Amendment."

I'm usually more cautious about telling someone where I work, but Trent is Silas's stepbrother. And even though Silas isn't a fan, so far, Trent has been nothing but nice to me. I'm thankful he came to our table and rescued me.

"That's awesome. I have a few friends who order from 21st Amendment."

"What about you? What do you do? Tell me about yourself."

"I work for an athletic talent agency. We represent and find deals for athletes."

"Oh. That's cool."

He pauses, a moment of silence passing. "Did you and Silas ever date?"

"Nope," I quip.

Please don't ask if we've hooked up.

I don't know if my inebriated brain can figure out the best way to lie.

He nods. "I just don't want to touch something that's his."

My head snaps up. "I'm not someone's property."

"Shit, that's not how I meant it." He grimaces. "I don't want to ask you out if you and he have been together."

I shake my head. "We're friends."

Silas made it clear we're nothing.

So, nothing is what we'll be.

Trent blows out a long breath. "How can I make the birthday girl smile?"

I smile timidly. "You're already helping."

He grins. "Glad I'm doing my job."

We talk for over an hour.

About our jobs, families, hobbies.

He enjoys cooking. I don't. So, he offers to cook for me sometime.

We're both homebodies and only go out for special occasions.

Silas isn't brought up again.

Trent seems nice, so why is Silas holding a grudge?

I'll need to ask him when I'm done kicking his ass. Even though what he did was wrong, I'll let him explain. If he wants to make up for what he did tonight, he needs to tell me what his problem is with my birthday.

When it's time to call it a night, Trent walks me back to my friends. Silas, Grace, and Finn are the only ones gone while the others are chatting. I don't ask where Silas is because I don't want them to know his behavior hurt me as deep as it did.

Trent walks me out of the club with the others and waits outside for the valet to bring our rides. He has no problem with introducing himself and making conversation with everyone.

Before I get into Lincoln's car, he asks for my number.

And I give it to him.

———

I HAVEN'T HAD a hangover this intense since college.

I do a once-over of the room I'm in. It's Archer's old

bedroom. Technically, it's still his current bedroom, but he and Georgia rarely sleep here. Archer owns the penthouse, and after Lincoln was released from prison, he moved in with him. Not too long ago, Archer surprised Georgia and bought a house she'd liked. Now, Cassidy and Lincoln stay here since Finn is crashing in Cassidy's old bedroom. It's all one big roommate web.

Me? I'm not a roommate kind of person.

I enjoy my space too much.

I'm here because Cassidy said she was in no way allowing me to go home alone last night. She mentioned something along the lines of choking on my vomit even though I told her I wasn't near that drunken stage. I argued for a good five minutes until I gave in because I was too exhausted to care at that point. All I wanted was a comfy bed, water, and a toothbrush—and thankfully, they had a spare one.

As I stretch in the bed, my head throbbing, flashbacks of last night worsen my headache. Silas made it the worst birthday I've ever had. I don't know what's going on with our friendship, but it's changing. At first, I wasn't sure if it was good or bad, but after the whole lap drop, it was bad.

My mouth is dry as I reach across the bed and collect my phone from the nightstand. I shrink back against the pillow as I scan the texts on my screen. Georgia. Grace. My mother. Trent. *Silas.*

My body feels heavy as I open his text first. He sent it last night, after I went to bed.

Silas: I'm sorry. So fucking sorry.

His message seems so … dead … nothing like our usual texts. I normally wake up to *good morning* texts from him, not apology ones. I haven't felt this lonely, this forgotten, in years.

I ignore Silas's text, answer my friends, and then open Trent's message last.

Trent: Good morning. I hope your hangover isn't too bad this morning.

His message brightens my mood.

I immediately reply.

Me: I'm never drinking again.

Trent: We've all said that before.

Me: True, but this time, I really mean it.

Trent: Let's go out and have a birthday redo since yours wasn't as great as you'd wanted.

Me: I'd like that.

———

THE FIRST THING I order at brunch is a mimosa—my whole *never drinking again* plan long gone.

Do I need a mimosa with this hangover?

Definitely not.

Everyone else does the same, except for Grace and Cassidy, who opt for a lemonade.

Our birthday-brunch tradition started in high school. It began with milkshakes, and then we graduated to mimosas once we could drink. Jamie, Cassidy, and Sierra have joined in as well. I chose a small bistro, and since the sun is shining and the humidity is tolerable, we're sitting outside.

"First things first," Georgia says after the server hands over our drinks. She plays with the straw in her hand, and it's like the drink gives her the confidence she needs to start her questions. "Lola, we need to know what the hell happened last night."

I push my oversize black sunglasses up my nose. "First things first. I'm hungover, and I'll talk about anything but that."

"Come on," Georgia groans. "What pissed off Silas so much that he acted how he did?"

"I've never seen him like that," Grace says. "He threw you off his lap."

I grab my mimosa. "Silas doesn't like it when I drink that much."

I shrug, hoping they believe that lie. Silas has never encouraged me to be sober.

"There's no way he was that mad over you having a few drinks," Georgia argues. "Not to mention, you looked like you wanted to jump his bones."

"It was actually hot," Cassidy adds. "Until the whole *dropping you on your ass* part."

I wince, remembering it so clearly. "Sorry, but I'd prefer not to talk about my best friend rejecting me. It was dumb on my part, smart on his."

"What about his stepbrother?" Jamie asks. "You two looked chummy."

"He's nice," I reply. "We exchanged numbers. He walked me to Lincoln's car, and then he and Cass took my drunken ass home." I give Cass an appreciative nod.

"He was a gentleman," Cassidy says. "With how Silas described him, I expected him to be a jackass. While we waited for Lincoln's car, he chatted with us. I think Silas was jealous of him buying Lola a drink."

Everyone seemed to like Trent, and he didn't give off any douchebag vibes when he wasn't around Silas. Maybe they bring out the worst in each other.

"Is it weird, though?" Grace asks. "With him being Silas's stepbrother?"

"They're not close," I answer. "Their parents didn't start dating until their senior year of high school, and they never hung out. Silas's dad left his mother for Trent's mom. I understand Silas not being a fan, but Trent had nothing to do with what his mom did. According to Trent, Silas has hated him since the day they met."

"As bad as it sounds, I get his anger," Sierra says. "I was pissed when I found out my father had an affair and secret child. I took it out on my brother's girlfriend for a while since she had something to do with it."

I nod. "My father was the king of affairs. It's why I don't trust men."

"Since Lola won't share anything, let's move on to Grace and

Finn," Georgia says, and I smile at the subject change. "Finn looked ready to kill Silas for what he said about you getting pregnant because Finn was a wuss."

When I woke up this morning, Cassidy filled me in on what had happened after I left and how Silas and Finn argued.

I guess Silas decided it was asshole day.

Grace blushes as she plays with her straw. "I'm happy he did. It knocked sense into Finn." A slow smile builds along her face.

Georgia gapes at her. "What?"

"Now, this is a much better conversation." I lean back in my chair and suck on the orange from my drink. "Did you fuck?" *Sorry, not sorry for my straightforwardness.*

"We didn't ... have sex ..." She trails off as if searching for the right words. "Just messed around."

"First base?" Georgia asks. "Second base?"

Everyone happily stares at Grace.

It's about damn time they got together.

"What base is tongues?" Grace asks, always my somewhat-innocent friend ... who also got knocked up by the principal ... so she doesn't seem as innocent as she once did.

There isn't one person at the table who doesn't show a sign of excitement.

"How was it?" Cassidy asks.

"It was amazing," Grace replies, looking on top of the world. "I could spend the rest of my life having him ... go downtown on me."

"Cheers to that!" Georgia says.

Everyone raises their glass and clinks them together.

"Does that mean you're dating now?" Sierra asks.

"I don't know." Grace's smile somewhat drops. "His feelings for me might change after the baby is born. I'm going to get fat—"

"Shut the hell up with that attitude," I interrupt, hating that she's feeling insecure about that. "Finn worships you. He isn't going anywhere."

Now, if only Silas were the same.

More of my friends dating each other.

Silas and I are the only ones left in our circle who aren't getting together.

One by one, they're finding men who are into them.

And day by day, Silas and I are only growing more and more apart.

Our happily ever after isn't with each other. Just our friends ever after.

And everyone, myself included, needs to start accepting that truth.

CHAPTER TWENTY-SIX

Silas

I WAKE up on the couch, my muscles sore, and regret immediately hits me.

My behavior was out of line last night.

With Lola. With my friends. With everyone.

Finn should've kicked my ass. I would've deserved it.

I slept in until midafternoon and wince at the countless texts on my phone.

Most from my friends.

Not one from Lola even though I texted and apologized to her last night.

She's the first person I text.

Me: Please answer me. Want to get dinner? Hang out tonight? Let me make up for my asshole behavior.

Five minutes pass without a reply.

Closing out of her text, I hit Finn's name.

Me: Can we talk?

Unlike with Lola, my phone immediately beeps with a response from him.

Finn: If it's about last night, I get it.

I blow out a breath of relief. Finn probably gets it because he's gone through the same battle with figuring out where things are in his relationship with Grace. He's also protective over her. I saw his reaction, the hurt on his face, when he found out Grace was pregnant with another guy's baby. It hurt him like no other. Watching Lola walk away with Trent out of all people matched the same hurt he'd felt.

Me: Are you with Grace?

I need to apologize to her too.

But I also need to talk to Finn alone.

Finn: Nah, she's at the birthday brunch.

Oh yeah, their annual birthday brunch.

Hopefully, Lola is at least enjoying herself there. Although she's probably experiencing one hell of a hangover.

I hit Finn's name to call him.

"I was an asshole last night," I say as soon as he answers. "I wish I could blame it on the alcohol, but that's obviously not the case."

"Nah, dude," he replies. "I'm buying you dinner for helping me get my head out of my ass."

Even though I'm having a day from hell, a flicker of a smile presses against my lips. "Does that mean you finally told Grace how you feel?"

"Sure did."

At least one good thing came out of last night.

Sometimes, you just need a jackass to point out the truth.

And I was that jackass.

"How'd that work out?"

"Pretty damn good."

"I'm happy for you, man." I chuckle. "Looks like you do owe me dinner."

"Now, it's time for you and Lola to do the same. You're the last couple in our group who needs to get their shit together."

"Lola and I are … more complicated than Grace and you."

"Trent was hitting on her. You need to make your move before she gives him a chance." Finn knows some about Trent because he's been with me other times when I've run into him.

I scoff, my stomach filling with dread, "Lola isn't that fucking stupid."

No way will she fall for his bullshit.

He mocks my scoff. "Do you remember what you did last night?"

I stay silent for a moment.

"You dropped her on her ass on her birthday," he says as if I don't fucking remember. "She walked off with Trent. We both know it wasn't only a friendly gesture from Trent."

"I have to go. I'll talk to you later, man."

I end the call.

As if with perfect timing, as soon as I hang up, another call comes through.

Trent.

That motherfucking jackass.

I hit Ignore and throw my phone across the room.

I scrub my hand over my face.

I need to talk to Lola.

I need to apologize.

Before I lose her.

CHAPTER TWENTY-SEVEN

Lola

I'VE IGNORED Silas all weekend. I need time and space to get my thoughts in order and am second-guessing everything about our friendship.

I cracked open a chunk of myself for Silas. He knows about my family, my father's affairs, my failures. But him? I'm learning he didn't reciprocate. He only told me the basics while keeping anything deep hidden. He never told me about Trent, about their high school rivalry, or that his father had an affair with Trent's mom. I never expected him to give me his life story, but being someone's best friend means sharing your life and experiences with them.

Was I a bad friend for not asking?

But it's not like I could read his mind and know his childhood hadn't been as peachy as he played it out to be. The only characteristic Silas has that maybe things weren't perfect is his sobriety. When I asked if alcoholism ran in his family, he told me no and that his parents barely drank.

I pause my *Desperate Housewives* episode when the doorbell rings and get up to answer it. Looking through the peephole, I find Silas on the other side, shifting from one foot to the other.

I grip the door handle when it rings again. My hand is sweaty as I slowly turn it and then pull away.

"Lola," Silas calls from the other side. "I'm fucking sorry, okay? Just let me explain myself."

Another knock.

Another plea from him to open the door.

I stare at him, one eye shut, and the small hole isn't providing as much view as I want.

His voice breaks, nearly pleading, on his third, "I'm sorry."

That is what breaks me.

I never wanted this to happen to our relationship.

The spinning has returned, and I answer the door before changing my mind.

"Thank you," he breathes out when I do. Sweat has built up along his forehead, and his eyes are red.

"Hey," I say while avoiding eye contact.

If I look at him, if our eyes meet, I might break.

I've kept myself together to avoid bursting into tears. With how my heart is sinking, I'm not sure if I'll be able to keep it that way. I'm shocked I've made it this long without crumbling. I credit it to the tough exterior I always put on. It helps when you always fake you're okay.

My mom sweeps back into my thoughts.

Then it wanders to Silas.

He's faking it. I'm sure of it.

I was blind to it before, but after last night, after faking it myself, it's become clear that he's broken in ways that many people aren't.

I sniffle and turn my back to him, hoping that I can compose myself while walking into my living room. He follows, his footsteps heavy and loud on our short journey.

Silence lingers in the air. There's none of our usual cracking jokes or arguing over what movie we'll watch. All that playfulness has shriveled up and died. I'm angry about what happened last night, about his secrets, about why he can't open up to me. There's no pretending today.

We sit on opposite ends of the couch. There's never been so much distance between us. Snatching a pillow, I pull it into my lap, hugging it to my stomach as if I were a young girl and this was my favorite stuffed animal, and I just woke up from a nightmare.

I don't speak.

He said he wanted to explain himself, so that's what I'm allowing him to do.

Neither one of us has looked at the other.

As I peek at him, I catch him massaging his temples.

"How pissed are you at me?" he finally asks.

Something in me snaps. Instead of telling him how pissed I am, I'm going to show him. He deserves to witness the pain and humiliation that have been my sidekicks since the club.

I shift to face him, to stare him down, so he can see the pain on my face. "Gee, I don't know, Silas." Heat spreads across my face like a blanket. "Tell me how pissed you'd be if I threw you off my lap in public *on your birthday!*"

I expect him to look away, but he doesn't. His tired and worrisome eyes are settled on me.

When he speaks again, his words are strangled. "Do you remember what you said that night?"

"I wasn't *that* drunk."

"So, you remember asking me to fuck you?"

It's a struggle not to wince, not to pull back and react to his words. I could lie and say no, but I want him to know I remember every single thing he said and did. I remember and will always remember everything that happened last night. From what each shot tasted like to the excitement I had when he arrived and then to the despair I felt when he stood up, and I slid off his lap.

Do I regret asking him to fuck me? Absolutely.

I wish I'd never said those words, wish I'd never climbed

onto his lap, wish he never knew that I'd gladly take a relationship with him that exceeds more than friendship. But it happened, and there's no taking it back.

"I do." I clear my throat, and my voice is hoarse. "I apologize for that. I wasn't thinking clearly, but it doesn't excuse what you did."

"I'm sorry," he croaks, rubbing at his watery eyes. "I reacted without thinking."

There's heartbreak and regret on his face. I'm sure mine shows something similar. Our bond had been so strong, so deep, and one night snapped it into something that feels almost forced now. It's like we never knew each other.

He's sorry. His apology is genuine. I've seen fake apologies. My father handed them out like candy to my mother.

I soften my voice. "You could've done it differently, though. You could have moved me, carried me somewhere else so we could talk, anything other than what you did." I try to swallow back the tears that match my mother's when she heard those fake apologies. "You completely humiliated me, and more than that, you hurt me."

"I was already trying to survive the night before I even got to the club." He squeezes his eyes shut as if being hit with a memory. "When you climbed onto my lap, I wasn't thinking clearly."

"Why?" I whisper. "Why is my birthday such a problem for you?"

"It's not your birthday that's the problem."

"Then what is it?"

His shoulders move as he roughly shakes his head. "It doesn't matter."

I drop the pillow from my hold, tossing it to the floor, and scoot in closer to him. "It does matter." I slap my hand against my chest. "Why won't you open up to me? We're supposed to be best friends and know so much about each other, but I didn't even know you had a brother."

Our eye contact shatters when he turns his head to stare ahead at the paused television screen. "We're best friends, but if I told you everything about me, you wouldn't want to be my friend any longer."

I flinch, and my response comes out in a stutter. "What?"

He rubs his hand over his tortured face, and it's halfway covered when he peers back at me. "Can we please ... I'm begging you ... talk about something other than this?" When our eyes meet, his are filled with sorrow, and he gives me the same broken, "*Please*," that convinced me to open the door.

Shutting my mouth, I stay quiet while contemplating what to do. We need to talk about this because if we don't, it'll only cause more tension. Nothing good comes out of running from conversations that need to be said. Unspoken words lead to broken relationships.

He grips the couch, not giving me a chance to say something, and raises himself to his feet. "I'm going to go."

He's leaving.

Walking away.

Not even giving us a chance to break down our feelings from last night.

You're just like your mother, Lola.

Loving a broken man.

"Trent asked me out," I blurt as if I'm trying to even the score with him leaving.

He stops in his tracks, his shoulders pulling forward. "All right then. Learn he's an asshole yourself."

My words didn't cause him to break down and deliver the truth to me. He only shakes his head, staring down at the floor, and heads toward the door.

Before he leaves, he turns to look at me. "You're my best friend. I love you in ways I've never loved anyone else. Don't ever forget that."

He gives me no moment to digest his words, to take them in

again, before he hurries out of my house as if he'd committed a crime and the getaway car was waiting.

If he loves me in ways he's never loved anyone else, why won't he give me more than what he gives everyone else?

As soon as the door clicks shut, the tears pour down my cheeks as if they were at the surface, waiting to find out Silas's next move.

He chose the cold shoulder.

Silas is choosing to break us.

I'm scared our relationship is on its last round, and we're going to lose.

CHAPTER TWENTY-EIGHT

Silas

LOLA WENT on a date with Trent.

It could've been some random guy, but no, it had to be him. I don't know where they went, how it went, and I don't want to know. The thought of them together haunts me. Finn broke the news. He didn't do it to be a dick. He did it to knock some sense into me. I've already lost two people who meant the world to me, and now, I'll lose Lola.

Lola and I went from talking nearly daily to checking up on each other every few days since the night I left her house. A few times, I've almost texted and asked if she was hanging out with Trent to get back at me, but I always stop myself. Lola isn't spiteful like that.

She's changing. *We're* changing.

Tonight will be the first time I'll see her since I showed up at Lola's place after her birthday. Lincoln and Cassidy are throwing a get-together at their place, and everyone will be there. As much as I don't feel like socializing, I need to see Lola.

LOLA IS ALREADY THERE when I arrive at their place, sitting on the leather sectional in the living room. Jamie, Georgia, and Cassidy are with her, and they're chatting away. Georgia's hand gestures, waving through the air, tells me they're talking about something she considers dramatic.

If it wasn't for the birthday disaster, Lola and I would have ridden here together. There are so many what-ifs that could've gone differently on her birthday. I could've gone about rejecting her in a different way. I could've not shown, and she'd never have met Trent. That night was just a complete nightmare.

I say hi to the room, waving at them, but fasten my gaze on Lola. She stares at me, her eyes tired as if she hasn't been sleeping well either. I hesitate, wondering if I should go to her, but the guarded expression on her face stops me from doing so. Not wanting to put her on the spot, I slip past them and meet the guys in the kitchen.

"Sup, chickenshit," Lincoln says when he sees me.

There's no question as to why he called me that. Other than at the bar, I haven't been around my friends much since Lola's birthday, but when they do see me, none of them have a problem with calling me out.

Cohen shakes his head and lifts his beer. "I second the chickenshit and raise you a dumbass."

"Fuck off," I say, shooting them both the finger.

"We're just trying to help you out," Lincoln says.

Grace and Finn walking through the front door interrupts our conversation, and I exhale a breath, happy at the opportunity to take the attention off me. They're holding hands and sporting bright smiles.

"It's about goddamn time," I call out, cupping my hands around my mouth.

"Another couple," Lincoln adds with a smirk. "Four down." He casts a glance at me. "One to go if you quit being a dumbass."

I flip him off again.

At their arrival, the guys and I venture into the living room as Grace sits down. She's smiling, but there's a hint of exhaustion on her face. The other day, Finn mentioned the pregnancy has taken a toll on her energy. Luckily, she has him, and he's making sure she doesn't have to lift a finger.

Georgia squirms next to her. "I'm really happy for you."

"Remember how we bet on who'd get pregnant first?" Lola asks.

I smile, realizing how bad I missed her voice.

Georgia laughs and points at Lola. "And we all said it'd be you."

Whoa. Didn't expect that.

If I had my guess, Grace would've been the first. She's a teacher, and she likes kids.

"Pfft," Cassidy says. "You thought *Lola*, the commitment-phobe, would be the first?"

I rest my back against the wall, shutting my eyes, and imagine a pregnant Lola. She'd be a gorgeous, glowing mom-to-be.

"We damn sure didn't think it'd be Grace," Georgia argues. "And I wasn't about to jinx myself in high school."

Grace laughs. "Me neither. That's why we voted on Lola."

Lola delivers a red-lipped smile. "Come to think of it, I don't know why we didn't put our money on Grace. She's always loved kids."

"Now, who's the next to get pregnant?" Jamie bounces a cooing Isabella, her baby, on her knee. "Two down—me and Grace."

"Uh …" Cassidy hesitates before slowly holding up her hand. "That'd be me." She inhales a quick breath before continuing, "Well … not next since I already am."

Everyone's attention flashes to her. Mine is quick, a simple glimpse, and then my eyes return to Lola, studying her. She's all smiles for her friend.

"I'm sorry," Cassidy tells Grace. "I've kept quiet because I didn't want to outshine your moment. I wanted to try to find the right time to tell you … and I guess this is the right time."

Grace squeals, all the tiredness on her face fading. "Really?"

Cassidy eagerly nods, her blond ponytail bobbing in the air. "Like you, I was totally shocked."

"I guess that makes it three down," Georgia says, scooting down the couch to hug Cassidy.

"Congrats, girl." Lola blows her a kiss. "We're going to have a shit ton of baby shopping to do."

I take the two steps to Lincoln, smacking his stomach. "Why didn't you tell me, asshole?"

He looks like he's on top of the world. "I've been waiting for when she was ready. If I had it my way, I'd have hung fucking flyers all over the bar and streets."

He winks at me before joining Cassidy, wrapping his arms around her from the back and kissing her neck. She squirms, throwing her head back and laughing into his cheek.

I tune them out, staring at Lola in concern, as my mind drifts to the night we found out about Grace's pregnancy. That was the night Lola told me she was lonely. I clench my teeth at the thought of Trent making her *less* lonely.

———

LOLA RODE with Georgia and Archer to Lincoln's, so I asked to drive her home at the end of the night. We need to talk, and I miss being alone with her.

Dammit, I just fucking missed her.

It's like I'm missing a piece of me—an organ I could survive without, but it'd make my life easier if it were still there, like a lung, a kidney, a limb.

She didn't immediately jump for joy. She paused, hesitation on her face, but then nodded and said, "Okay."

"How are you doing?" I ask, focusing on the road ahead of us.

"Good." She plays with the strap of her purse. "Busy with work."

I nod, sneaking a quick glance. "You okay after Cassidy's announcement?"

She tilts her head. "Yes. Why?"

"When I took you home the night after Grace told everyone about her pregnancy, you were happy for her but told me you felt lonely at times." I clear my throat. "Do you feel the same tonight?"

"I'm happy for Cassidy."

"But are *you* happy?"

"I have a good life, good friends, and a good family. For the most part, I'm happy. As far as lonely-wise, I'm not sure how I feel anymore. For so long, I believed I was wired differently. I refused to see a relationship as something that could brighten my life because I was scared that it'd end up as nothing but my mother and father's. But maybe I just needed that time to figure myself out." She lowers her voice. "I don't want to be alone for the rest of my life … don't want to be *single*."

"I get that."

And I do.

At times, I look around my empty home, knowing it'll never be filled with more. No children running around like Cohen's. No lovemaking like at Archer's. No holidays with presents sprawled around the living room floor while my child shows me all the cool shit Santa brought him. I've thought about having it —*smiled* while thinking it—but then I snap myself together.

The inside of the car turns quiet as I digest Lola's words. My turn signal has never sounded so loud as I veer onto her street. I brake, putting the car into park, and bow my head, wishing I had the right words to assure her she'll never be lonely because I'll always be at her side. But as far as her not wanting to be single, that's something I can't provide.

"Eventually, you'll find the right one, and she'll capture your heart." Emotion overflows her voice.

"Trust me," I say around a raspy laugh, "I don't have much heart to keep myself going, let alone to give someone a part of it."

"That's such a bullshit excuse."

I refuse to look at her. "No, it's not."

"You could …" Her voice turns pained. "You could try to give your heart to me. I promise, I can work with even a sliver of it." There's a hint of hope in her voice at her last words as if she's been waiting to get that out and she's proud of herself for doing it.

"And what, Lola?" My reaction is embarrassing. The coldness in my tone is out of line. "Take *a sliver* of yours, only to destroy it later? I refuse to do that to you."

"We can have a happily ever after just like our friends if you'd just quit thinking so negatively about yourself." That hope dissipates. "You've never hurt me in the years that we've been friends."

"Exactly. *Friends* being the key word."

"You're in love with me." She says it with certainty, with agony, yet with fear. "I know it. You know it. Everyone knows it."

I wince at her words—at the truth. "I do love you."

"In what *way* do you love me?" She says the words, but it's as if she needs the confirmation from me—for me to tell her exactly the love I have for her zipping through my veins, as if she were embedded inside me.

I'm thankful for the darkness surrounding us, happy that it's here to cover the lies I'm about to feed her. "As a friend." My heart putters in my chest, this time reminding me that what I say will change our entire dynamic. "I'm sorry, Lola, but I can't be anything more than your friend. That's all I can give you. If you're looking for love, I hope you find it."

"What broke you?" she whispers. "*Who* broke you?"

I give her silence. A refusal to answer. A refusal to crack myself open and pull out the answers, my secrets, my darkness.

Lola wants to take a chance at love. If I were the person she took that leap with, she'd learn that our love would be so like her parents'. I'd break her as much as her father did her mother.

Unlike her selfish father, I refuse to do that.

"All right then." She grips the door handle.

Reaching out, I touch her arm, stopping her. "I love you, Lola."

"Just not enough to do something about it."

CHAPTER TWENTY-NINE

Lola

"SO, THE BABY SHOWER WAS A DISASTER," Trent says
from across the table when I finish telling him my story.

"Literally like something out of a movie," I reply.

"Or out of Grace's worst nightmare."

Georgia, Grace's sister, and I threw Grace an amazing baby
shower. Everything was going well—minus Silas and me hardly
talking once he found out I went to dinner with Trent—until
Grace's *real* baby daddy showed up. He made the announcement
to everyone that Grace and Finn were faking it.

The thing the asshole didn't know was that maybe they lied
about who the biological father was, but Finn has been more of
a partner to Grace than him. Grace and Finn love each other,
and as far as Finn sees it, he's the baby's father.

He's the one who's been there for her throughout the
pregnancy—the doctor appointments, setting up the nursery,
parenting classes, being an emotional partner for Grace. Not the
douchebag who hid his marriage, his children, and that his wife
was also pregnant.

Finn was also there for Grace when the douchebag's wife
went to Grace's work and made a scene. It was all a mess and put
her through emotional hell. It took some damage control on

Finn's and Grace's sister's part, but they've managed to control the idiot now.

This morning, I'm having a coffee date with Trent at the local coffee shop before we go to work. We've gone out a few times. The first was a dinner. Then we attended an Italian festival, where I ate enough food to keep full for days. And this is our third coffee date before work. Trent is fun, carefree, and easy to talk to. At first, I was worried that he'd asked me out to get back at Silas, but he hasn't mentioned him once. Then I thought he'd asked me out in hopes of hooking up, but we haven't had sex or gone any further than a simple good-night kiss.

Trent raises his coffee. "Can I interest you in an event that isn't a disaster?"

I raise a brow. "What's that?"

"My mother and stepfather throw this annual charity event to help the local homeless shelter. Want to be my plus-one?" He playfully smiles. "I promise you, there will be no secret baby mamas of mine showing up and making a scene."

"Ah, man." I dramatically frown. "That sounds way too boring for my liking."

"A little normalcy helps balance out the drama."

I shake my iced coffee. "Oh boy, is this meeting the parents?"

Trent chuckles, shaking his head. "I promise, it won't be uncomfortable. It always has a large turnout, so you won't be put on the spot."

"Will Silas be there?" I pluck a chunk of my banana bread off and drop it into my mouth, hating that I asked that before committing. I don't want to show up and catch Silas off guard.

Trent shakes his head. "Silas doesn't attend anything family-related. If he knows I'll be there, he's a no-show. It seems he only attends events with you and your friends, not us." He directs his gaze downward, and he quickly scrubs a hand over his face.

He's also usually a no-show on my birthdays too.

I frown. "That's sad."

I hate that for him, but as I think about it, I believe Trent. Silas hardly talks about his family.

"We've tried everything," Trent continues. "I've apologized for my wrongs, but he can't seem to get past it."

"Get past what? Some ridiculous teenage rivalry?"

"He hasn't told you about Sienna?"

Sienna?

I straighten in my chair and shake my head.

"Figures."

"Who is Sienna?"

"That's his story to tell. Not mine." He takes the last swig of his coffee and slowly swallows it down, his Adam's apple bobbing in the process.

"But if it involves you, why can't you tell me?"

"I only played a small part."

"I hate when people do that—give you a crumb of something but not provide more."

He blows out a breath. "I told someone what Silas was doing behind his back."

"That's why he hates you so much?"

"That's why." He checks his phone. "We'd better get going. Don't want to be late for work."

I have a feeling there's more to the story than that.

———

"MEETING THE FAM?" Georgia practically shrieks. "Um, that's a pretty big deal."

I roll my eyes. "Quit being dramatic. It's some charity-banquet thing."

She turns her gaze to Archer. "Is it a big deal for a guy to invite a girl to go to some charity-banquet thing where the family will also be?"

Archer shrugs, pulling himself up from the couch. "I

wouldn't know. You pretty much showed up to all my shit, uninvited."

She throws a pillow at him. "Shut up. You loved it."

"Will Silas be there?" Archer asks.

I shake my head. "Trent said no."

He raises a brow. "How does *Trent* know Silas's agenda?"

"He doesn't show up to anything family-related."

"Can Trent get a plus-two?" Georgia asks. "If Silas does show and it turns into chaos, I need a front row seat."

"What *you* need to do is have my baby since it seems all our friends are getting to be dads but me," Archer says.

"Then *you* need to get to work on a nursery."

He throws his arms up. "I'm not building a nursery before you even get pregnant."

Georgia grins. "You know I like to be prepared." She shifts to me. "Just like you'd better prepare yourself in case you walk into some family drama."

———

I DEBATED on whether to cancel with Trent.

Back and forth like a teeter-totter.

My head spinning as if I were on a Tilt-A-Whirl.

I enjoy spending time with him. Go figure, the one other guy I click with has to be the stepbrother of the only man who's ever truly known me. No, it couldn't be a random man. Leave it to me to get wrapped up in a mess like this.

I have no idea where things will go with Trent, but as someone who's gone on some terrible dates, Trent has by far been the best in years.

At the end of the day, I said yes. If Silas wants to live his life in misery, if he wants to keep me at a distance, then that's his choice. And I'll turn in the other direction to find myself happiness. At least, that's what I tell myself as I clasp the strap of my stiletto around my ankle.

———

"WOW, THIS PLACE IS NICE," I say, staring out the window, admiring Trent's parents' home.

The driveway is large enough to be considered a parking lot, and it's crowded with cars. With so many people here, Trent was right—I won't be put on the spot.

Trent stops at the valet—the three of them dressed in black suits with funky polka-dot ties—and hands his keys over.

Something I've never understood is how exactly these types of parties work. Tens of thousands of dollars are spent to throw an affair like this, but why not just donate that money? Do they make more in donations than what the party costs? Or do they consider it a write-off?

My father holds charity events for work sometimes but definitely on a smaller scale: donate fifty dollars and wear jeans to work for the month or donate to be entered into a raffle for an extra vacation week. Something that always ties in with work.

Trent takes my hand, holding it tight, and leads me toward the door, where two men—same ties as the valets—are holding trays of champagne with fake smiles.

"Your parents sure know how to throw a party," I comment.

"My mom likes to go all out." Trent grabs two champagne flutes and hands one to me. "You should've seen my birthday parties, growing up. Craziness and way overboard."

I smile. "Are you a big birthday person too?"

He squeezes my hand. "I love birthdays. Blame it on my father."

"Same. Silas hates them."

I slam my mouth shut, wishing I hadn't brought him up. I planned for it to be a Silas-free night—free of speaking about him and thinking of him. I'd have given him a chance, been willing to leave every other man alone, if that was what he wanted. But he didn't. He told me no, turned me down as if he hadn't been sending mixed signals our entire friendship.

Trent ignores my Silas comment. "Your birthday? What day is it again?" He squints as if trying to remember the date of when we met.

We squeeze around a couple of people arguing over who donated the most money tonight.

"June twenty-third."

Trent freezes, causing me to stumble ahead of him, and I grip the handle of the flute tight, relieved I didn't spill it all over my dress. And even though I told myself I wouldn't think of Silas, his reaction reminds me of how Silas reacts anytime my birthday is mentioned.

"Do you ..." A prickle sweeps up my neck. "Do you know someone else with that birthday? Does that date mean something?"

Trent drops my hand, and just as I think he's going to pull away, he curls it around my waist. "Nope."

Trent is a sucky liar.

Classical music, played by an orchestra, fills the room. This is much fancier than some charity raffle I'm used to. I knew Silas had money, came from money, but nothing like this.

"There's my stepdad and mom." Trent points toward a crowd of people, not exactly singling anyone out.

His hand rests on the indent of my back while we head toward them. The group breaks apart, splitting in different directions.

"Trent," a man says when we approach them, smiling, deep laugh lines forming around his mouth. "I'm glad you made it, son. And I see you brought a date with you." His tone is inviting, cheerful.

I wouldn't think this was a man who had left his wife for his mistress.

This is Silas's dad.

After years of friendship with Silas, I'm finally meeting his father but not with him.

I stare at him, taking in the familiar features he and Silas share. The shape of their faces, their hair color, the way their cheeks lift when they smile.

I hold out my hand, returning the smile. "I'm Lola."

His hold is light, not businessman-like, when he shakes it. "Grady Malone. It's nice to meet you. Thank you for coming."

"Oh, wow. She's gorgeous," a woman says, appearing at Grady's side. She presses her hand to her chest before lightly brushing my arm. "I'm Janet, Trent's mother."

I smile and introduce myself to her.

"One request: you need to improve your nonalcoholic beverages at parties if you want me to come."

And just like I know his features, I know his voice.

It stands out in every room, in every crowd, around anyone.

I stiffen and do a double take as Silas steps to his father's side. I hold in a breath, watching him narrow his eyes at Trent before glaring at me.

CHAPTER THIRTY

Silas

THE ONE TIME.

The one time I show up to an event to appease my father, it turns out to be a bigger nightmare than I imagined. Just like the night of Lola's birthday, I didn't want to come. I need to learn my lesson that when I get a sense of dread while walking into something, I should turn and abort mission.

The reason I kept walking?

My grandmother called and begged me to come—something she hadn't done in years. The last time was my grandfather's funeral, which I attended. She only asks when it means a lot to her because she knows it's hard on me. I couldn't say no to her. I also didn't have anything else to do, so I figured I'd go and at least be able to see my grandmother. If Trent did show, I could dodge him. *Or* tell him to stay away from Lola.

Lola is rapidly blinking as if attempting to process that she's not imagining me. Trent's rubbing his forehead, his shoulders tight. My father glances between us, curiosity in his eyes.

"Oh, hey, Silas," Lola finally says. "I didn't know you'd be here."

My father signals back and forth between Lola and me. "You two know each other?"

Lola nods. "We're friends."

"That's how Lola and I met," Trent says as if wanting to save Lola from the awkwardness. His arm is casually draped around her waist, causing me to snarl. "I ran into them at a club, and Lola and I hit it off."

"Lola," my father repeats the name as if it's finally dawning on him. "This is *the* Lola?"

Lola has been brought up in our dinners before when my father asks how I'm spending my time since I hardly visit my family. His brows are furrowed as he stares at Lola, and it's not like I can lie and say no with Lola standing right there. Lola appears as if she'd prefer I'd say no—the color gone from her face as she averts her gaze from everyone.

I tap my foot, trying to stop myself from walking away from everyone. "It is."

My father angles his concentration on me, a look of understanding on his face.

My thoughts are racing. To stop focusing on Trent's hand on Lola, I glance from one side of the room to the other, back and forth, as if searching for a lost person in the sea of overdressed people.

"I'm going to go say hi to someone," I lie before turning on my heels and walking away from them.

I place the glass on a random table and storm up the stairs to my old bedroom. Slumping onto the edge of the bed, I rub at my throbbing temples, the image of Lola and Trent together burning through my brain.

I need a minute.

A minute to prepare to see them together again.

Or I could just leave.

No one would expect anything different from the son who caused chaos in the community.

Resting my palms against the bed, I brace my fingers against the black duvet and pull myself to my feet.

If this is a game Trent is playing, I won't let him win.
I'm staying to make sure Lola is okay, to keep an eye on her —and to also torture myself. I move down the stairs at a slow pace and keep my head down until I'm close to where Lola and Trent are talking to my father and the man he founded the charity with.

I crack my knuckles, watching them, and jerk back at my father's voice.

"You're in love with her," he says, stepping to my side. "Which is why I'm lost as to why she's here with Trent and not you."

"Like she said, we're friends," I mutter.

"I'm familiar with wanting someone thinking you can't have them. I know what it looks and feels like."

"Don't." I glare at him. "Lola and I are nothing like you and Janet."

"I know, I know." He sighs. "You'll lose her to him if you don't get your head out of your ass."

I avoid eye contact with him and stare directly at the couple. "Are you telling me to go steal Trent's date?"

"Is it stealing if she's already yours?"

"I thought you wanted Trent and me to make amends?"

"I do, but I also want you to be happy."

"And I want her to be happy, but that won't be with me," I say before walking away.

I stand to the side, watching them from afar. A few people stop and say hello. It annoys me because they're taking my attention off Lola. Everyone views me differently here. In my new life, in my circle of friends, I'm the life of the party. But in this world? I'm the kid who created tragedy.

"Trent said you usually don't attend this stuff," Lola says, stepping up next to me. "Otherwise, I wouldn't have come."

My mood softens when I look at her. Her dark hair is down in loose curls. Her cocktail dress is different than her usual style

—a light pink, shimmering with butterflies. I smile, remembering another time she wore it. It was a work event, and I told her as much as I loved her wild, dark side, it was nice to see her sweetened up.

She punched me in the gut and asked, "How was that for sweet?"

We shared a hotel room that night, sleeping in separate beds, but those were the days when shit wasn't weird between us.

"I don't, and tonight is a reminder of why it's smart not to."

My mouth is dry. I stare at the champagne glass in her hand, watching the bubbles dance together. Even though I don't drink, something would be damn good right now to help erase seeing them together. I start to ask her where her little date is but stop myself.

The less I see her with Trent, the better.

Her lips open into a smile as if attempting to cheer me up. "Your family seems nice. I'm glad I got to meet them."

I can't stop myself from scoffing. "I'm glad Trent did that for you because I couldn't."

"Wait," she snaps, holding her palm toward me. "Are you angry with me for coming?"

I cross my arms. "You don't think it's fucked up that he brought you here, knowing you're *my* friend?"

She stares at me in disbelief. "No one thought you were coming, and considering I'm *your friend*, shouldn't you be happy to see me?"

I drown everyone out and focus on just the two of us.

"I'd be happy to see you if you weren't out there, playing around with a man I despise."

"Is everything okay here?"

With the worst timing ever, Trent reaches us like he was watching and made his way over at the sight of my anger. I hate being angry with Lola and her being angry with me. It rarely happened in the past, and now, it seems like we can't escape that cloud lingering over our friendship.

"Everything would be okay if you left," I bite out, my nostrils flaring and every muscle in my body tensing.

"Whoa," Trent says, stepping closer to Lola. "No one thought you'd be here. Lola is your friend. Why do you care if she's here?"

It's as if he and Lola rehearsed that statement on the ride here, just in case I showed.

My pulse speeds, my heart pounding, and I raise my voice. "I care because you're using her to get back at me."

"Get back at you?" Trent yells, his upper lip snarling. "I didn't even know you'd be here, asshole."

My brain isn't processing what I'm saying, and I swing my attention to Lola. "You're both doing this to get back at me."

"Excuse me?" Lola asks, retreating a step from me.

"Dude, talk shit to me all you want, but leave her out of this," Trent demands, and the way he goes to Lola, blocking me from her, is so familiar to what I did at the club.

He thinks he needs to protect her from me?

From me?

Her goddamn best friend?

The man who's looked out for her for years and always been by her side?

"Lola didn't do anything but accept an invite," Trent goes on, and Lola peeks over his shoulder at me, her face brimming with embarrassment as people around us watch.

Trent stares at me, stone-faced, waiting for my next move.

I point over his shoulder to Lola. "She'll be another woman you ruin, just like the last one I cared about."

"Oh, you want to go back to that?" Trent says, loosening his tie, and I do the same. "You always seem to forget the part you played in it too." He steps forward, our faces inches away from each other. "You seem to forget that she questioned how you felt the same way Lola does."

"Trent," Janet yells from a distance.

"Silas!" screams my father, stomping in our direction, aware a fight is about to ensue.

The anger I felt for him that night returns like a bad nightmare.

Before anyone can stop us, I swing my arm back and punch Trent in the jaw, knocking him back a few steps.

CHAPTER THIRTY-ONE

Lola

I'VE NEVER SEEN Silas like this.

Sure, he's been angry before. He's punched a few guys for grabbing my ass or disrespecting me, but this? This is much deeper. Silas punches him, his face filled with so much fury it's as if he wanted to kill Trent.

Seconds after being punched, Trent snaps back, wiping the blood dripping from his nose and onto the expensive rug underneath them, and lunges back at Silas. Silas grunts when he's pushed into the wall, and a full-on fight ensues. Silas scores another jab to Trent's face, and Trent responds by drilling his fist into Silas's eye.

Finally, a group of men successfully breaks them apart.

I avert my eyes to the rug, staring at the blood, knowing that everyone thinks the fight is my fault. But then I quickly raise my chin. *I won't act like this affects me.*

It's not my fault these two are having some pissing contest. Something deeper brought on the war between Silas and Trent.

Three men stand between Silas and Trent, ready as if waiting for one of them to start round two. Trent is blocked from my view, so all I see is Silas. His face is burning, and he wipes his arm along his face to collect the blood before he rips his suit jacket off his arms and throws it onto the floor. Blood falls, staining his white button-up, but all he does is stare straight ahead as if he has tunnel vision and only sees Trent.

"Just wait," Silas says. "I'm going to kill you. It's what you deserve."

A light whimpering sounds from behind me, and I turn to find Janet. She meets my gaze, giving me an apologetic nod, and tenderly cups my shoulder.

Trent huffs, raising his voice so Silas can hear him. "It's what I deserve?"

Guys yell as Trent circles around them to get back to Silas, but he holds up his arms as if saying he means no harm.

Trent thrusts his finger in Silas's direction. "Do you not remember what happened that night? Do you remember *who* went upstairs with Sienna? Because it sure wasn't me. Sienna is dead because of the secret you two hid."

"Fuck you," Silas screams, and I swear his voice is so powerful that the sparkling chandelier vibrates from it.

"Enough," Janet yells, moving around me and stalking toward them. "Both of you!" She swings her arms in the air. "Enough!"

Silas stands straight, his chest heaving in and out so deeply that I'm shocked he's not hyperventilating.

I rush to his side, frantically grabbing his arm. "Calm down. *Please*. Let's go talk."

Janet shoots me an appreciative head nod.

"You have no idea who he is." Silas seethes, baring his teeth. "You shouldn't have come. I shouldn't have come. We don't belong here."

He grabs my drink, chugs the remainder of the appletini, and throws it onto the floor. The sound of glass shattering echoes through the silence of the room.

"I'm out of here," he says before squeezing past me and

pushing his way through the people who are watching—slack-jawed, bug-eyed, and hands covering their mouths.

I don't realize tears are running down my cheeks until I no longer see him.

CHAPTER THIRTY-TWO

Silas

I HADN'T HAD a single sip of alcohol since I was eighteen.

That changed tonight.

And as I charge into Twisted Fox, it's about to be more than the sip I had of Lola's nasty-ass apple-something. Whoever my stepmother hired to bartend needs to be fired ASAP.

I ignore hellos, ignore those who try to make conversation and ask why I'm a bloody mess, and head straight for the bar.

Pointing at Lincoln, I say, "Vodka. Make it a double."

Lincoln freezes, taking in my appearance. "Good one. What the fuck happened to you?"

"I'm not kidding," I grind out, licking caked blood from the corner of my lip.

"Dude, in case you forgot, you don't drink." He says it as if I'd just come out of a coma and asked who I was.

I clench my fists, noticing the broken skin on my knuckles, covered in Trent's blood …and possibly mine as well. "I drink now."

"Not happening. I won't be the one responsible for breaking your sobriety. You're upset about something, so sit your ass down, and we can talk about it."

Ignoring him and his request, I storm behind the bar and

snag a bottle before he gets the chance to stop me. "You don't want to serve me? I'll do it my damn self then."

Customers gasp as I twist off the cap, drop it onto the ground, turn the bottle up, and lift it to my lips. Even though I finished off Lola's drink, straight vodka is nothing like a watered-down martini. It hits me harder, nearly knocking me on my ass, and I stumble back against the liquor shelves.

Just like that, in a matter of seconds, after years of saying no, I broke my vow. I stomped on the one thing I'd said would stay with me for the rest of my life.

The liquor burns, going down, but it's a sweet burn, a satisfying one, a reassurance that I'll forget everything about tonight.

"Jesus," Lincoln hisses, spinning on his toes and yelling for Cassidy as she walks by, not noticing the shit show I've started.

She whips around. "What's up?"

Lincoln jerks his head toward me as I take another swig. "We have a problem."

"Yes," she says, drawing the word out. "I'll get Cohen …" Her voice lowers. "And call Lola."

"Don't bother calling Lola," I yell, playing with the bottle. "She's with Trent, meeting our parents."

Cassidy freezes, no longer going to get Cohen, and Lincoln does the same before a customer calls out, "Enough of the pretty-boy dramatics. I need a drink."

I hold up the vodka and take a gulp in a *there ya go* gesture.

Cassidy scurries off, disappearing down the Employee Only hallway, and I take another desperately needed drink.

Lincoln ignores the customer and keeps his attention on me. "Man, I know you're upset about Lola, but you're going to regret this when you're in the right state of mind." He shakes his head in frustration, and his words slowly leave his mouth as if he's not sure I'll process them if he says them any faster. "Put the bottle down, have a seat, and we can talk."

I wave off his Dr. Phil speech. "Nah, I'm good. I don't want to talk about anything."

"Too damn late," Cohen says harshly, appearing out of damn nowhere. Taking me off guard, he steals the bottle from me. "My office. Right now."

"Piss off," I grumble. This time, it's me taking him off guard as I re-collect the one thing that can help me leave behind thoughts of Lola and Trent. In fear of him stealing it back, I take another swig of the vodka.

"Jesus fucking Christ," Cohen mutters before glancing back at Cassidy. "Call Lola."

Why are they saying, call Lola?

Like she isn't on a date with another man at the moment.

Fuck it. Let them call her and ruin it.

"Lola," I whisper her name into the bottle before taking another swig.

Was it a mistake, hiding pieces of myself from her?

I'm unraveling, the darkness seeping through those openings, showing my friends who I really am. They don't know the real Silas—the one who struggles with who he is and is ashamed of the things he's done.

Standing there, gripping the bottle as if it were my lifeline, I draw in deep breaths as if I don't know if the next one will come.

Cohen grabs my elbow, jerking me away from the shelves, and Lincoln grabs my free elbow.

"Watch the bar, babe," Lincoln tells Cassidy, and she gives him a thumbs-up, worry lining her features.

I'm overpowered as they walk me through the bar, people pointing at me and talking about my swollen eye. I'm talking shit, telling them to mind their business, as I'm shoved down the Employees Only hallway. Just as we're passing Archer's office, the door swings open, and he appears in front of us.

He eyes me, raising a brow, taking in my beat-up appearance, a bottle hanging from my fingers. "The fuck is wrong with him?"

"Lola," Cohen answers, pushing me into his office while curses leave his mouth.

He and Lincoln roughly sit me down in a chair while Archer slams the door shut behind us.

"Shocker," he grumbles.

Pulling away, Cohen slams his hand on his desk, causing shit to rattle and papers to slide off. "Jesus, why do I always have to deal with your guys' relationship issues here?" he groans. "I'm about to ban all of you from this damn bar."

"I never thought he'd be a depressed drinker," Archer comments, shaking his head in disapproval. "It makes sense, though."

I slump down in the chair, my head spinning, regret hitting me as hard as the vodka. Surprisingly, no one attempts to take the bottle from me again. They watch me as if I were a child playing with a dangerous object they were scared to take away because it'd provoke me further.

CHAPTER THIRTY-THREE

Lola

I HURRIEDLY WIPE tears from my eyes as Trent darts toward me. "I need—" I'm struggling to catch my breath. "I need a break … need to get away from these …" I motion toward the nosy crowd. "Everyone."

Trent nods, his lip busted, and takes my hand. He holds it tight as if he's reassuring me that everything will be okay, that he'll protect me the best way he can. Our pace is frantic, and I nearly stumble up the stairs he leads me up. We rush down a hallway and into a bedroom with bare walls and a strawberry smell—one of those plug-in scents.

When Trent releases me from his hold, I stare at my hand, fastening my gaze on the blood.

Whose blood is it?

Trent's?

Silas's?

Both of theirs?

A light across the room flips on, showing off the attached bathroom, and Trent rifles through the drawers. He turns on the faucet, wetting a washcloth, and slowly treks back to me. I'm shaking as he carefully guides me onto the bed. Dropping to his knees, he takes my hand, flipping it over, and starts cleaning off the blood.

"No," I stutter, sniffling as I attempt to grab the washcloth from him. "You're the one covered in blood."

He chuckles—an attempt to appear lighthearted, but it's forced and phony. "That wasn't the first time Silas and I have fought. After what happened tonight, it might not be the last either."

"That doesn't make it right," I mutter when he grabs my other hand. "I'm not the one bleeding."

"And I'm not the one who just had to endure the embarrassment of that."

"That wasn't your fault. Silas was—"

"He was hurting," Trent says for me as if he doesn't want me to think negatively of the man who just started a fight with him.

Should I have gone after Silas?

Yes.

The moment he finished my drink, I should've stopped him. But I was shocked, frozen on my feet, when Silas stormed out of the party. Had I tried to chase after him, I'd have face-planted and endured further embarrassment.

When Trent finishes and there's not a speck of blood on me, he allows me to clean his face. He winces as I carefully remove the evidence of his earlier brawl. He already has a fat lip, and a bruise is forming under his eye. When I'm finished, I stand, walk to the bathroom, and deposit the washcloth into the sink.

As I return, I find Trent on the floor, his back against the bed, and his head is bowed. "I'm sorry. If I had any idea that would happen, I wouldn't have invited you."

"I shouldn't have come," I whisper, sliding down next to him, our thighs touching as we stretch out our legs.

I need to talk to Silas, but right now, I'm so angry with him. He embarrassed me again, and at this point, I'm not sure how much more I can take. If Silas doesn't open himself up to me, if he doesn't explain why he's had this sudden shift in his character, we might not be friends any longer.

"Do you want me to take you home?" Trent asks.

"I think that's a good idea."

He stands before helping me to my feet. "Do you want a change of clothes? I'm sure I have some old high school clothes that will fit you somewhere in here."

"This was your room?"

He nods. "It looked cooler when I lived here, I promise."

I smile, grateful for him trying to make light of our situation and not as weird. "Sure."

As he opens a drawer, my phone rings. I fetch it from my bag to see Cassidy's name flashing across the screen.

I quickly answer. "Hello?"

"You need to come to Twisted Fox, like, right now." Her sentence almost sounds like one word because she says them so fast. "Silas is here."

I press a palm to my heart, thankful he's in good hands. "Thank God."

"He's here, *drinking*."

"Oh my God."

"Exactly what everyone here thinks. If you can, please get here ASAP."

"I might be the last person he wants to see right now, but I'm on my way." I look at Trent. "I need you to take me to Twisted Fox. It's a bar not far from here."

"I know where it's at. Let's go."

I don't bother changing clothes. If I need to calm Silas, I doubt me showing up in Trent's old high school gear would help the situation.

———

"WILL you tell me what's going on?" Trent asks fifteen minutes into the ride.

We snuck down the back stairwell and into the garage, and Trent snagged the keys to his Grady's BMW—he said he wouldn't mind. I shrugged. It sounded better than having to wait for the valet to bring Trent's car around.

"Silas is there and upset, so they asked me to come." I withhold the information that Silas is drinking.

He nods. "You're a good friend to him."

"Contrary to what you've seen recently, he's a good friend to me."

He peers over at me. "Is that all you two are? Just friends?"

"That's all." I try my hardest to sound confident in my words even though it's the last thing I feel about our friendship.

He nods again. "Even with our issues, Silas is a good guy. He went through some tough shit in high school, and it seems he might never fully recover from it."

He keeps telling me the same thing—Silas went through something tragic in high school—but it's driving me crazy that no one will elaborate.

"Why doesn't he drink?"

"I'm not sure. My guess is, he's punishing himself."

"Do you have something to do with that?"

"I had a part in what destroyed him, but even if he thinks so, it wasn't all my fault."

Cassidy texts again, asking if I'm coming, and I tell her yes before asking her to keep me updated if things get worse. I texted Silas a few times, but he hasn't replied.

When we pull up to Twisted Fox, I'm ready to jump out of the car and see Silas. He might've hurt me, but I need to make sure he's okay. He's drinking—something he's never done, upset or not.

Clutching the door handle, I peer at Trent when he steers into a parking spot. "Thank you for the ride. I can have one of my friends take me home."

He unbuckles his seat belt. "I'll walk you in."

I hold out my hand. "That might not be a good idea."

He shakes his head and opens his door. "Neither is letting you walk into whatever you're about to walk into alone."

"My friends are here."

He steps out, not saying another word, and I do the same. Together, we walk into Twisted Fox, and I'm unsure of what we're about to discover. My heartbeat turns sluggish as I scan the bar, frantically searching for him with Trent on my heels.

"He's in Cohen's office," Cassidy says when she sees me before her eyes shoot to Trent, and she raises a brow. "Not a good idea."

I shrug. "Neither is Silas drinking."

Cassidy's comment doesn't change Trent's mind about tagging along, and I storm toward Cohen's office. The door is closed, but I don't bother knocking before swinging it open. I gasp, taking in the sight of a drunk Silas hunched over in a chair as if he's in time-out.

Silas's hand is tightly gripped around a vodka bottle, and his eyes are bloodshot as they slowly travel to me. I'm unsure if it's from drinking or crying, considering it appears he's done his fair share of both. He hasn't cleaned himself up, so he's still sporting blood on his face and white shirt.

"You motherfucker," Silas snarls.

I stiffen, shocked he'd talk to me like that, but then I follow his gaze over my shoulder to Trent standing behind me.

Silas's attention swings back to me. "Not only are you going on dates with him, but now, you're also bringing him here?"

Trent steps to my side. "She needed a ride here to take care of you, dumbass. You've already ruined our night, so there's no coming here to have fun."

"Hey, man," Archer says in warning to Trent.

Silas stands, shifting his body back and forth to catch his balance, and I'm surprised our friends aren't helping him.

No, wait, I'm not.

They're going to make Silas deal with the consequences of how he's acting tonight. Silas isn't wasted. He can still stand on his own, and his words aren't slurred, but it's also been a while since he drank. He's more angry than anything.

He blinks rapidly while focusing on me. As he does that, Archer swipes the bottle from his hold, causing Silas to glare at him. Archer shrugs because he couldn't care less about Silas's anger.

"You brought her here, huh?" Silas scoffs. "*Now,* you care about people's well-being? You sure didn't care about Sienna's."

I wince at her name, wishing I knew who she was.

Trent blows out an exasperated breath. "We were in goddamn high school! Quit blaming it all on me because you're too scared to realize you played a bigger part than I did. I did something shitty, yes, but I'm not responsible for their deaths. Neither of us is. Kenny is who we should blame. He's the one who killed Sienna."

Kenny?

Who the fuck is Kenny?

Now, we have a Kenny thrown in with a Sienna that I know nothing about.

My attention is moving back and forth between the two, trying to process their conversation and take in every word I can, searching for clues between each one of them.

"Don't say their names," Silas yells.

Trent shakes his head. "No one told you to sleep with her."

"Fuck you!" Silas screams, and I'm sure everyone in the bar heard him.

"No one told you to race after them either," Trent continues as if he wants to rub salt in the wound. "You made that decision."

CHAPTER THIRTY-FOUR

Silas

TRENT'S WORDS are a knife to my gut, twisting the memories and truth into every muscle and vein.

I try not to blame Kenny for what happened.

How can you think bad of your dead best friend?

I swallow down Trent's words.

Swallow down the truth.

I made the mistake of getting caught with Sienna, of secretly hooking up with her, but Trent made the mistake of ratting us out. Even if he didn't know what would happen, I'll never forgive him for it.

He took Sienna from me.

And now, he's taking Lola.

No one here, other than Trent, knows what happened that night—what changed me. And I hoped to keep it that way.

Of course, he's fucked that plan up too.

Cohen stands, staring at Trent. "It might be time for you to go before it makes the situation worse."

Trent nods, looking away from me to Lola. "You're a good person." He motions toward me. "He's poison. Don't let him drag you down with him. It'll only end up with you being hurt."

"Oh, fuck off," I yell, my pulse speeding as I tremble,

fighting to control my anger. "The only person who's poison is *you*."

Trent ignores me, as if I no longer exist to him, and stares at Lola. "Are you sure you're good? I can wait out in the car until you figure this out."

"She's fine," Lincoln says. "Trust me, we got her."

Trent nods. "Call or text me when you get home, okay?"

"Okay," Lola whispers.

I clench my fist, hating that he's speaking to her, that he's acting protective—like he cares about her as much as I do. I should be in that position, not him.

He goes to kiss her cheek but then suddenly stops, realizing the bad timing.

How strong are their feelings for each other?

Stronger than ours?

No way. Lola and I have years of history.

Trent could never match that.

But he does have something I don't—the ability to be in a relationship.

After what happened, everyone blamed me.

Not him.

I was the one caught with her.

Trent doesn't say another word before turning around and leaving.

"What the hell is wrong with you?" Lola screams at me before grabbing the bottle of liquor from Archer's hand. "Why did you do this? This isn't you!"

My throat tightens, and my words are strangled as I say, "Maybe you never knew the real me."

CHAPTER THIRTY-FIVE

Lola

"MAYBE YOU NEVER KNEW THE real me."

I want to collapse and sob at Silas's words because they're the truth. I don't know the true Silas, but in my defense, he only allowed me to know what he wanted. He gave me the lighthearted Silas—the one who wore a smile as a daily uniform and hid his secrets so deep that it was as if it were a second skin.

My best friend—the man, albeit he's being a total jackass at the moment, I wanted to spend the rest of my life with—just said I don't know the real him. The guilt is strong right now.

Cohen and Archer are staring at me for answers as if I'll know what to do about the drunken Silas standing in front of us. Even though my heart is tugging to comfort him, my anger also has me frozen in place as I think about my birthday, for the stunt he pulled at the party, and for pulling away from me. This Silas—the one who's finally coming to light—his main job seems to be hurting me.

Is this the Silas he's been scared to show?

That he's this bitter man, doused with resentment?

His breathing is rushed, nearly coming out in pants, and with each exhale, the liquor on his breath becomes more potent. He'll regret his actions in the morning.

"Silas," I whisper, forcing myself forward, closer to him. "Why don't we go talk in private?"

"No." His tone is clipped, his answer short, concise, and harsh. "Trent was right. I'm no good for you. Even though he isn't either, he might not be as fucked up as I am. Hell, he seems like he's doing just fine, even after what he did."

"What did he do?" I yell, the power to keep my voice low gone.

He shakes his head violently. "There's a reason I don't drink, why I can't see you on your birthday, or commit."

"*Please*," I beg. "Let's talk in private."

If he doesn't want to explain it in front of Archer and Cohen, I get that, but he needs to with me.

"I'm good." His eyes are blank, unreadable, and I groan when he stalks out of Cohen's office—too fast for anyone to stop him. Storming down the hallway, he pushes the exit door open and walks out into the darkness.

Cohen, Archer, Lincoln, and I crowd into the hallway, and when Cohen goes to follow, I throw my arm out to stop him.

I pat his shoulder. "I got this."

Cohen's eyebrows draw together. "He's in pretty rough shape."

"Which is why I need to be the one to talk to him."

If there's anyone who can help even just a little, it's me. They might not think so because he's so angry with me, because I showed up with Trent, but even with the issues we're going through, my bond with him will never break.

"Whatever you do, don't you dare get in the car with him," Archer demands.

I nod. "I won't."

It's chilly when I step out, and the guys stand at the open door as if they were watching their firstborn attend her first prom, their eyes glued to me. I shiver at the breeze and see Silas turn the corner of the building toward the parking lot. Even though it's a struggle with my heels, I speed up my pace.

Damn heels.

I would've taken Trent up on his *change of clothes* offer if I had known I'd be playing chase tonight.

"You can't drive," I yell out into the night.

Silas freezes as if my words were a barricade in his path and stares back at me over his shoulder. I can see his face from a distance, somewhat clear, because the parking lot lights are bright—something Archer and Cohen required when they were installed.

"I'd never drink and drive," he sneers. "Not after what happened."

He flinches. Those words weren't supposed to make the journey out of his mouth and into the public, not supposed to come out around me. I add them to my mental notes, to the words Silas and Trent have provided that I've begun piecing together while trying to figure out what could've happened in my head.

There was a girl involved: Sienna, who's now deceased.

A guy: Kenny.

Something happened with drinking and driving.

And Silas blames himself.

Was he drinking and driving?

Is that why he doesn't drink?

No. I can't wrap my head around that.

Wouldn't he be in jail?

That's a manslaughter charge.

Cohen would've known when he looked up his background check upon hiring, so that can't be it.

Then what is it?

"Go back inside, Lola," he yells, scuffing the toe of his shoe into the ground. "It's dark, and this is a bar. It's not safe for you."

I cross my arms and continue in his direction. "If you're out here, then I'm out here."

He turns and returns to walking, but his pace is slow, allowing me to catch up with him while also not making it obvious. He's not stumbling, he doesn't appear too wasted, but I'm sure we look childish. If someone were to drive by, they'd assume we were a drunk couple arguing, but I don't care. I'm not leaving Silas alone and hurting like this.

Maybe that's why he's kept his past buried for so long. He didn't have someone to help fight those demons with him.

If only he'd tell me, if only he'd open himself up, I'd be there at his side the rest of the way.

He peeks down at my shoes when I reach him. "Your feet are going to kill in the morning. I don't want to get a text with you blaming me for that."

"Does that mean you plan to talk to me tomorrow? Or will you be too hungover?" I frown at his lack of answer as he stares ahead into the night. "Or you might be dead since you're walking in the opposite direction of your house that's *twenty miles* from here."

Coming to a halt, causing me to nearly trip, he bends down. I stare down at him as he unties his shoes and takes them off.

With a shoe in each hand, he holds them out to me. "Put these on."

I stare at them with wide eyes. "Huh?"

"Put my shoes on." He shoves the shoes closer. "If you must follow me, I don't want your feet to hurt."

"Thank you," I whisper.

He takes my hand and helps me sit on the curb. I thought he wanted to escape me, but here he is, waiting for me to change my shoes. I ignore the thought of my dress getting dirty, unstrap my heels, and replace them with his shoes. I tie them as tight as I can, but they're still too big.

I'm about to look more childish with my Ronald McDonald shoes, but I'll make do.

He stares down at me, despair in his eyes, before assisting me to my feet. I sigh when he takes my heels. Without a word, we return to our walking. As bad as I want to question him, there's a possibility that doing so might cause him to close up and tell me to go back inside.

A bright light forms behind us, and a car slows down, going at our pace.

The window rolls down, revealing Cohen.

"Look, guys," he calls out from the driver's side, "let me drive you home, and you can talk about this in the morning."

I nod, hoping Silas agrees so we can take Cohen up on his offer.

Silas shakes his head, his shoulders slumped, my heels smacking against his leg. "Take Lola home, but I'm good." He peers over at me with wet eyes. "Get in Cohen's car."

I cross my arms. "Nope. If you're staying, then I am."

"Jesus," Cohen hisses. "Talk it out and text me when you're ready for a ride. I'll wait in the parking lot."

He pulls away, and as bad as my feet are already killing me, I refuse to go. This man needs to be assured that no matter what war he's battling emotionally, I'm there for him. He's okay. *We're* okay. At least, we're on the verge of being okay.

Is this my fault?

My stomach churns.

Did me being with Trent trigger something inside him?

Does my happiness cause Silas's darkness?

I considered Silas to be one of my best friends, but I was dumb.

Grace and Georgia are my best friends. We don't share romantic feelings. I don't want to hand them my heart and go to sleep in their arms.

I want all of that with Silas.

Silas isn't my best friend. He's my everything.

I'm unsure of how much time has passed when I finally say, "Are you ready to tell me what drove you to drink tonight?"

CHAPTER THIRTY-SIX

Silas

"ARE you ready to tell me what drove you to drink tonight?"

Chills run up my spine at Lola's question. I kick my toes against the small rocks along the sidewalk, feeling them jam through my sock and into my toe.

There's so much that drove me to the bottle tonight, but I focus on one.

"I can't stand seeing you with him."

We stop as if we were in a movie and needed a dramatic pause to amplify our emotions. I've wanted to say that for so long, so my confession deserves a minute since it's taken too many to tell her that.

"Silas," she whispers, shifting us until we're facing each other. Her face is just as broken as my heart feels, as if she's mourning the downfall of our friendship as much as I am.

I'm exhausted. Hopeless. Fucking shattered.

My voice shakes as I continue, "I thought I'd be okay, seeing you with someone else, but seeing you with him, out of all people, it rips me apart, and that's why I drank."

"I'm sorry," she says, slowly reaching out to rub my shoulder.

I've never been vulnerable with anyone.

Only Lola.

She makes me want to be a better man.

She makes me want to be more than this damaged man who cuts out anyone if they get too close.

When I took my first drink tonight, I hated myself. Hated myself for breaking the pact I'd made so long ago, hated myself for the pain on Lola's face as I made a scene, and I was embarrassed at the humiliation on my family's face. As I sat in Cohen's office, waiting for Lola to arrive as if she were picking her child up from the principal's office, my mind focused on the last time I'd turned to the bottle, the last time I'd used it too much to numb me.

Her birthday is what triggered me.

Triggered this to come out.

On her birthday, that's when the depression, sadness, and regret always kick in. But I usually give myself the day to soak in my pity. This year, I didn't in fear of disappointing Lola again.

"Now, please, for the love of God, let Cohen take you home." I squeeze my eyes shut, her touch a calming effect—almost as strong as the vodka.

"I told you," she says softly, "I'm not going until you do."

"*Please.* I need some time." My lips tremble. The fear of breaking down in front of her is strangling me. "I won't do anything stupid, I promise."

"Can you take that time in Cohen's office? Anywhere but out here?" She sniffles, and I know she's just as close to crumbling as I am. Mascara blotches sit underneath her eyes, and her face is red and puffy.

"I promise, I'll be okay." I pull my phone from my pocket and call Cohen. When he picks up, I say, "Lola is ready to go home."

"Got it," Cohen replies, and I hang up.

"Silas—" Lola starts.

"We're not having this conversation here … like this." Dropping her shoes onto the ground, I take her face in my hands as she still rests her fingers on my shoulder and cup her cheeks as if I might never see her again. "We will, though. I promise. I will break down and tell you because I don't want to lose you. I will give you every piece of me if it means you're still in my life."

Tears fall down her cheeks, hitting my thumbs, and I choke back my own emotions. Just as she opens her mouth to reply, Cohen pulls up.

"Please," I beg with sorrow in my voice. "Get in that car, and I swear, I'll be fine."

"Lincoln is over there," Cohen says as if reading our minds even though we're hunched together, our voices low. "He'll keep an eye on him."

I frown that I've been assigned a babysitter, but I get it. I'd do the same if my friends were falling apart, so it makes sense they'd do it for me.

I rub my thumb over Lola's cheek and catch her tears before slowly pulling away.

"At least text me tonight," Lola says, our faces only inches apart. "If you don't, I'm getting in my car and driving here. Do you hear me?"

I slowly nod. "I hear you."

She kisses my cheek, her lips so close to the edge of my lips, and my shoulders slump.

"Here." As she pulls away, she bends down, untying my shoes.

I shake my head, stopping her. "Keep them."

"You're barefoot."

"Consider it an insurance policy that I'm not going to shut you out."

"Okay," she whispers.

I help her into Cohen's car, not paying him a glance, and when she pulls away, I sink down onto the curb. Shutting my eyes, I allow the memories of what happened that night to surface. I sit there, in my own regret, wishing I'd been a smarter man back then.

CHAPTER THIRTY-SEVEN

Lola

"GIVE HIM TIME," Cohen says on the drive to my house.

If this wasn't Cohen, I'd struggle to mask my tears, but he'd never judge me.

"I don't know what to do anymore," I say with a sniffle. "I'm just ... so confused. And I feel selfish that I never realized Silas was suffering through this internal hell. I'm a bad friend for not catching on to it."

"Don't. I've known Silas for longer than you, and I had no idea. He was good at playing the part."

"Until he couldn't any longer."

"Until he was afraid of losing you." His voice is soft, calming, but also sure of himself.

I sigh, my throat tightening at the thought. "He'll never lose me."

"We know that. The problem is, he doesn't."

"I'm in love with him." My last word comes out in a sob, and I cover my mouth. I'm not sure if it's to stop my tears or that I'm shocked. Because for the first time, I've allowed myself to reveal my feelings for Silas.

Even though I'm saying it to the wrong person, it feels good to finally release it. To speak my truth.

"I know. We all know. *Silas* knows."

I peer at Cohen. "Just because someone knows you love them, that doesn't mean they have to love you back."

"He tries to hide it, but there's no doubt in anyone's minds that he doesn't love you. He's scared, and sometimes, it takes us seeing our worst nightmare to figure out what we want in life. His worst nightmare was seeing you with someone else, so you being with Trent was the push that he needed to get out of it."

"Is that …" I play with my hands in my lap. "Is that how you felt with Jamie? That you were going to lose her?"

He nods. "The same with the other guys. It made us wake up. Silas is getting there."

When we pull up to my house, I find Trent sitting on my front porch steps.

I pull in a heavy breath, unsure of what to do.

"You want me to talk to him?" Cohen asks, shifting the car into park.

I shake my head. "No, I got this."

I'm the one who started hanging out with Trent, so I need to be the one to figure it out with him.

"I'll be sure Silas gets home safe. You two are going to be okay, Lola."

"Thank you." I tip my head down. "Give the kiddos a kiss for me."

"I will. Think about what you want, okay? Not what anyone else wants, only *you.*"

I nod and step out of his car.

Trent stands as I approach him, and he runs a hand through his thick hair. "I hope you don't find this weird. I was going to wait a little longer, and if you didn't show up, I would have gone home. I was just worried about you."

I give him a gentle smile. "I'm okay. Thank you. I appreciate you checking, and I'm sorry tonight turned into a mess."

He shakes his head, holding up a hand. "Don't apologize. You had nothing to do with what happened tonight. That was a long time coming, and you just got shoved into the middle of it. I'm sorry for my role in it." He pushes his hands into his pockets, and I notice he hasn't changed out of his bloody shirt either. "What happened when I left?"

"Silas and I talked for a minute, but he asked for space, so Cohen brought me home."

"You want me to stay, keep you company?" He stops and rushes out his next words. "I'll sleep on the couch."

I press my hand to his chest, knowing that this will probably be the last time Trent and I have a face-to-face conversation. Guilt coils in me for bringing him in the middle of Silas's and my problems.

"Thanks for the offer," I whisper, "but I'm okay."

"I understand." He stares at me, his face brimming with concern. "You said Silas and you were just friends. Is that the truth?"

I can't look him in the eye. "I don't know."

"I think you do, but you're scared of it." He brushes his lips against my cheek before stepping to the side, allowing me better access to my front door. "Good night, Lola." He waits until I walk in before leaving.

———

THE TEARS RELEASE as soon as the door shuts behind me, and I slouch back against it, allowing my emotions to overcome me. I plod to my bedroom, checking my phone with every step, praying for something from Silas.

It's not even midnight, yet this feels like the longest day of my life. I get ready for bed and change into my pajamas, and just as I'm about to leave Silas's shoes on the floor, I tuck them underneath my arms instead. I keep them there as I slide into bed, and as gross as it seems—especially since I don't even allow dirty clothes near my bed—I situate them next to me, hugging them to my chest. I need something related to him to comfort me.

I keep my phone in my hand, gripped tight as if it were my lifeline. I check my messages in case I missed something from him and slump my shoulders when I see I haven't. Scrolling through our text messages, past the ones before my birthday, I read our history—our past of how we once were.

Two weeks ago:

Silas: Rise and shine to my favorite girl! I'm on my way with your fave breakfast, so get your cute ass out of bed.

One month ago:

Me: Tinder is gross. Vomit.

Silas: That's because you haven't swiped right on my profile.

Me: I swiped left as soon as I could once I read your profile that said, "Lola has my heart." I thought you were talking about another woman you were hung up on.

Silas: Nah, there's only one Lola who'll ever have my heart.

Me: It might not be the smartest to make that known on Tinder.

Silas: Why? They need to know you're my girl before everything.

I swipe away tears, missing us, and take in every word of the happiness we once had. My sob-fest is interrupted when my phone rings, and as much as I love Georgia, my tears come out harder when I see her name instead of Silas's.

I clear my throat, snap my fingers in front of my face, and shake my head—all attempts not to sound as broken as I feel. I'm not the girl who gets swept up in her emotions, and before all this happened, I stupidly believed I wasn't the girl who'd cry over a broken heart.

"Hello?" I'm proud of how strong my voice sounds.

"Hi," Georgia says—no chirp, all seriousness. "Archer told

me what happened. I'm about to leave now, and I should be there in about ten minutes."

"You don't have to do that. Stay home. It's late."

"I want to be there for you."

"I appreciate that, and thank you." I sigh. "I think I just need a moment to myself."

"Okay, call, and I'll be right over if you need me," she says softly before briefly pausing. "You love him, don't you?"

"I do." I lose what little control I had.

She releases a long breath. "Swear to God, there's just something about brokenhearted men that get us every time."

"Yes, and then they break our hearts."

"Not always. Sometimes, they grow hearts."

CHAPTER THIRTY-EIGHT

Silas

"GO AND MAKE THINGS RIGHT," Cohen says, stern and parent-like, when we pull up in front of Lola's house.

It's late, but I texted to make sure she was okay with me coming over.

After she'd left Twisted Fox, I'd stayed outside for a good hour, pitying myself. Lincoln silently stood in the distance, waiting for me to get myself together until I'd called Cohen and told him I was ready to talk to Lola.

Cohen didn't lecture me on the drive. All he said was, he was here if I needed to talk. That's Cohen—the only father in the group and the father to the group.

Today has been a shit show. I finally snapped—the deep-seated emotions I'd controlled for so long had become uncontrollable, fighting their way into my new world. I hate myself for the pain I caused everyone, including my father, Janet, and my grandmother, for my actions at the charity event. And my friends for my behavior at Twisted Fox. None of them deserved any of that.

But especially Lola—for her birthday, the party.

I've been pushing the person who means the most to me the

farthest away. I need to apologize for how stupid I've been acting the past few weeks.

I miss her.

Miss us.

Even though she's expecting me, my heart pounds when I knock on her door, not knowing what to expect. The door swings open, and she stands before me, wearing one of my old tees and pajama shorts. Her face is clear of the makeup stains she had earlier, and her hair is in a messy ponytail. Unlike me, she's pulled herself together. Even with all that, her eyes are still puffy, still red, and I know that's because of my actions.

"Hi," she says shyly, touching her cheeks as if making sure her tears are gone.

"Hi," I say in response. I don't want to say the wrong thing. I want to make things right with Lola, so I need to be careful.

I turn briefly and wave at Cohen, telling him all is good—that Lola didn't slam the door in my face. He rolls down his window, gives me a thumbs-up, and drives off.

If only I had the confidence he has in me.

"First things first," Lola says, waving me inside. "We need to get you cleaned up."

I step inside, slow, my body tight.

"I can't believe you haven't changed out of this bloody shirt." She peeks down at my feet. "At least you found some shoes."

I scratch my head. "Cohen had a spare pair in his trunk."

This isn't Lola and me.

We're never like this—so hesitant with our words, so careful with every move we make, for fear it'll upset the other.

She takes my hand, and I lace our fingers together, holding her tight, as if I never want to let go, never want to lose her. I shuffle my feet as she leads me through the house and into her master bathroom. Her bathroom smells like her—like the citrus shampoo she uses and her perfume.

Gripping my shoulders, she settles me onto the lid of the toilet seat. She waits, making sure I'm stable, before pulling away and grabbing supplies from her drawers. I focus on her as she opens the cabinet for her first-aid kit. Shame rocks through me. After all the embarrassment I caused her, she's still here for me.

"I'm sorry," I say, my voice shaking.

When she drops to her knees, our eyes meet. I painfully stare at her in desperation, praying she sees the apology over this beat-up face of mine.

If she does, she doesn't tell me. She grabs my chin, supporting it in her hand, and inspects my face while hers is unreadable. I'm not sure if it's that way because she's over my shit or if she's trying to hide from me. She's given me her all so many times, told me how she felt, and I turned my back on her. Maybe she's done with handing me something so precious, only for it to be stomped on.

She situates her supplies at her feet, and I wince when she starts cleaning my face even though I deserve the pain. She's deep in concentration as if desperate to remove all evidence of what occurred tonight. I treated her terribly, and now, she's taking care of me.

"What's going on, Silas?" she finally asks, her voice as difficult to read as her face.

I stare at her, leveling my breathing, and I lick a remnant of blood she missed from my lip. "I don't know."

I came here to explain myself, and that's all I'm giving her?

That won't do with Lola.

Just like me, it's difficult for her to find the right words. In front of her is a man who has been so involved in her life and is now pulling away. I don't blame her for doing the same.

She stares at me, her face pain-stricken. "You don't know …" Her voice becomes shaky. "Or you don't want to tell me?"

I'm going to lose the woman I love if I don't crack myself open and hand her the section of me that only she can fix. She will walk away, tired of my shit, as if she has no choice. She'll take the sliver of happiness I have with her. I'll crumble more with every waking day.

That's why, as I sit in the bathroom, her nursing me from a fight with a man who threatened to take her from me, I sit in anguish, conflicted with myself on what my next move should be.

To open myself up and find love.

Or to shut down and be lonely.

Those are my only two options in this life with her.

Fuck that. Losing her isn't an option.

I will unlock every secret and open every door that is me to keep her.

"I'm struggling," I whisper.

She has no idea how even those two words were a war to get out.

Please, God, help me get through this battle.

Help me keep her.

Her eyes are tired as they meet my despaired ones. She runs a single finger over my busted lip. "With what?" Her tone is soft and soothing—a side of Lola no one else sees. A side of her I haven't seen until tonight.

I relax into her touch, take a deep breath, and do something I never thought I would. "With my feelings for you."

And with those five words, our entire relationship is about to change.

Whether it's good or bad, I'm unsure.

Her finger freezes in the middle of my lip. "What do you mean?"

Don't have a change of heart.

Tell her, dumbass.

Tell her who you really are.

The things you've done.

My heart rattles in my chest, as if nervous to give itself away, but I force myself through it. "In high school, I made a terrible mistake that cost two people their lives."

I've gained her full attention, but she doesn't say a word, as if terrified I'll stop if she does.

I rest my hand over hers, not only because I'm scared of her pulling away but also because her skin against mine will give me the push that I need to get through this.

I gulp.

And do it again.

And again.

And she waits with patience, never once pushing me.

"I can't get over it. Their deaths are why I don't date, why I don't drink, and why I can't go out on your birthday."

"Silas, I'm not understanding." She cups her hand over mine, the one that's resting on hers. "Please tell me."

I nod, squeezing my eyes shut, and for the first time ever, I tell someone exactly what happened.

CHAPTER THIRTY-NINE

Silas

High School: Senior Year

SNEAKING AROUND with someone is a pain in the ass.

Especially when it's around your best friend's back.

Sienna and I have been hiding our relationship from everyone—including her twin brother, Kenny—for months. We didn't mean for it to happen, and when it did, we said it'd only be one time. But one time wasn't enough, so we swore it'd only be two. Then two wasn't enough, and I wanted to be around her every second of the day. Which is hard when you're hiding your relationship.

But lately, anytime she brings up going public, I insist we need more time. Kenny is protective of her, and so are her parents. Given my reputation of being a *player*, they'd force her to stay away from me. It's better to be together in secret than not to be together at all.

Tonight, we're at a friend's party. Kenny is grounded, and we've been drinking, so Sienna's and my inhibitions are lowered. We're not being as careful as we typically are. Not only have I been touching her all night but I'm also attempting to make up for arguing last night. She asked if we were going to prom, and I hesitated, knowing it was more complicated than a simple *let's go to prom together.*

But now, she seems to be over our fight—until the next time she gets unhappy.

I'm gripping her hand as we hurry up the stairs, and she giggles when we enter a bedroom. Her mouth is on mine as soon as I click the lock on the door. I love kissing her, I love tasting the strawberry bubblegum she always chews, and I love wrapping my hands in her curly hair.

She raises her arms as I pull her shirt over her head, and I toss it onto the floor while leading her to the bed. As I hover over her, I tickle her waist, causing her to giggle more.

"I love being with you," I say against her lips before sticking my tongue between them.

As I start kissing her neck, she pulls me back.

She strokes my shoulder. "What are we, Silas?"

I raise a brow. "What do you mean?"

It's a stupid question because I know what she means, but it gives me more time to come up with an answer.

"I hate feeling like a secret," she whispers, looking away from me.

I move a curl away from her eyes. "You're not a secret, babe."

"Then tell Kenny. Stop being scared."

The erection I had is starting to shrivel from the conversation I hate more than anything.

I level myself onto my elbow to meet her eyes. "I'm not scared. I just know it'll cause issues. With him, with your parents, with my parents. Your parents look at you like you're innocent, and I'm the *playboy,*" I say the word in their mocking voice. "Once they find out we're dating, once they find out we're having sex, all hell will break loose. Your parents might not even let us see each other. I don't want that. That's what I'm afraid of. I'm afraid of the truth making me lose you."

She shuts her eyes. "Do you love me?"

I'm quiet.

"Silas," she stresses. "Do you love me?"

I'm eighteen. Do I even know what love is?

Instead of answering, I kiss her hard, my tongue diving into her mouth, not giving her the chance to continue our conversation. I slide my lips to her ear, nibbling on the skin behind it, knowing it's her sensitive spot. She melts underneath me, and long gone is the *what are we* talk.

When I move my lips to her mouth, she moans into mine. I slide my hand up her skirt—slow and careful because even though she isn't the first woman I've been with, she's the one I want to please more than anything. She's soaking for me, and I think back to the night she gave me her virginity. Moving her panties to the side, I slowly press a finger into her warmth, loving that she's always ready for me.

That we're always ready for each other.

I've hooked up with other girls before, but I've never felt such a pull to them—never wanted to please them, be with them, never craved them as much as I do Sienna. Even though we haven't gone public, she's still mine, and I'm still hers. I've been committed to her in every way—not even thought about touching another girl.

She lifts, dragging my shirt over my head, and I'm unbuckling my pants when the door is kicked open.

One second, I'm on top of Sienna, and the next, I'm being dragged off the bed. Chaos erupts, and my head spins as I'm thrown to the ground, two sets of feet kicking me. As I pull myself up and push them off me, I look forward, look for Sienna, but my view of her is cut off by people.

I attempt to push through them but am held back by the two guys who kicked me.

"Get your fucking shirt on, and let's go," Kenny yells to Sienna.

With all my power, I grit my teeth and elbow each guy, causing them to let go of me.

Fucking traitors.

"Don't you dare talk to her like that," I seethe, getting a quick glimpse of Sienna as she holds the sheet to her chest and reaches for her shirt.

I cringe at the embarrassment on her face, wanting nothing more than to tuck her in my arms and protect her from it.

My nostrils flare as I turn my attention to the crowd, hoping to direct their attention away from her to me. "All you motherfuckers! Get out!"

"Out of all the chicks you could've messed with, you chose her?" Kenny screams, clenching his fists. "My sister isn't one of your stupid whores!"

"We were going to tell you," Sienna sobs, tugging her shirt on.

Kenny snatches her wrist and drags her out of the room.

Anger roars inside me, and I fight my way through the crowd, following Kenny and Sienna while yelling their names.

People scream at me, calling me names, asking how I could betray my friend like that. Being Kenny's friend for so long, I know how he gets when he's angry, how he doesn't ask questions before he goes crazy.

"Let her go, or I swear to God, I'll knock you out." I jump over the staircase, growing closer, and that's when I see Kenny slap Trent on the back.

"Thanks for the heads-up, man," he says while on his way out the door.

They disappear through the front door, and Trent smirks at me. Grabbing the collar of his polo, I slam Trent against the wall. A picture falls to the floor and shatters.

"What the fuck did you do?" I scream in his face, spit flying onto his cheek.

Trent laughs. "I just let the truth come out."

"I'll deal with you later," I snarl, letting him go and sprinting outside.

Kenny is across the yard, shoving Sienna into his Mustang,

and it's still a struggle to work my way through the crowd. He peels out, his wheels spinning before driving off.

How many people are fucking here?

I can't run fast enough to keep up with a car, so I jerk my keys from my pocket, sprint to my Camaro, and drive. I don't see them, don't see their taillights in the darkness, but I trust my instincts and drive toward their house. When I finally catch up with them, Kenny is speeding around a sharp curve.

He doesn't make it around that curve.

Brakes squeal, and the car flips before sliding to the side of the road, flames shooting from the car. I feel like my life is flashing before my eyes. And even though it's not my life being taken, I'm losing the person who was my life. I cover my ears, the car alarm screaming into the empty air as I sprint toward the wrecked Mustang.

I never told Sienna I loved her because I was scared.

June twenty-third will haunt me for the rest of my life.

CHAPTER FORTY

Lola

MY VIEW of Silas is blurry from my tears, and I slide my hand up, touching his cheek. Slowly, I swipe away the tears that have fallen down his splotchy red cheek.

I've cried during movies.

Cried while reading books.

But nothing has ever shattered me like Silas's story as I witness the raw pain, seeing this broken man before me.

In the span of one night, I've met parts of Silas I never knew existed. The angry side. The sad side. And now, the heartbroken and torn side. I once viewed this man as flawless, as perfect, as not having a care in the world. I never knew he carried this heavy weight of history on his shoulders. Not only did he lose people he loved, but he also witnessed them losing their life. He saw the very thing that killed them and could do nothing to stop it.

Something like that breaks a person.

I don't know how he's been strong, how he's hidden from it all these years. I get the secrets, the reason he held it in—because he was terrified of losing us. But what Silas doesn't know is that it'd have only helped us understand him, to be there for him and hold his hand along the way.

Rising on my knees, I pull him into my chest, cradling his head, and allow him to hide himself. I'm an emotional shield, giving him privacy to let go, to release the pain he's been keeping inside. I hold him tight, tears streaming down my face as he sobs against me, as he drains his hurt and hands it to me, giving me what I've been asking for all along. And I'm fulfilling the promise I gave him—that I'll always be there, no matter what.

This is the man I'm in love with.

Broken, not broken.

Happy or soaking my shirt with his tears.

He's my everything.

And now, I can give him what he needs to heal from this.

We sit there, and I lose track of time. Even as my knees go sore against the tiled floor, I'm willing to sit here all night if it's what he needs. When he pulls back, his face is almost lifeless, as if he's given all he can give for the night. As much as I want to know more, to dig out every detail, he looks exhausted enough.

I kiss the tip of my thumb and trace it along his mouth before pressing it to his lips. His shoulders curl over his chest, his entire body shaking. He inhales deep breaths, calming himself. He offers a pained stare, no longer hiding from me, and his eyes glisten from his hurt.

Sliding my hand down, I slowly unbutton his shirt, and as I undo each one, I massage the now-exposed skin with the same thumb I touched his lips with. He's silent, still, tears swimming in his eyes. After dragging the shirt off his shoulders, I ball it up in my hands and toss it behind me. I drop my hands, fingering the hem of my shirt, and peel off my tee—*his* tee that I stole one night.

I'm standing in front of him, wearing only a sports bra, as my chest heaves in and out.

"Here," I say, unsure if my word is even audible through my tears. "Put this on."

He shakes his head but grabs it, and I take a step back when he stands.

"No, I like seeing you in it."

I shiver when he reaches out, pulls me closer, and slides his chilly hands up and down my arms before slowly lifting them. I sigh at the loss of his touch as he pulls at the neck of the shirt and carefully slips it back over my head.

"DOA," he says, his voice clearer than it has been all night. He stares above my head, toward my shower, as he speaks. "That's what the paramedics said as I stood there and watched them carry their burned bodies out of the car." He draws in a breath. "Everyone blamed me. I was the reason Kenny was so pissed. I was the one who got into my car and chased them." His tears land in my hair. "When I got home, I found Trent sitting on the porch. My friends later told me that Trent messaged Kenny that I was upstairs with Sienna. All Trent said was that he was sorry, and if he could take it back, he would. I told him he was the one who deserved to be dead … and then he said no one would be dead if it wasn't for me. And even though his words hurt like a bitch, they were the truth."

"He was wrong. They were all wrong." I press my hand to his chest, over his heart, and feel his frantic pulse.

"If I'd never touched Sienna, if we'd never gotten caught, they'd still be alive."

"You were teenagers in love. Her brother's recklessness is what caused their deaths. I know there's guilt, but you don't need to wear the burden of it being your fault. You tried to stop him, tried to stop it from happening."

"I was banned from their funerals." His voice hardens with that statement.

"They needed to find someone to blame because their son, the one who was responsible, was gone. Them needing someone else to blame in their grieving was unfair to you."

His lips move to my ear, and goose bumps cover my arms. "Now, do you see why I think I'm no good for you? Look what happened to the last girl I loved. She's dead, Lola." His voice breaks, hurt ricocheting with every word. It's as if he believes his confession might cause me to walk away from him. "I don't deserve you for what I did."

"Stop punishing yourself." I cup his neck, dragging his head closer to mine, and it's me now whispering in his ear. "You deserve happiness just as much as I do … just as much as anyone. No matter what, I'll always be at your side. I'll always be your friend."

He flinches, pulling back as if I'd slapped him. "I hate that word."

"What?"

"Friend." Desperation is on his face. "I'm fighting with myself, Lola. Even though I say I don't deserve you, I also don't want to lose you."

I sniffle. "I don't want to lose you."

"I'm in love with you."

I stare at him, wide-eyed, words catching in my throat.

"I'm in love with you, and I wanted you to understand why I am the way I am. What I just told you is why I've been fucking terrified of crossing any lines with you. I can't do that anymore. I came here, risking our friendship, to tell you I'm as lonely as you told me you are. When Sienna asked me if I loved her, I was scared to believe that love was real because I didn't know what it was. But with you, I know exactly what it is because it's how I feel about you. Words can't explain the emotions I feel when I'm with you, the happiness, the fact that I never want to be with anyone else. It's love."

I'm quiet, still scrambling for words, as my head spins.

Taking my hand, he walks me into my bedroom and sits me on the bed. Dropping to his knees, the same way I did with him in the bathroom, he cups my neck, drawing me close to him.

"I'm sorry," he says through quivering breaths, "for the pain that I caused. But I'm not sorry for opening myself up to you, for giving you all of myself. You have me, Lola. All of me—my anguish, my fears, my past, and my nightmares—because I know I'm in good hands. But you also have my heart, my soul, my everything … because you're my everything."

CHAPTER FORTY-ONE

Silas

HAVE you ever had something happen that makes you feel a thousand pounds lighter?

Told someone something that was way overdue?

I'm showing Lola all my weaknesses, but I'm also giving her all my strengths.

That balances itself out, right?

She can have this broken man, and in exchange for taking him, she can also have his heart.

Is that considered a fair deal?

Everything that's happened in my life—the good, the bad—has led me to Lola. She is the woman who was sent to heal this brokenness inside me, just like I'm there to show her real love—that a man can stay committed, that he can give a woman his heart unconditionally and never make her feel lonely.

Without Lola, I'm not sure where I'd be, but I know it'd be somewhere low.

Unhappy.

Drowning in my pity.

With Sienna, I was young and dumb, but I know right from wrong now. My biggest regret from my past is not telling Sienna that I loved her. She died, uncertain of my feelings. She died, not knowing if the man she loved, loved her back. I failed Sienna, failed to keep her safe, and I've learned that lesson. I've grown, and I won't make that mistake again. I refuse to allow another woman I love question my feelings for her.

I was scared to tell Lola, scared of losing her, but just like with Sienna, if I hadn't told her my true feelings, I'd have lost her.

Lola's tears have returned as she bows her head and stares at me, her eyes gentle yet also confused. "Will this ruin us?"

"Possibly." I'm giving her all the honesty I have inside me. "But it could also make us the happiest we've ever been. I just need to know you feel the same way."

I release her when she nods, wanting a better view of her face, of her eyes so I can see the truth in them. I hold in a desperate breath, a life-changing breath, and wait for her to tell me what the next road in my life will be.

Her hands are shaking, her lower lip trembling, and then slowly, her face somewhat relaxes. "I love you. With all my heart. With everything that I am."

She's spilling her heart out as much as I am mine. And even though I'm reminded of the pain from my past, even though I'm angry with myself for drinking and taking my sadness out on her, hearing those words shines a light over all of that.

My and Lola's relationship has been based on timing. We weren't meant to be together romantically years ago. Neither of us was ready for something that strong. Had we tried, I'd have broken her heart … if she'd even been ready to give it out. We needed that time, those years to find out who we were and what we wanted in life. Our friendship allowed us to build the foundation that constructed our love.

I don't regret the time it took us to get here, don't wish this had happened sooner because I was a different man back then.

A man undeserving of her.

A man who wasn't ready to face his demons.

Us becoming friends to lovers is how our story was always meant to be.

Us being side by side in our journeys without expectations is what we needed.

And now, our story has reached the end of its friendship and the beginning of more—what all this time has been preparing us for.

I didn't love Lola the minute I saw her.

There was no love at first sight for either of us.

But now, there's love with every glance at each other, love with every conversation we share, and love every time we touch.

And just like I fought like hell not to fall in love with her, it's now time I fight like hell not to lose her.

She runs her hands through my hair. It's soothing, relaxing. "Now, you need to get some sleep."

I nod. "Sleep sounds amazing."

She wraps her arms around my neck. "I've missed you."

Our eyes meet.

And there's no hesitation before our lips do the same.

It's slow. Intimate. And worth all the years we waited.

CHAPTER FORTY-TWO

Lola

POURING your heart out to someone can be exhausting.

We're mentally and emotionally drained and in dire need of rest.

Especially Silas. He got into a punching match with Trent, drank, walked down a dark street for an hour, and then came here to reveal his truths, his inner demons, to me.

But I have a feeling we'll sleep better tonight than we have in weeks.

Rest easier.

Now that the weight is off our shoulders.

The truth is out.

When Silas notices his shoes in my bed, he points at them, raising a brow. I tell him not to ask and toss my pillow at him. I hand him a pair of old gym shorts I stole from him, and then we get into bed.

I turn on my side to stare at him. It's surreal, different yet familiar at the same time. We've loved each other as friends for years, but now, we're opening our hearts for a deeper connection.

"Come here," he says around a yawn, dragging me into his side while he's on his back.

I cuddle against him. He stares down at me, his eyes heavy, and I can't believe he hasn't passed out yet. His eyes shut and then open back up.

He kisses my forehead, mutters a quiet, "Good night," and doesn't make it a few seconds before drifting to sleep.

I do the same not even minutes after.

———

WE SLEEP IN LATE.

The rest much needed.

I'm still spooning his side when I wake up, my head resting against his chest, and I can hear his heartbeat. It's different than last night—relaxed, calm, not frantic. As I slowly pull away, I cringe when I see the drool I've left as evidence of my being there.

Um, gross.

I stare at him, uncertain of what to do, and wonder if he'll wake if I clean it.

"It's not the first time you've drooled on me," he whispers.

I draw back, startled at his voice, and I cast my gaze on him. He has one eye open, focused on me, and yawns.

I smack his chest. "How the hell did you know what I was thinking?"

"I was watching you."

I shove my hair behind an ear. "With one eye?"

"Yes, I can only halfway take the sunlight in your room." He grins up at me. "You're a drooler. It's cute."

"I'm *so* not a drooler." I wipe up the evidence of the drool with the back of my hand. "You're a snorer."

"Hey now, I never said I didn't *like* your drool. It's like a trinket of you being here, a memento that I had you close enough to drool on me."

To change the conversation of me apparently being a drool

monster, I reach out and trace my hand along his jawline. "How are you feeling? Hungover?"

I love how we can touch each other like this now.

Be so intimate.

He rubs his forehead with two fingers. "I forgot how bad hangovers suck. I don't miss this shit."

"What made you stop drinking before?"

I'm treading into dangerous territory. He opened himself up last night, gave me pieces of him, and I don't want him to think I'm asking for more too soon. We might've reached a new space in our relationship, but it's fresh. Like twelve hours fresh.

He opens the other eye, and sorrow flashes in them as he adjusts his gaze on me.

"You don't have to tell me," I rush out. "I don't want to push you."

I start dragging my hand from his face, but he clasps my wrist to stop me and lowers it to his chest, on his heart—the same spot where my head was sleeping … and my drool decorated.

His skin is warm, and his heartbeat picks up. It's not as relaxed as it was when I woke, but it's not almost leaping from his chest like last night.

He shakes his head, fighting back tears. "I was banned from their funeral, but I went anyway. I sat in the parking lot with a half-gallon of cheap vodka and got drunk. It was stupid, but I was so fucking hurt that not only did I lose them, but everyone was also pointing the finger at me. Saying I killed them. Their cousin came out and threatened to kick my ass if I didn't leave. I told him to go ahead. But instead of physically fighting me, he broke me down with his words, saying I didn't deserve to numb myself with liquor and needed to suffer for what I'd done. My parents showed up, forced me into their car, but their cousin's words haunted me on the drive back. When I got home, I grabbed all the liquor I had stashed in my room, flushed it, and vowed to never drink again. I kept that vow until last night."

"I'm sorry what I did made you break your sobriety."

I lose my touch on him as he rises, pulling me up with him. He rests his back on his headboard while pulling me to my knees so that we're facing.

He strokes my cheek, and I quiver. "It's not your fault. It's mine. For the first time in years, I felt like I needed to numb myself."

"From what?" I gulp. Guilt consumes me, but his touch relaxes me. "Wanting me?"

"Yes."

"Did it work?"

"I wouldn't have shown up here if it had. I could never drink away my feelings for you. They're so deep that they're untouchable. You're inside me, Lola. A part of me that there's no getting rid of. Last night, even when I tried to drink you away, it didn't work. All it did was make me realize that if I didn't man up, I'd lose you." His hand freezes on my cheek, and he doesn't break eye contact with me. "I never want that to happen."

He's surrendering his secrets to me.

His feelings.

Everything that is him.

"I'm not going anywhere." I drag his hand to my lips and kiss his palm. "I'm all yours."

He smiles.

"But I need something from you."

"What's that?"

"Tell me if something isn't easy for you … like my birthday. You can't give me you and then pull away later out of fear that it'll upset me."

He nods. "I promise you."

"No one ever said falling for your best friend was easy."

He lightly chuckles, pulling me closer until I'm nearly sitting on his lap. "It's actually harder."

"I don't know about that. We skipped a lot of steps. We already know so much about each other. Already comfortable."

"We can do this now." He presses his lips to mine, and this time, it's my heart pounding. "And this." His hand disappears under the sheet, and he caresses my thigh, playing with the hem of my shorts.

I stop him when he goes for another kiss. "I have morning breath."

He cups the back of my neck. "Yeah, and I don't give a fuck about that."

"I do." I laugh. "I need to shower."

He groans, and as I slide off him, the hint of an erection presses against my leg. I grin, loving that I have that effect on him. I'm surprised when he follows me.

"Guess what," he says.

I peer back at him from over my shoulder. "What?"

"I'm in need of a shower too." He comes up behind me, tickling my waist, and I double over, laughing. "Want to clean me up again?"

I escape his hold and head toward the bathroom, swaying my hips from side to side, my intent to make his erection unbearable. The tiles are chilly underneath my bare feet as I collect the trash and the first-aid kit from the floor, turn on the water, and grab a towel from the closet. I can feel his eyes pinned on me, but I act like I don't notice.

"You going to grab me a towel too" he asks, his voice raspy.

I peek a playful glance at him. "Why?"

"Lola," he groans, and his tone turns pleading. "Can I please join you for a shower?"

I turn on my heel, pointing at him with the towel. "You can wait your turn."

"What?" he stutters.

"Did you think I wouldn't get back at you for dropping me on my ass at the club?" I smirk and brush my hand along his arm as I walk past him. "I'm showering. If you want to watch me while you wait your turn, be my guest."

"What?" he repeats, as if he's struggling to process my words.

I strip off my shirt. "You can watch me shower or go back to bed and wait until I'm finished."

He gestures to his waist, to the outline of his bulge. And as much as I want to see it, I give myself a pep talk to hold my ground.

"Are you trying to torture me?"

Yes. Yes, I am.

"Call it a consequence for your actions." I wiggle out of my shorts, tugging them down my legs with my panties, take off my bra, and step into the shower.

The door is glass, giving him a straight view of me, and I tip my head back, water droplets falling down my bare chest.

Trying my hardest not to make it obvious, I sneak a peek at him.

He leans back against the vanity, his arms crossed, his gaze latched on to me. "Am I allowed to … what are the rules here?"

I smile. "The only rule is, you can't touch me."

He removes his shirt, dropping it to the floor. "Oh, I can easily join you in the shower without touching you."

"Correction: you can do anything but touch *or join me.* Other than that, do what you please."

"I always said you were the damn devil."

"The devil always gets her payback."

CHAPTER FORTY-THREE

Silas

FROM THE MOMENT I met Lola, I knew she loved a good revenge.

Now, I'm on the other end of that.

And it sucks.

I'm intoxicated as I watch the hottest show I've ever seen.

Lola's wet body. Water dripping down her perfect curves. Plump breasts that I'd give a kidney to have my mouth on.

I watch her, fixated, and my dick grows harder and harder.

She lathers shampoo into her hair, paying me no mind, as if torturing men like this is something she does on the regular. Tipping her head back, she rinses it from her hair, and releases a slow moan while grabbing the conditioner. While conditioning her hair, she peeks over at me for my reaction.

I tighten my fists—an attempt to stop myself from pushing down my shorts and stroking my cock while she rinses her hair again. If Lola wants to play games, I'll tap in, stopping her from seeing how bad I'm aching to touch her.

Teasing me seems to be Lola's favorite foreplay.

I'll have to remember that … and then give her a piece of her own medicine.

I have a feeling Lola and I will have plenty of push and pull, of teasing, and it's exactly what I expected being with her would be like.

"You doing okay over there?" she asks, trying to sound as innocent as possible.

"I'm good," I croak. "Just a normal day in the office. Nothing new I haven't experienced in a bathroom."

I shut up.

Not the smartest thing to say, dumbass.

You want her to allow you to join her in the shower, pleasure her in the shower, not drown you in it.

"Oh, really?" She spills body wash onto a loofah. "You've watched other women shower before?"

"Fuck no. Only you."

"I don't believe you." She glides her hand between her breasts, slowly cleaning herself with the loofah. "I'll be getting you back for that as well."

"Bullshit," I groan, my knees feeling weak, and grip the edge of the vanity to hold myself up.

She covers every inch of herself with soap, and the sweet scent of her body wash drifts through the room. The steam of the shower fogs the glass and interferes with my view of her.

"I'm trying …" I stop, catching up with my breathing. "I'm trying to be a gentleman over here."

But you're making it really fucking hard. The same with my dick.

I groan when the shower door opens, and Lola steps out, water dripping from every inch of her perfect body. As much as I'm trying to be the gentleman I said I was, I can't stop myself from slipping my gaze down her body. I lick my lips, my breathing a mixed pattern of shallow yet quick, as she leaves the water running.

"And now," she says with a twinkle in her eye, "it's time to stop being one."

I take one long stride toward her, circle my arms around her waist, and glide her back into the shower. The water is hot as I press her against the shower wall. She gasps, a mischievous smile on her face.

When I place a hand to each side of her head, her eyes meet mine as I slowly lower my mouth to hers.

"I still have morning breath," she says, inches from my mouth.

"And I still don't give a fuck."

It seems almost dramatic.

In slow motion.

As our lips connect.

She opens her mouth, morning-breath thoughts long gone, and thrusts her tongue into my mouth.

This isn't our first kiss, but it's our first passionate one.

Our first mouth-devouring, *I need you right now* kiss.

The kind of kiss I craved to share with her.

The one I never thought would happen.

She sucks on the end of my tongue as her hands frantically push down my shorts, and they pool at my feet. Grabbing my ass, her nails digging into my skin, she draws me closer to her. The moment my bare cock hits her thigh, she moans. I move my lips to her neck, lapping up the water as I rain kisses along it.

"Wrap your legs around me," I say, unsure if the words sound demanding or shaky as they leave my mouth.

She hooks her leg around my thigh, and I carefully open the shower door. As I carry her out of the shower, she quickly turns it off, and I deposit her on the vanity. I make sure she's stable and drop to my knees, fully ready to worship every inch of her.

I spread her legs open, the space perfect for me to fit between, and caress her thighs. She shivers, her face burning with desire as her eyes meet mine.

"This okay?" I whisper.

She grins, tipping her hips so that they're closer to my face. "Let's consider it an apology for what you did at the club."

"Oh, babe, this is just the start of the apology." I kiss each of her thighs, slow and precise. My gaze drifts back and forth from her face to her pretty pussy, soaking the view of her turned on in both places.

When I take my first lick, I smile against her slit, and she shivers above me. I give her my tongue, lapping her up, and don't add my fingers until she moans. With two fingers, I slowly stroke her before adding another, curling my fingers inside her warmth as I gently suck on her clit.

I start a game, just like she did with me.

I slide my hand out of her pussy and then slowly play with her clit.

I stop playing with her clit and return to pleasuring her with three fingers.

I could eat her out for every meal and still never be fully satisfied.

She rocks her hips, getting closer, her moans growing louder, and she grips the back of my neck, pinning my head between her legs, not letting go until she's arching her back and her legs are shaking.

I don't stop as she comes into my mouth.

No, I wrap my arms around her thighs, dragging her quivering thighs closer, and devour her harder. Suck her clit faster.

She wanted to play games.

I'm not showing her any mercy as she pants above me, asking for more yet also saying she can't take any more.

When I'm fully satisfied that she's fully satisfied, I stand, licking my lips, lapping up every taste of her that I can.

"Remember when I said I wanted you to fuck me at the club?" she says through ragged breaths.

I nod, sliding my body between her legs, and brush her wet hair from her face.

"I want you to fuck me."

"You sure you're ready?"

"Absolutely." She points at the drawer below us. "Condoms are in there."

My hands are nearly shaking as I pull one out, rip it open with my teeth, and roll it onto my cock. I don't have to stroke myself, don't have to get myself hard, because my dick is throbbing to feel her, throbbing to feel what my tongue did as it dived into her pussy.

My head spins as I align my cock with her entrance, curl my arms around her waist, and slowly sink into her.

I do what Lola asked me to do at the club.

I do what I've dreamed of doing.

I do what I want to spend the rest of my life doing.

And even though we're wet, even though it's messy, there's never been anything more satisfying than being inside the woman I love, to watch my cock move in and out of her, owning her in ways I never thought that I would.

Angling my head down, I nip at her lips before fully kissing her, our tongues dancing together. Her ass is nearly off the vanity as our hips move faster, and she meets me thrust for thrust, moan for moan. When she's close, she shoves her face into my neck, and I groan when her teeth sink into my skin as she comes undone.

Waves of pleasure push through me harder than I'm thrusting into her, and I don't make it two more pumps until I'm exploding into the condom, feeling on top of the world.

CHAPTER FORTY-FOUR

Lola

OUR SEX MIGHT'VE BEEN the hottest sex I've ever had, but now, we're a wet, freezing mess.

Silas and I had sex.

Holy shit.

When last night's craziness happened, I thought our friendship was doomed.

We went from fighting to crying to fucking.

I'll take it.

Only next time, none of the first two and more of the last.

"We're so dumb," I mutter, attempting to get my pulse under control as he carefully eases the condom off his cock and tosses it into the trash.

On his way back to me, he snags my towel from the hook. Sitting on the counter, I lick my lips while taking in the gorgeous sight of him. With everything that happened earlier— his lips and fingers between my legs—it was impossible to think about anything else.

Sure, I've seen him shirtless plenty of times—each time a turn-on but me acting like it wasn't—but now, I can admire all of him. And I'm thoroughly impressed.

I study him, water dripping from his body but him not caring, as if I might be quizzed on every inch of him later. My gaze drops to his cock—thick, long, a slight curve to it, and the biggest I've ever been with before. Thank God I was incredibly turned on and wet. Otherwise, I'd have had an issue with letting him go as deep as he did, allowing him to give it to me as good as he did.

Our sex was passionate.

Steamy.

Everything I'd imagined it'd be with him.

"Huh?" he asks, opening the towel to dry me off.

"We're so stupid," I repeat, my eyes still on his cock but losing the view when he steps closer to me.

He grimaces, and his words are rushed. "I'm sorry. I didn't mean for our first time to be on the bathroom counter. One thing led to another—"

I press my finger to his lips to stop his words. "It was perfect. Was it short and sloppy? Yes. But I loved it."

He frowns. "Short? I mean, it'd been a minute since I'd had sex, but I wouldn't say it was *short*."

I laugh. "I didn't mean it *that* way. It was everything I'd hoped, and if you had drawn it out, if you hadn't been thrusting into me so hard, I probably would have complained because I was so desperate for your cock and an orgasm. Just like you, it'd been a while since I'd been with anyone."

He smirks, drying me off, lowering the towel and sliding it between my thighs. "Been a while, huh?"

I sigh breathlessly when he spreads my thighs wider and gently rubs the towel over my clit. "I appreciate you trying, and I don't want to hurt your feelings, but three orgasms in a row isn't going to happen."

"Oh, really?" he asks in challenge.

Suppressing a moan, I nod. "Really."

He's careful as he caresses my sensitive nub, and his breathing turns ragged as he stares down at where he's playing with me. "Since it's been a while what have you been doing to get yourself off?"

"What have *you* been doing?"

"Jacking off to thoughts of you."

Heat radiates through my chest at his response. "You're lying."

"I'm not." His voice is level, calm, as he dips the towel between my folds. "I thought of all the things I'd do to you if I ever got the chance."

God, that's so hot.

I tilt my waist up to meet his touch, almost frantic for it.

"Did you ever think of me when you touched yourself?"

"A girl never masturbates and tells."

I grind against the towel, and with his free hand, he cups my ass, bringing me to the edge of the vanity.

He chuckles, his lips hovering over mine. "How many fingers did you push inside yourself when you thought about me?"

I stay silent and groan when he drops the towel.

"Was it this many?"

My back arches, and I nearly come off the vanity when he slides his long fingers inside me.

He easily finds my G-spot, as if it were something he did on the regular. His eyes are wild yet also concentrated as they meet mine.

Using his free hand, he catches my chin between his thumb and forefinger. "Is this about to be a third orgasm, baby?"

"I …" I'm struggling to find the word to answer him, struggling to focus on anything but his fingers working me so precisely, so skilled.

"You what?"

"I think so," I rasp—at least, I think I do.

He chuckles. "Who's the only one who can give you this many orgasms?"

"You," I manage to moan out.

His face burns with desire as he pleasures me—so good, so deep, so perfect. "And who's the one you think about when you finger this pretty little pussy?"

"You," I sputter, sweat forming along my forehead, my bathroom suddenly feeling like it's a hundred degrees.

"That's right. Always me."

I gasp at the feel of his erection brushing against my leg as he works me.

The thought of having him in my mouth excites me.

I'm fucking his hand.

Wanting more but not wanting him to stop to give me more.

I'll get this third orgasm and then drop to my knees and suck him.

The thrill of doing that sends a ping of excitement through my veins.

I want this man—emotionally, physically, in every way he'll give me.

And with just his fingers inside me, his thumb on my clit, I fall apart.

He catches me as I collapse into his arms. I tuck my face into his chest, drawing in deep breaths, until he tilts my head up to look at him.

"I love watching you lose it at my touch," he grits out. "I love *you*."

I grin a cheesy, bright grin that's never crossed my face before.

An orgasmed grin.

A *this is the happiest day of my life* grin.

"I love you." I lick his cheek before pressing my lips to his. "Now, it's your turn to shower."

"You going to join me?"

"Absolutely."

As soon as we get into the shower, I drop to my knees and take his thick cock into my mouth. He gathers my hair in his hand, gripping me tight, and I expect him to direct me on how he wants it. Instead, he lets me set the pace, allows me to suck him in a way I feel comfortable.

I do.

Fast.

Then deep.

And I don't stop until he comes in my mouth.

———

"HOW SHOULD WE TELL OUR FRIENDS?" Silas asks.

We're orgasmed out.

We ordered takeout.

Now, we're snuggled on the couch with Netflix playing in the background, but instead of watching a show, all we've done is talk. He's sprawled on his back, and I'm on my stomach, resting my chin on his chest to get a good view of him. Our legs are tangled together, and my body is halfway on his.

We're back to being the old Silas and Lola, talking about anything and everything. But now, we have a bonus of venturing into territories we never did, roads that weren't open before.

He explained why it was hard for him to go out on my birthday. My stomach curled as I thought about all the times I'd texted, only to be ignored, and how he always had to lie to me. I remembered how angry I'd been at the club and how I couldn't piece together why he looked so pained. In the back of my mind, I always thought it was me.

He told me about Sienna, about Kenny, about his troubles with Trent.

I loved the playful Silas, the friendly Silas, the one who never had a care in the world.

But this one?

That love is deeper now.

So deep that it can never be pulled out of me.

I can't wait for what our future has in store for us.

I smirk, tapping my fingers along his cheek. "My vote is, we just start making out in front of them."

He throws his head back, laughing. "Swear to God, you come up with the craziest shit. I wish I could crack open that brain of yours, my little name-swapping devil."

"Hey, we have to keep it entertaining, spice it up from the other ways our friends have done it."

Us making out would be the least of their worries after last night. I woke up to multiple texts from our friends, both the girls and guys, asking if I was okay, if I'd talked to Silas, if he was okay. I texted them back, saying we were fine, that he was here, and I'd talk to them about things later. The guys said good luck, and the girls sent me their love. Silas also had texts from everyone.

"Oh, I think I've kept it entertaining enough for how I acted last night." His lips press tight into a grimace. "They're going to have a shit ton of questions, and I have a lot of apologizing to do to them and my parents."

I caress his cheek, hating the sudden pain in his eyes. "Everyone figures it was because I was with Trent."

Reaching out, he grabs me from under my armpits, moving me until I'm straddling him.

He pushes my hair from my face and runs his hand through it. "I'm not blaming you for my childish behavior."

I relax into his touch. "It's fine. Once we tell them we worked it out, they'll be happy. Trust me." I laugh, stroking his hand in my hair. "Like, literally, *worked it out.*"

He cracks a smile, twisting a strand of my hair around his finger. "Is this how it'll be, dating you? Dirty comments and sexual innuendos?"

I rest my palms on his chest, giving him my weight. "Is that any different from when we were friends?"

"Yes, now, we can follow through with them."

I squeal when he playfully squeezes my waist and run my hand through his hair. "I'm serious, though. Blame it on me. I know they're our friends, but if you don't feel comfortable telling them, don't. They're concerned because they care about you."

He blows out a heavy breath. "I'll talk to them."

I need a plan on what to tell our friends, but for right now, I have no problem with blaming it on Trent and me. If and when Silas is ready to talk about his past, then I'll be open about it too. I have his back until then.

"We're really doing this, huh?" Silas asks.

I raise a brow. "What do you mean?"

"We're really going to be together?"

My heart speeds just at those words, at the mention of us being together. "As long as you're serious, then yes. I can't have us start, and then you go back on it. If you have any hesitation, let me know now. It won't change our friendship."

"There is no question. This is what I want, Lola. You're what I've always wanted."

CHAPTER FORTY-FIVE

Silas

"HEY, MAN," Cohen shouts when I stroll into Lincoln's penthouse.

The other guys—Finn, Lincoln, and Maliki—all call their own form of greetings.

Three days have passed since I acted a fool at Twisted Fox, and I haven't been back since. They texted me, making sure I was okay, but I needed time to clear my head before going out again. I've spent all my free time with Lola—either crashing at her place or her at mine.

And even with spending so much time together, we can't get enough of each other. We wake up in each other's arms every morning and go to bed together every night. We have electrifying sex nearly everywhere.

In our beds. The shower. Random furniture. On the floor.

It's like we just discovered sex.

Or discovered sex with the right person.

Lincoln invited me over for poker night, and I know there will be questions on why I turned into a different person that night. None of them have given me any strange looks as I move into the penthouse and find the living room couch shoved into a corner, a poker table in its place.

"I ordered pizza," Archer says, tossing his phone onto the kitchen island. "Should be here in about ten minutes."

When I walk into the kitchen, I notice the lack of alcohol lying out. Usually, on poker nights, the guys have drinks. My guess is, that's intentional ... because of me.

Finn updates us on Grace and the pregnancy. I hate the shit they had to go through with Grace's baby daddy, but I'm glad they got it sorted out. The guy signed over his rights, and Finn plans to be the father when the baby is born. Finn is a good guy and didn't deserve the shit I said to him on Lola's birthday.

Then Lincoln questions him on what to expect with Cassidy's pregnancy. Maliki and Archer then argue over whether Georgia or Sierra will get pregnant first. Maliki already has a daughter from another relationship, but he'd like to have another with Sierra.

After devouring the pizza, it's time to play some poker. I'm not a great poker player, and we usually lose to Lincoln—apparently, you get a lot of practice playing cards in prison.

As soon as we sit, I start my apology, cringing inwardly at what I did. "I want to say sorry for my dumbass behavior lately." I pay each of them a remorseful glance. "What I did was messed up."

Cohen, sitting in the chair next to me, slaps my back. "We've known you long enough to know that's not you."

"Yeah," Lincoln says, shuffling the cards. "We've all had bad days ... gone through some dark times."

Finn nods, smiling at me. "We just want to be there for you. If you need anything, call ... text ... show up. Whatever."

I nod as each one speaks. "I appreciate that, guys."

Not only would I feel lost without Lola, but it'd hurt to lose my friends too. The girls and guys. They came into my life when I needed them the most, and they've provided me with some of my brightest times. And even though I haven't been the best person to be around, they still invited me tonight.

"Do you want to talk about it?" Maliki asks, taking a drink of water.

Do I?

Or should I blame it on Lola, like she said I could?

Do I keep hiding from the truth?

No.

It's time I stop hiding.

I massage the back of my neck, giving myself a silent pep talk. "I dated a girl in high school who passed away ... the same day as Lola's birthday."

"That explains it," Lincoln says under his breath.

My head buzzes as I continue, "It always hits me pretty hard around that time, and I guess, this year ... it was worse for me."

"Worse because you went to Lola's birthday party?" Cohen asks at the same time Finn asks, "Because she was with Trent?"

"Both," I say with no delay.

The mention of that night causes my mind to drift to thoughts of Trent and Lola. I know they went out a few times, but I haven't asked her any questions. I don't want to know. It wouldn't be fair for me to ask her if they did anything, hooked up ... or for me to be upset with her over it. If I hadn't acted how I did, they'd never have even talked or exchanged numbers.

"Are you and Lola good now?" Archer asks.

"We're good." I scratch my cheek. "Working everything out."

"I'm happy to hear that," Maliki says. "We've been waiting for you to get your head out of your ass and wife her up before another lucky bastard did. But I have to warn you, the smart-ass ones are always the hardest to handle."

Maliki's girlfriend, Sierra, reminds me of Lola in some ways —loud, doesn't give a shit, and does what she wants.

I chuckle. "I've handled Lola enough to know how she is."

"We all have a past," Archer says, surprising me since the dude hardly talks. "I struggled for a while, but then Georgia came into my life—"

"Georgia *pushed* her way into your life, giving you no

opportunities to run," Finn says with a laugh.

"Pretty much," Cohen says. "My sister has a way of doing that."

"She might've been a pain in my ass, but she helped me through it," Archer continues. "There's something about having someone by your side that makes your struggles easier to get through."

"Hear, hear," Cohen says.

We all cheers with our waters.

They don't ask more questions, only make it clear that if I need anything, they have my back.

We play five rounds of poker.

I win once.

And then I go home to my girl.

———

"HOW HAVE YOU BEEN?" Trent asks as he stands next to me.

Tonight is the first time we've seen each other since the night of the charity event—when I punched him.

Two days after, I texted him a quick, *Sorry for punching you,* after Lola insisted it was the civil thing to do.

I groaned but did it even though I can't stand him. But she was right. I shouldn't have punched him.

I'm here, at one of my grandmother's dinners, as part of my apology for my behavior that night. I sent my grandmother flowers. Lola and I took my father and Janet to dinner—Lola being introduced as *my* date this time. That felt damn good. My grandmother asked for one more thing as part of my apology— to attend one of her dinners. Thank fuck she also extended that invite to Lola, so she could come with me.

I brought Lola, and Trent brought a date too. That helped it not be as awkward. Dinner went well, no punches were thrown, and we managed to put our differences aside for our family. My grandmother took Lola and Sylvie, Trent's date, on a tour of her new flower garden, leaving the two of us alone.

That was either a good decision or a stupid one.

We can make small talk or work out our differences.

Or we could fight again.

"Good," I reply, watching my grandmother point out flowers to Lola.

He tips his head toward them. "I'm glad you and Lola worked it out."

I shoot him a skeptical look. "Are you?"

"I'm not going to lie and say I didn't like her." He brings his drink to his mouth but doesn't take a sip. "But after that night, I knew I didn't stand a chance. Lola sent me a pity text the next morning and said she couldn't see me anymore."

I can't stop myself from smiling at his last statement—at him backing off, but her also making it clear she'd never be his. "I see you moved on quickly, though."

He chuckles. "Sylvie and I are friends who go to shit together when we don't have dates."

"Lola and I did the same thing for years." I crack a smile at the memory, watching Lola throw her head back and laugh at something my grandmother said.

Now, we no longer have to pretend.

Janet already took me aside when I went on a bathroom break to tell me how happy she was that Lola and I found each other and that I'd better not mess it up and lose her. Her eyes watered when I told her Lola knew everything and still loved me.

Trent blows out a harsh breath and drains his drink, and out of nowhere, he says, "She was with me too."

My gaze flashes to him. "Lola?"

"Sienna," he immediately corrects. "Sorry, should've done better at clarifying that."

I furrow my brow. "You and Sienna had a thing?"

He nods, staring straight ahead, as if reliving the memory.

"On and off."

"When?"

"Right when I moved to your school, Sienna and I started talking. Then after you two started your secret relationship, she blew me off. But the night before the party, she texted me, mad at you. We met up at the park, and she swore she was done with you and sick of being a secret. But then I saw you and her walk upstairs. It pissed me off, so I texted Kenny. I had no idea he'd do what he did." He squeezes his eyes shut. "Their deaths fucked with my head, too, and it took me some time to work through it because even though you think I didn't care, I knew I had some blame."

It makes sense. Anytime Trent saw Sienna and me together at school, his attitude always got worse when we got home that day. He'd start fights in front of her, but I always thought it was because he hated me.

And as I stare ahead, watching my grandmother and Lola, watching Lola talk with Sylvie, I realize that maybe I'll be okay. I'll never forget about Sienna or Kenny, never forget the role I had in their deaths, but each day, I'm healing from the emotional wounds I've suffered from it.

Even after, with all the confusion of Sienna and me, deep down, I hope she knew I loved her. I hope she knew, as I chased them, I tried to save her.

I clear my throat. "That night was just mistake after mistake."

"Agreed." He holds out his hand. "Truce?"

I hesitate before shaking it. "Truce."

Love causes people to do spiteful things.

It makes us act before thinking.

Trent and I will never be best friends.

We'll never have poker nights or hang out solo.

Maybe years down the road, that'll change.

But for now, since we're both healing from our mistakes, we can be better men.

CHAPTER FORTY-SIX

Lola

"I CAN'T BELIEVE Grace had her baby," I squeal from Silas's passenger seat.

Silas hangs a right into the hospital parking lot and searches for a spot. "You can't believe it? She was pregnant. It was inevitable."

"Shush." I smack his arm. "You know what I mean. It seems so real now. Like, she had a baby come out of her, and now, that baby is out in the world to have Grace as a mom." I relax in my seat. "Grace will be an amazing mom."

I'm so happy for her and Finn—that they found their way to happiness. Even though Finn isn't the biological father, he's stepped up in every way a father should. He loves Grace and that baby girl as if she were his own. He's texted us picture after picture, over the moon to finally be able to hold her. They have so much heart, and I know baby Millie will be loved.

"I'm thrilled they worked it out," Silas says while parking.

I clasp my hand over his. "Just like us."

We might've been the last of our friends to make it official, but we were one of the firsts to fall in love. We just needed our timing to be perfect, and timing is a hell of a thing. Silas had some growing to do, some demons to fight, and I had to convince my heart it was okay to be put on the line. I trust Silas with my heart, with my everything. And one day, maybe that'll be us, sending picture after picture of our baby.

Silas leans across the console, taking my chin in his hand, and smacks a kiss to my lips. "Just like us."

I love that we can do that anytime now—that we can kiss, touch, make love without questioning if it'll change our dynamic. Our friendship, our relationship, our love have grown so much stronger. We're discovering so much about each other, falling in love so much deeper, and I can't imagine him not being by my side as I go through life.

All the fear of handing him my heart, only for our relationship to end up like my parents', is long gone. He'd never hurt me, never look for someone who wasn't me, and I trust him more than anyone.

And the sex?

Holy hell. It's amazing.

The man hardly touches me, and I come apart.

We're in a normal relationship. Him hanging out with my family. Me with his. Our families hanging out together. We've even been around Trent a few times, who said he was happy we finally pulled our heads out of our asses. I thanked him for being what Silas needed to take a stand and fix himself. Otherwise, we would've fallen apart as friends and never had the chance to be together.

I grab my gift—well, *gifts* because I tend to go overboard.

Silas and I walk hand in hand into the hospital, and when we step into the elevator, he looks at me with intent. "Do you think you'll ever want to have babies"—he pauses, as if nervous—"with me? Together?"

I hit the floor button. "Well, I don't know who else I'd have them with."

He chuckles. "You know what I mean."

"If you're game, then I'm totally game," I answer with no

delay. It's something I've never said, but apparently, it's something my brain knows I want.

His face lights up. "That's a very romantic response from you."

I shrug. "Look, the only romance we need is in the bedroom … where we can do said baby-making."

"You'd be an amazing mother." He takes a step back, resting his chin in his palm. "If it's a girl, she'd probably have a smart mouth like you, and we'll be in trouble."

"And if he's anything like his daddy, he'll be just as troublesome as you. But also, a little heartthrob."

He grins wildly, takes a step closer, and wraps his arms around my waist. "I love this."

I settle my palm on his chest and peer up at him. "What?"

"Talking about our future kids." He rests his forehead against mine. "Our future."

The elevator dings, the door opening, and we hurriedly step apart. An older nurse stands in front of us.

"Oh, don't you two worry," she says with a wave of her hand. "You're not the first couple who's made out in the elevator on the way up here." She shakes her head, a large smile on her lips. "Something about visiting babies makes people want to have babies."

For the first time in years, I grow flustered and quickly shake my head. "We weren't making out."

"Oh, honey, but you were about to." The woman winks.

"She's not lying," Silas whispers into my ear, and I nudge him with my elbow before we step out.

The nurse's smile doesn't waver as she takes our spot. As we walk toward the heavy doors of the maternity unit, we find Georgia, Archer, Lincoln, and Cassidy standing near the waiting area, talking.

Cassidy rubs her belly as if she's as close to bursting herself. She's the first to notice, and she waves us over. "We're making bets on who's next to have a baby."

"Um, you," I answer, pointing at her belly.

She smiles. "Let me rephrase. Who will be the next to announce a pregnancy?"

"Like you guys did in high school, I bet on Lola," Lincoln says.

I motion toward Archer and Georgia. "Um, they've been together way longer and are *engaged.*"

"How long you've been with someone doesn't dictate how ovaries work," Cassidy says, resting her palm on Lincoln's shoulder and giving him some of her weight. "Archer and Georgia have been together longer than Lincoln and me."

"True," Georgia cuts in. "I guess it's really a matter of whether Archer's or Silas's sperm is faster."

"Really, babe?" Archer asks, shaking his head.

"Jesus, I'm terrified of a little Georgia," Lincoln mutters.

I cock my head. "But not of a little Archer?"

Silas smirks. "Nah, a baby Archer will just sulk in the corner."

Archer flips him off.

"I vote Silas and Lola," Cassidy says. "Something just tells me."

"I vote me and Georgia," Archer says with a shrug. "Maybe that'll manifest, and it'll happen."

"Same." Georgia wraps her small arm around his muscular one. "I like betting for myself."

Silas shoots me a glance. "Should we do the same then? Bet for ourselves?"

I nod. "Yep."

Everyone gawks at us for a moment. Georgia and Archer are engaged and have talked about a family. Archer is ready to be a father anytime. But Silas and I haven't mentioned anything like this to our friends.

"Speaking of babies," Georgia says. "Let's go meet the new addition to our family." She claps her hands, nearly jumping for joy.

I smile. While I'm happy for Grace and Finn, I don't allow my emotions to bleed out as much as Georgia. That girl doesn't wear her heart on her sleeve. She wears it as a damn badge.

We stroll down the hall, Silas's hand finding mine again. As soon as Georgia knocks, Grace calls for us to come in. We walk in, sanitize our hands, and see Grace in the hospital bed. Finn is next to her with Millie in his arms.

"Where is my goddaughter?" Georgia sings before holding up a gift bag. "I have presents on presents on presents to give her."

I nudge her with my elbow. "I think you mean, *my* goddaughter."

Grace laughs. "How many times have I said that you're both the godmothers?"

"Is that a thing?" Georgia asks. "Can there be two? And if there are two, who's number one? If so, I'm number one."

I playfully roll my eyes as we settle our gifts onto the small couch where others sit. Millie is going to be one spoiled girl.

Cassidy waddles in behind us, Lincoln resting his hand on her back, and she looks directly at Grace. "Don't tell me any horror stories, please. Lincoln has made me watch birthing pregnancy videos, and I'm terrified."

Finn chuckles. "Prepare yourself for war, Lincoln."

Georgia is the first to hold Millie, and I'm sure had someone tried before, she'd have pushed them to the side. Grace is nervous as Finn carefully settles her into her arms as if he's sad to even let her go.

Finn has always been a good man.

But Finn as a father? It's indescribable.

It's an entirely different level.

Silas sits by my side as I hold Millie. "She's awfully wrinkly for being so young."

Finn shoves his shoulder. "Jealous you're not as cute as her?"

"Her wrinkles are adorable," I say, tracing her tiny forehead with the tip of my finger.

Silas leans into me. "I wonder how wrinkly our baby will be."

I laugh, shaking my head. "I'm sure after that comment, she'll have her fair share of them."

As I hold Millie, my thoughts drift to the night I told Silas I was lonely. My heart needed something, but I was clueless about what that was exactly. As I look around, that question is answered.

It's this.

Friends. Family. Love.

It's seeing Grace having a baby and me wanting the same. It's glancing at Georgia's engagement ring and seeing me doing the same with one Silas picked out.

People can grow up in dysfunctional homes, witness toxic relationships, but if they find the right person, it'll give them hope. Silas gave me that. And I want to give that to our children … with a man who's currently discussing baby wrinkles.

————

AND GETTING to the baby-making is what we do when we get back to my place.

We're undressed in minutes. I squeal when Silas grabs my ass, hoisting me up, and I wrap my legs around his waist. His cock is hard, and I rub against his erection as he carries me to the bedroom.

"Can we work on winning that bet?" he asks before slamming his mouth onto mine.

Panting into his mouth, I say, "Absolutely."

He tosses me onto the bed, and before I can catch a breath, he's peeling off my pants and panties. Without bothering with his, he spreads my thighs, making room for himself.

He licks me.

Sucks me.

Finger-fucks me.

Until I'm falling apart beneath him.

There has never been a man who's cared about my orgasm more than Silas.

Hell, he even cares about it more than I do.

As I catch my breath, coming down, my heart still beating wildly, Silas strips off his clothes. I shove him onto his back and straddle him. Just as quick as he had his head between my legs, I tease him at my entrance before lowering myself fully on his hard cock.

I freeze.

Even though we talked about baby-making, it doesn't mean it has to happen right now.

Me? I'd be totally fine with it.

And even though Silas said he wants to win that bet, I don't move.

"You're not wearing a condom," I whisper, settling my hands on his chest to hold myself up.

He stares up at me, unblinking. "Are you okay with that?"

I slowly nod.

"Then so am I." He grips my waist and grinds into me. "This is about to be the best sex of my life."

For the first time ever, we have sex without a condom.

It feels more intimate.

Closer.

I ride his cock, switching from slow to fast to rough to soft.

Wanting to draw it out for as long as I can.

"Fuck," he moans, swiping my hair from my face and pulling my head down to kiss me. "You give it to me so good, baby."

It doesn't take long until I gasp his name and then collapse against him. He grips my hips tighter, driving into me until it's time for him to moan out my name in release.

CHAPTER FORTY-SEVEN

Silas

I WAS NEVER a fan of weddings until I found someone I wanted to marry. In fact, I only attended two weddings before today—my father and Janet's, and my mother and her new husband's. The first one, I was forced to attend, and I sulked in the back row and spit spitballs at the back of Trent's head.

Today has been nice. Georgia and Archer had a small, intimate ceremony in Hawaii—which I was game for because a vacation with Lola sounded like a damn good time. A vacation with *all* our friends since all of us were able to attend.

Call it rude, but during the ceremony, I paid more attention to Lola. I imagined marrying her, of me standing where Archer was and her walking down the aisle. We'd say our *I do*s and live happily ever after. It sounds cheesy, but hey, when you know, you know.

Cohen walked Georgia down the aisle, and Archer attempted to hide his misty eyes as he stared at her.

Archer had been right when he told me to get my shit together as I debated on whether to attend Lola's birthday. Not that the advice was good timing, given the disaster that happened, but his words stuck with me. Georgia had changed his life and helped him heal from the past. Lola has done the same for me.

"Is your stomach still upset, baby?" I ask around a yawn as we walk into the hotel room.

The reception was fun, but Lola hardly ate, only drank sparkling water, and whispered she was nauseous as she saw the newlyweds cut their cake.

"It's a little better," she says around a stressed sigh, reaching for the back of her dress.

I stop her, helping her with her dress, and massage her tense shoulders as the beige bridesmaid dress pools at her feet.

Tipping her head back, she relaxes at my touch.

Sweeping her soft hair off her shoulder, I slowly rain kisses along her neck before whispering in her ear, "Do you want me to order you something from room service to help with the nausea? Or run to the store?"

She shakes her head, her voice timid as she says, "I'm okay."

"Do you think it's the flu? Jet lag?"

"Um ..." She draws the word out for what seems like a minute.

I freeze, my heart falling into my stomach even though I have no idea what it is yet. "What?"

"I think it might be ..." She pauses, turning to face me, and chews on her plump lower lip.

My eyes widen as I go into panic mode.

Is she sick?

Cancer?

Done with my ass?

"A baby," she whispers.

"What?" I stutter out again, my heart now in ultimate panic mode.

"A baby," she says clearly as if she's practiced it in the mirror a few times.

We haven't talked about a baby since the hospital, but we also haven't been careful. When we want to have sex, we have sex, not giving a care in the world about protection. Hell, I don't know if there's even any in either of our homes—even though I wouldn't consider my home mine anymore since I sleep at Lola's nearly every night.

"I missed my period. I've googled pregnancy symptoms, and I talked to Grace about it." She shivers, goose bumps popping along her arms. "What I'm feeling, what's happening with my body, is similar to what she experienced."

I clasp her hand, settle her onto the bed, and grab her pajamas from the suitcase. I unstrap her shoes, tossing them to the side, and slide the tank over her head. I fall at her feet to slip her shorts on.

"Have you taken a test?"

She shakes her head. "No … not yet. I thought I'd give it more time. It could be stress from the trip, helping with the wedding, something. But my body seems off, and I haven't had my PMS phase either."

"We need to get a test."

She stops me from standing, resting her hand on my chest and playing with my shirt buttons. "What are your thoughts about this, Silas? How will you feel if it's positive?"

"Baby"—I soften my voice and grab her hand, running my thumb between hers and her pointer finger—"I want everything with you." I raise her hand and bring it to my lips. "Do you want me to go get a test?"

"It's late."

"There's a store in the lobby." I kiss her hand, then her forehead, and then her mouth—drawing that one out longer, tasting the small slice of strawberry cake she had before saying she couldn't eat another bite or she'd vomit. "If they don't have one there, I'll catch an Uber. Otherwise, I'll be up all night, thinking about it."

"Okay." She blows out a breath. "I'd tag along, but I'm so tired. I don't know if I would make it to the lobby."

"I got this, baby."

I pull back the blankets and tuck her in before walking out of the room. I don't find a pregnancy test on-site in the hotel, so I take a quick trip to a convenience store that has them. When I return to the hotel room, Lola is sleeping. As much as I want her to take it, to find out at this very moment, she looks so peaceful. Instead, I place it on my nightstand and undress. Careful not to wake her, I snuggle to her side, spooning her to me, and grin.

I wanted Lola the moment I saw her at the bar, but I never thought it was possible. Finding love again was never on my radar, but here we are, in love. Everything good I thought would never happen has.

Anticipation spirals through me.

A baby.

I might be a father.

If it's negative, that'll be fine.

It's not our time.

My and Lola's relationship has always been about timing.

Maybe it's our time for a baby.

———

"SORRY," Lola says the following morning, flipping onto her back in bed to peer up at me. "I fell asleep on you."

I grin at her. "You had a long day and needed the rest." I bow my head to kiss her. "Good morning. How are you feeling?"

Even though the bed was comfortable as fuck, I hardly slept. It was like I was a kid waiting for Santa. All I could think about was the news we'd find out this morning. But I won't rush her to take the test. It'll be when she's ready.

"Tired, but better now that I broke the possible new development in our lives to you ..." She trails off, rubbing her hand through her hair. "Did you get the test?"

I nod. "I did, but you can wait until you're ready to take it."

Her eyes are wide, concern in them. "How would you feel if it's positive?"

"Damn good."

"And negative?"

"I won't lie and say a little disappointed because I got my hopes up, but I'd have the woman I love, so still, damn good."

She reaches up and caresses my face. "You're the best thing to ever happen to me, you know that?"

"Trust me, I know the feeling because you're what saved me." I rest my forehead against hers. "You're what gave me life again."

We lie there for minutes, our breathing heavy.

We know that when she takes that test, our lives might change.

———

"YOU GO LOOK at it because I can't," Lola says, tapping her foot, staring at the bathroom door like a monster is going to come out.

She took the test, and the stick is in the bathroom, lying on the counter, front and center. The star of the show. The most precious item we have in this room.

I brace my hand on her leg to stop her foot. "Why don't we look at it together?"

"Why don't you just do what I said?"

I chuckle. "There's my girl coming out."

I don't take her words as an insult because she's been a nervous wreck all morning. She fidgeted and dropped the stick five times before peeing on it.

I drum my fingers along her thigh. "You really want me to do it without you?"

"Yes," she groans. "Ugh, I don't know."

"We can wait for as long as you want." I scrunch my brows. "They don't time out, do they? Like we have ten minutes before it goes away?"

"How would I know?" she shrieks. "I've never taken a pregnancy test before!"

"Really? There's never been a time you thought—"

"Nope. I always used a condom, except for you, took birth control, prayed to the pregnant gods."

"Oh, but what about with me?" I sit up straighter as if I'd just been served an award.

She grins. "With you, I told the pregnancy gods to do with me what they will."

I kiss her forehead. "I love you. Let's see what the pregnancy gods have blessed you with."

"Love you too," she whispers before squeezing my hand and slowly standing while releasing a slow breath. "Let's do this."

It's a short walk to the bathroom, and her hand is sweaty as it grips mine. My chest swells with hope when we grab the test with shaking hands. Our eyes meet, our focus solely on the other as if trying to read what's on the other's mind.

I drop a quick peck to her head. "You ready?"

Her hand, her chin, her body are trembling. "Ready."

We count down from three, and as soon as we look at the stick, the bathroom goes silent.

I blink at it, focused. "I'm pretty sure that means positive."

We should've read the directions.

"I'm pretty sure you're right," she replies.

It takes a moment for the news to dawn on us.

"Holy shit," Lola finally yelps. "I'm fucking pregnant."

Her eyes are wide as they look at me, and my entire body relaxes.

"Baby!" I yell, not caring if everyone in the hotel hears me. *Let the whole damn world know.* "We're having a baby!"

She jumps into my arms, the stick still in her hand, and I don't give a shit as it hits my neck. Just like Archer, I attempt to hide my tears, but it doesn't happen.

I'm going to be a father.

Call *The Guinness World Records* because I'm the happiest damn man alive.

CHAPTER FORTY-EIGHT

Silas

I WOKE with a sense of determination today.

Got out of bed—a rarity on this particular day.

A smile on my face—the first time in years.

It's Lola's birthday, and I'm going to give her the best damn birthday she's ever had. It's wild that a year has passed since the club disaster. It's also wild that we're having a baby.

We took all the tests in the box that day.

Then when we got home, we took more.

Then went to the doctor.

It was confirmed.

We're having a baby, and I couldn't be happier.

But before tonight's festivities, there's something I need to do.

I'd come here when I was depressed, when guilt was eating me alive, but now, I'm here to cleanse myself, to help myself heal. Lola offered to come with me, but it's something I need to do on my own. She's helped me move on so much, but this final step needs to be done by me.

I'll always have guilt over what happened with Sienna and Kenny.

Always know that I played a part in their deaths.

But I also know that I tried to protect her and stop them.

The morning air is sticky yet chilly as I step out of my car and walk through the cemetery entrance. I've sat outside the gates countless times, but today is the first time I've gained the guts to walk through them.

I know where their gravestones are because I watched the funeral from afar. I watched their family break down, people hold their mother up as they were lowered into the ground.

I'm not sure what I'll do when I get there since I didn't plan anything out, not knowing if I'd go through with it.

They're buried side by side, sharing one headstone.

Sienna and Kenny Jenkins
Taken too soon and will always be remembered.

THEIR FACES FLASH through my mind, memories of the times we shared together coming next, and I squeeze my eyes shut.

When I open them, I stare at the headstone, taking in every curve and slant of their names, and whisper, "I'm sorry."

I'm sad.

Yet I'm also angry with Kenny for putting Sienna in danger and killing her.

I stand there, unsure of how much time has passed.

As I'm about to leave, a timid, soft-spoken voice says, "I'm sorry."

It's nearly the same way I said it that night at the crash scene —guilt mixed with sadness and anger.

Looking over my shoulder, I see their mother behind me. I hold in a breath, waiting for her to tell me to get the hell out of here.

"I'm sorry," she repeats, her eyes on me, not the headstone.

I rub my hands down my pant legs at the realization that she's talking to me.

This is the woman who told me she wished I'd rot in hell for what I'd done, who told anyone who would listen that I was the boy who'd killed her children, who'd taken advantage of their daughter. She ran my name through the dirt, even tried to sue me for wrongful death until my father agreed to pay them a settlement and keep it out of the courts. Mary Jenkins despised my existence.

And now, I have no idea what she'll do about me being here.

She can't sue me for being at a cemetery, but she can scream at me, smack me.

Is she apologizing because she's about to kill me or for the way she put a teenage boy through hell?

I gawk at her as she pulls her sweater tight around her body and steps next to me.

Silence passes between us until she says, "I'm sorry," again.

I stare at the headstone as if it had the answer for what's happening. "What do you mean?"

"I'm sorry for blaming you." Her eyes water as she shifts to face me. "You were a high school kid, and there we were, blaming you." She shakes her head. "We wanted to find someone to blame, but after time passed, after therapy, I realized you were the same age as Kenny. I asked myself how I'd feel if someone treated him like that had he been in the same situation. Kenny was the one who had forced Sienna into his car. He was the one who had driven recklessly, but it was hard to accept one of our babies had caused the death of the other one."

I came here, expecting to find peace with Sienna and Kenny.

I didn't expect to get it with their mother as well.

Would I have felt differently, not allowed the guilt to eat me as much, if they hadn't treated me the way they did?

There's no going back to know that answer.

And what happened, happened.

I blink at their headstone. "I understand."

She hesitates before slowly reaching out, putting her hand on my shoulder. "I hope you've found happiness now. I hope we didn't break you too much."

Her face is red when I finally direct my gaze to her. And a bit of warmth, of hope, spreads through me.

I offer her a polite smile. "I'm going to be a father."

I shut my mouth immediately after.

Shit.

Her children will never have that luxury. She'll never have the chance to be a grandmother.

"Congratulations." Her tone is genuine—no animosity coming from her at my news. "I wish you and your family the best. And I mean that, truly, from my heart."

MY FIRST TEAR falls when I get into my car to leave the cemetery, and I sink into my seat before smiling.

"I did it," I whisper.

I worked up the nerve to walk into that cemetery.

And Mary worked up the nerve to speak to me, to apologize.

Everything takes time.

"IS THERE a way to put more chocolate on this?" Lola asks, sitting next to me, holding a plate with a slice of birthday cake on it. "Or hot sauce? That actually sounds amazing."

"That sounds like the most disgusting thing I've ever heard," Archer mutters. "I don't know if I can hang out with anyone that weird."

"Just wait," Finn comments, shooting his attention to Archer. "Georgia will have the weirdest pregnancy cravings too."

"Nah, all my girl wants are burritos from Le Mesa. Swear to

God, I almost asked if I could buy stock in the business since we order takeout from there so much."

"Le Mesa does have some killer food, though," I say.

It's a regular spot for us to hang out when we have Taco Tuesdays.

It's crazy how much our life has changed. Here we are, having a birthday, where everyone is either pregnant or already a parent. Cassidy had their baby girl, Emma, and she and Lincoln have been on top of the world. She and Grace have been a giant help to Lola with any questions she has regarding pregnancy and birth. The guys have also been the same way with me.

Then Georgia and Sierra broke the news that they were expecting.

It's like getting pregnant runs in the water at Twisted Fox.

I caught on to the nervousness of everyone, worried I'd bail on Lola's party tonight. Even after Lola said we could stay in a hundred times so things wouldn't be hard on me, I felt fine, like I was a different man. So, I told her we'd do something simple, go to dinner, but instead, we drove to Cohen and Jamie's, where everyone was waiting for us.

They yelled, "Surprise," as soon as we walked in, and Lola gave me her angry pregnancy glare because she hates surprises.

But seconds later, she was smiling and laughing.

I peek over at the woman I love, thinking about how far we've come.

My gaze falls to her belly, taking in the bump, and I grin.

I did it. Created a life I love. Attended her birthday without dread.

This is my life.

Something I thought I'd never have.

I've made it to happiness.

We've made it to happiness.

And so have our friends.

————

"GOD, I've been wanting to do this all night," Lola says around a moan, her hands eagerly unzipping my pants. She places a quick kiss on my bulge over my jeans before roughly pulling them down.

Pregnant Lola is horny-as-fuck Lola.

We had plenty of sex before, but it's on a different level now. Not that I have an issue with it. I loved seeing Lola naked, thought it was the best sight in the world, but Lola naked and pregnant?

Holy shit.

My cock gets hard anytime I think of it.

There's the excitement that she's mine, that we're having a family and made it this far. We've discussed marriage but decided to take it slow because of how marriage has scared us in the past. Although I know I'd never do anything to fuck up a life with Lola—to hurt the person I love and committed myself to, like our parents did.

Lola also said she wasn't walking down the aisle while pregnant, but I have a ring for her for when the timing feels right. It's waiting—something I had custom-made that fits her in every way.

Chills climb up my spine when her lips wrap around my cock with no warning, and she sucks the tip before taking my entire length into her mouth. She doesn't gag while deep-throating me, only moans when I hit the back of her throat. I grip her hair, keeping a hold on her but allowing her to decide the pace. As I grow closer, I can't stop myself from tilting my hips up, feeding her more and more of my hard cock before pulling her head away from my lap.

"Time for you to fuck me now," I grind out.

She grins, her eyes bright, while climbing onto my lap and falling on my cock, pre-cum already dripping from the tip. She rides me rough and fast as I play with her nipples before reaching down to her belly, slowly rubbing it. It doesn't take long until she falls apart above me, collapsing against my chest, although it's harder now for her to do than it was before.

A few pumps later, and I'm throwing my head back, clenching my jaw, and busting inside her.

She rests her palms on my chest, and I lean forward to kiss her.

"I love you," she whispers against my lips. "Thank you for loving me"—she laughs, pointing at her belly—"and for impregnating me."

"Anytime, baby." I laugh. "I love you."

EPILOGUE

Lola

Twelve Years Later

"DO you remember when our lives were sane?" I ask the girls. "We had silence, freedom, no whining about losing iPads."

"Babe," Georgia deadpans, "our lives were never sane."

"Saner than this." I motion toward the kids running around the yard, yelling at each other, a few throwing balls while talking shit, like their fathers do. I stop to cup my hand around my mouth and yell, "Amelia! Don't you dare throw that drink on Jax."

Twelve years have passed since I found out I was pregnant, but it seems like an eternity. We have families, marriages, SUVs, and soccer practice schedules. Hell, Grace even convinced me to join the PTA.

Zero out of ten.

Still trying to find a way to bail myself out of that one.

I might be a mom, but I'm a cool mom, okay?

Silas and I married eight years ago when the timing was perfect. Even though we knew we wanted to spend the rest of our lives together, we had so much happening with being new parents and our jobs that we wanted to wait. Silas's mother, of course, insisted on the wedding planning and went all out. Silas even asked Trent to be one of his groomsmen since they'd started working on their relationship for the sake of his family. Amelia also likes playing with Trent's daughter.

Now, our circle, which was once a small group of friends, has grown.

Silas and I have Amelia.

Georgia and Archer ended up with twins—a girl and a boy.

We still beat them on the whole *who will get prego first* bet. Although she found out a couple of weeks later, so it wasn't by much.

Finn and Grace had a girl to give Millie a little sister.

Cassidy and Lincoln have two—a boy and a girl.

Jamie and Cohen added another to their family.

Sierra and Maliki have Jax.

Jax, for some reason, doesn't get along with my daughter.

Amelia, for some reason, has kicked him in the balls one too many times.

As everyone started to get busier, it became harder for Cohen and Archer to work as much. So, they asked Lincoln, Silas, and Finn if they wanted to become part owners of Twisted Fox. The guys were ecstatic, and Silas immediately jumped on the opportunity. Then I became the president of 21st Amendment after my father stepped down until I realized I didn't want to work as much either. So, I demoted myself and gave my position to Robby.

"Mom! He deserves to have the drink spilled on him!" Amelia yells. "And a kick between the legs!"

"Who?" Georgia asks, looking around the yard.

Amelia comes stomping toward us with Jax at her heels. "Jaxson! He's the biggest jerk in the world."

"Hey," Jax says, crossing his arms and glaring at Amelia. "Don't get mad at me because I'm better at everything than you are."

"You're not better at anything than her," Theo, Cohen and Jamie's son, tells Jax.

Jax flips him off, resulting in Sierra jumping out of her chair and scolding him. "Dude, mind your business!"

Amelia stomps her feet and raises her knee as if she's ready to give Jax a good kick. "Don't tell him to mind his business."

"Seriously, Jax," Sierra groans. "You are just like your father."

Jax smirks. "You're married to him, so is that supposed to be a bad thing?"

Even though we shouldn't, everyone at the table either laughs or smiles since we're obviously very mature. The guys join us to find out what the commotion is about.

"Sorry, babe, but he got you there," Maliki says, coming up behind his son. He throws his arms up when Sierra glares at him. "I'm just saying."

Georgia signals back and forth between Amelia and Jax. "Those two are going to get married one day. I'll put my money on it right now."

"Can we please not talk about marrying my daughter off?" Silas says. "Those two hate each other."

"*And?*" Georgia asks. "Archer and I hated each other. Shoot, Maliki kept kicking Sierra out of his bar, and now, they're married."

Jax's green eyes widen as he gawks at Maliki. "You kicked Mom out of your bar?"

"You hated Mom?" Roman, Georgia's son, asks Archer at the same time.

"Can I kick Jax out of Daddy's bar?" Amelia asks, swatting her dark hair—the same color as mine—out of her eyes while glaring at Jax.

Silas shakes his head. "Sure, honey." He turns his attention to Maliki. "My daughter isn't going to marry a kid who sticks gum in her hair."

Georgia clicks her tongue against the roof of her mouth. "Just wait and see."

"Babe," Silas says, glancing at me, "tell them you're only supposed to fall in love with your best friend."

"Amelia is my best friend," Theo says, narrowing his eyes at Jax. "Does that mean we're going to fall in love?"

"That means, it's time for you boys to mind your business and quit talking about falling in love with my kid," Silas says, and I crack up.

Silas comes up behind me, resting his hand on my back before caressing my neck. "Remember when I found out we were having a girl, and I say she'd be a little firecracker?"

I laugh, staring up at him, a bright smile on my face. "Oh, she's definitely our little firecracker."

Silas and I might've been the last to get our happily ever after.

To admit we loved each other.

But sometimes, the last round means everything.

If you enjoyed Silas and Lola's story, check out the other books in the Twisted Fox series!

Stirred
(Cohen & Jamie's story)
Shaken
(Archer & Georgia's story)
Straight Up
(Lincoln & Cassidy's story)
Chaser
(Finn & Grace's story)
Last Round
(Silas and Lola's story)

Enjoy the interconnected Blue Beech series!

Just A Fling
Just Exes
Just Neighbors
Just Roommates
Just Friends

ALSO BY CHARITY FERRELL

TWISTED FOX SERIES

(each book can be read as a standalone)

Stirred

Shaken

Straight Up

Chaser

Last Round

BLUE BEECH SERIES

(each book can be read as a standalone)

Just A Fling

Just One Night

Just Exes

Just Neighbors

Just Roommates

Just Friends

STANDALONES

Bad For You

Beneath Our Faults

Pop Rock

Pretty and Reckless

Revive Me

Wild Thoughts

RISKY DUET
Risky
Worth The Risk

ABOUT THE AUTHOR

Charity Ferrell is a USA Today and Wall Street Journal best-selling author of the Twisted Fox and Blue Beech series. She resides in Indianapolis, Indiana with her fiancé and two fur babies. She loves writing about broken people finding love while adding humor and heartbreak along with it. Angst is her happy place.

When she's not writing, she's making a Starbucks run, shopping online, or spending time with her family.

Find her on:

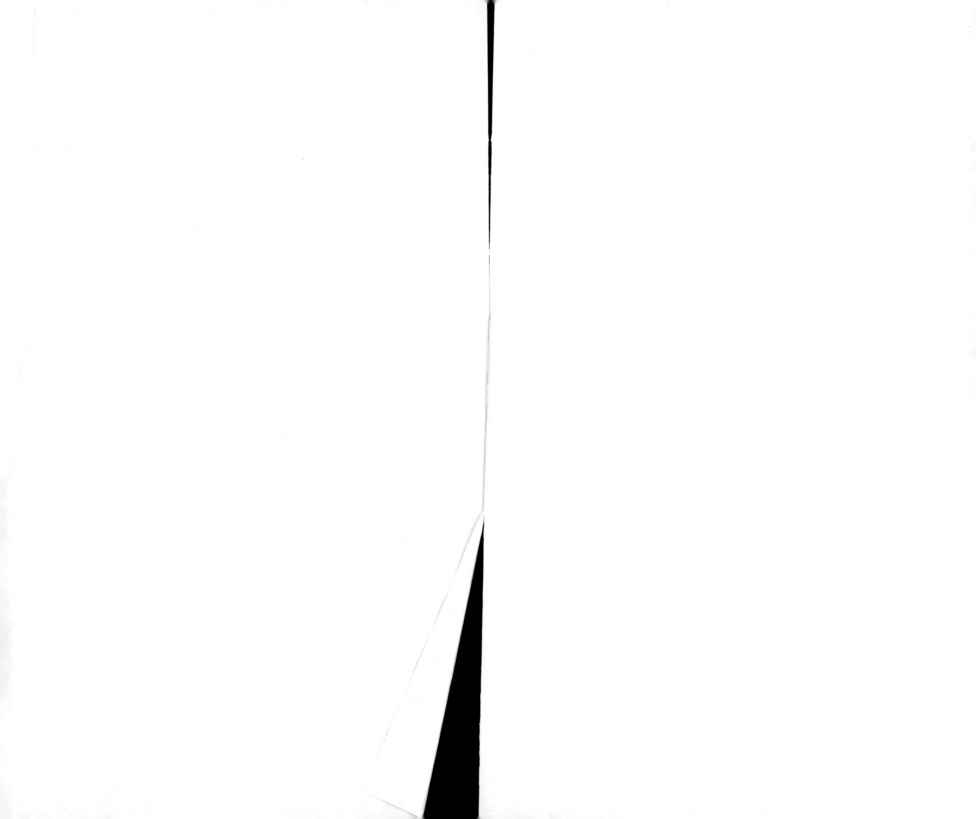

Made in United States
Orlando, FL
05 April 2022

16536747R10168